I0735378

THE BURNING DAYS

a dystopian tale

Judith Baller-Fabian

WORKBOOK PRESS LLC
187 E Warm Springs Rd,
Suite B285, Las Vegas, NV 89119, USA

Website: https://workbookpress.com/
Hotline: 1-888-818-4856
Email: admin@workbookpress.com

Ordering Information:
Quantity sales. Special discounts are available on quantity purchases by corporations, associations, and others.
For details, contact the publisher at the address above.

Library of Congress Control Number:
ISBN-13:   978-1-956017-05-2 (Paperback Version)
                978-1-956017-06-9 (Digital Version)

REV. DATE: 01/07/2021

To my beloved, patient, husband Allan,
who listened to *almost* every word.

Other books by
Judith Baller-Fabian
The Officer's House

Chapter 1

The Garden State

June looked over her shoulder. She was blond, tanned from the sun, and as she kneeled in the garden, her long, pale hair fell over her face. Upstairs in the farmhouse, a window curtain was quickly moved back into place and the dog, Sherpa, barked somewhere inside but was hushed.

How odd, she thought. Why?

She squatted down and picked up a handful of soil from the vegetable garden. Last year she had helped tend the gardens, and the earth had been moist and a deep brown. She had enjoyed the fresh vegetables all summer long and had stored root vegetables and cabbages for the winter.

But today, as the soil ran through her fingers, small puffs of dust floated up from between her sandals. The tender green shoots that appeared a few weeks earlier and forced their way up through the dry earth were dying in the hot sun.

She sighed and gazed out over the acres of farmland that belonged to the people upstairs – good people who gave her a living space in their basement and paid her to work on the farm. Sometimes they brought her honey or pastry, and the wife always took her to the village on Saturdays. This was home, now.

June was worried. A sepia haze hung over the horizon, coming closer every day, and heat lightning flashed far away. Last year's wheat chaff was burned black by the sun and lay in dusty heaps across the field. Every now and then, for no apparent reason, a small fire would start, little flames licking along the ground only to die as the dust smothered them. The cornfield was empty, and the bees that had scared her with their tiny, busy bodies were gone.

A crow gave a harsh call as it beat its way across the wheat field and then it was quiet again.

June looked back at the garden, lost in thought. She had seen this before, back home in the little town where she had grown up. First, the dry, bitterly cold winter, and then the endless sun, killing every growing thing, vegetables, fruit, wheat, corn … all gone. She felt a chill in the hot, still air. It was happening here, and she realized she would have to leave her little basement home, leave and head further north. She trembled at the thought. She would be a traveler again – just another lonely traveler on the road.

Chapter 2

North Carolina

The girl's name was June because that was the month of her birth. She had grown up with her mother in a small southern town. Her mother had told her it was North Carolina, but June didn't know where that was and didn't care. She didn't remember her father, and her mother wouldn't speak of him, only say he had died for the South in the American Civil War of 2045.

"When you were a little girl," she said when June begged. Then she would tighten her lips and look away. June remembered a tall man with a sweet, slow drawl who picked her up and sang silly songs. A man with eyes as blue as the sky. "Daddy," she would whisper, but the memory would fade away, and she would think she had just made it up because she wanted to.

Mother owned a shop called The Knitting Shop. It was filled with colorful knitting wool and other knitting and sewing notions, as well as the lovely hand knit sweaters she sold. By the time she was seven years old, June had learned to embroider delicate designs and knit soft sweaters and scarves, mittens and baby blankets.

During the day, June would sit by her mother's side in the little shop, needles clicking, their voices low and loving, surrounded by the rows of wool and knitted goods. In the evening, her mother opened her big Bible, and while she knitted, she taught June to read.

There had been no school in the little town since the war, and the only book that was allowed was the Bible, so this is what June learned to read. The words were often beautiful, and she loved the sound of them on her tongue, but there were some things in the pages that scared her. Then her mother would smile or gently brush back her hair.

"The Lord is a kind gentleman," she told her. "Just think of him as Sir … someone you can talk to if you're scared or alone, a good man."

The Knitting Shop was one of the small stores on Main Street. There was a hardware store, a grocery store, and a little coffee shop named *The British Tea Shoppe*. The lady who owned the shop was named May. She had seen some photographs and pictures of England and liked them. She had even hung a framed print of a fox hunt on the wall, and whenever June was in the tea shop, she gazed at it and wondered what had happened to the little fox. She hoped he had escaped, hidden in the bushes or behind the wall.

None of the townsfolk liked tea, just coffee, and cola, but *The British Tea Shoppe* was the only place in town, so they just called it the Coffee Shop and hung out there, drinking coffee and cola and trading gossip.

June was a happy child. On Saturdays, her mother would take her shopping and to lunch at the tea shop. There was lemonade in the summer and hot chocolate when it was cold. June loved her home. She believed it was the most beautiful place in the world. Big trees and weeping willows lined a river that rolled through the middle of town, and magnolias filled the air with their sweet perfume. June was allowed to play on the grassy bank, while her mother sat on a blanket nearby.

"Happy Child," her mother would always say, "stay this young and innocent." Then she would smile to herself and gaze out over the water. "Here, by the river, you will never grow old."

On hot summer days, she dressed June in her bathing suit, a tank top, and flouncy skirt and took her to the small beach the menfolk had made by trucking in loads of sand. Here, in the river, June's mother taught her how to swim. "You must know how to swim," she told her, "be friends with the water. You never know…"

June didn't know what "you never know …" meant but she took to the river like a sturdy little fish, dipping under the water and pushing hard with her hands and feet as she swam through the lazy currents, then popping up and tossing the water out of her hair. Sometimes she floated on her back and gazed up at the sky.

"Blue sky," she would sing, "blue, blue sky …"

Everyone who lived in town was friendly and gracious, and June knew them all by name. They smiled and passed the time of day with June's mother when they met, and Mother taught her to show respect to the gentlemen when they stopped to chat.

"That's Mr. Hannah," she would say, or "that's Mr. Grant. Dip your right knee just a tiny bit and bob your head one time. That will show respect and good manners. It doesn't matter how much money we have, not if we have good manners!"

June decided she was a very fortunate little girl to live in this beautiful place, and she never changed her mind. No matter what happened, she kept that hidden in her heart like a treasure.

Wealthy ladies with names like Miss Archibald or Miss Lee lived in the big mansions across The River. Miss Lee was very old with snow-white hair. She wore it in a braid on top of her head and walked with a cane. Over and over she would tell June she remembered what it was like *before*. Miss Lee would cock her head and tap the side of her nose. "Before," she'd whisper. "Shhh! Don't say a word!"

Her friends would always say "Hush, Daisy, "don't go putting ideas in her head. She's still a child, and at least we're safe here."

June always wondered what it was like "Before."

The Wealthy Ladies would come into the knitting shop and buy the items on display: designer sweaters and scarves, babies' and children's clothing for a grandchild. Sometimes, one of the ladies brought her dog in a shoulder bag: a small, creature with black shoe button eyes and a pink tongue. June was afraid of the little animal because it would show its tiny teeth and make a growling sound whenever she came near.

The ladies would twitter among themselves like birds and smile at June, diamond rings flashing as they held up the knitted goods to admire. They were the only people in town who owned cars and June could hear the electric motors purring softly when they parked outside. Sometimes she wondered where the wealthy husbands were. It was whispered they worked in Washington, D. C., but it remained a mystery.

When June was sixteen, her mother went south to visit her only sister, a jolly woman named Glory. June begged to go. She had heard such wonderful stories about Florida, how the sun was warm and palm trees grew tall. She had seen pictures of palm trees in her mother's Bible, and their fronds looked like giant green feathers.

June wanted to see the big ocean where there was no end in sight. Oh, and how she longed to swim in that endless sea. "Please take me with you," June begged. "I want to see that beautiful place and swim in the endless water."

But her mother shook her head. "You need to stay here and care for the shop. You're old enough to take the responsibility. I trust you."

June was disappointed, but she liked the sound of responsibility, and that was the end of the conversation.

Her mother packed some sweaters for her sister's family, carefully folding them into tissue paper before adding them to her suitcase. Before she left, she brushed June's hair back from her face, gazing at her for a few moments and telling her how to fend for herself, kissing her softly before she headed out.

"I love you," she said and was gone.

June stood at the shop's front window and watched as her mother walked across Main Street to the bus stop. In a way, she was excited to be on her own, and she gave a little skip.

"Responsibility," she whispered to herself. "I like it."

When the bus pulled up, her mother looked back, waved once and then disappeared inside.

A week later, the Great Flood of 2056 swept across the South. In the Southeastern Region, huge waves, fed by the last of the melted Arctic icecaps, rose out of the Atlantic Ocean, swallowing the land and killing everything and everyone as it moved inland. The flood swept westward with deliberation; it covered cities and towns, consuming everything in its path. It met the Pacific Ocean on the far western coast and sank back down.

When the sun rose the next day, half the country was under one vast ocean. The sea had taken back its own.

Rain poured down in North Carolina and ran down the streets; the river where June learned to swim overflowed its banks, swallowing the tiny beach and three magnolia trees.

It flooded River Road. Flood water covered the mansions' wide lawns and Miss Archibald's electric car. But the Great Flood stopped just short of town, leaving nothing but mud as far as the eye could see. Soon the sun dried the streets, and the river returned to its banks.

June waited in vain for her mother to return. She stood at the edge of the mud plain with the townsfolks: rich and poor, shoulder to shoulder waiting for someone, anyone, to come out of the drizzling fog.

Finally, little by little, the townsfolk gave up hope and started sad, nightly memorial services for The Lost. June stood with the others, frightened and heartsick. Every night she held a lit candle in her hand as the crowd sent prayers and hymns into the muggy night air, but she couldn't find the words.

As the months went by fewer and fewer people met at night, and fewer candle flames burned in the dark. Finally, everyone gave up hope.

Preacher Pride, the town preacher, said, "people live, and people die." Then he looked down over his glasses and said in a deep voice, "maybe somebody sinned." But the people were tired of talk of sin and salvation. They didn't believe it anymore, so they shrugged and went on with their lives. They tended their shops and farmed their lands. "People lived, and people died," they told each other.

Some said it was a tsunami and others said a huge super hurricane out of the Atlantic; but whatever it had been, it had changed their world.

That was the last rain they would see.

June went back to knitting and caring for her mother's little shop. It seemed to be the least she could do. She would sit in the evening light, knitting needles clicking, and wondering what was to become of her. The Wealthy Ladies would come in and shop, their faces sad, but they kept June secure with their ten, twenty, and fifty-dollar coupons. June spent some at the grocery store; the rest she saved in a jar hidden under the sink in the kitchen. Reverend Pride came by and said she should believe, but she shook her head. "You are doomed," he said and went on his way.

Chapter 3

A few months after the Great Flood a virus struck the people in the town. It spread across the country and raced up the East Coast. It was nothing like the Coronavirus Pandemic that had sickened the country in 2020, killing so many and causing such economic devastation: sheltering at home, face masks, social distancing, anything to stop the dying. No, this was chills and fevers that sent the townsfolk to their beds, and the glands in their necks became so swollen they could hardly move their heads without terrible pain. Men groaned and thrashed under their sheets as their private parts swelled. The town herbalist was mystified and turned to her oldest books of remedies. She even glanced at an obsolete list of vaccines: measles, mumps, chicken pox and COVID, but then she fell sick with the rest of them. Those are so old fashion, anyway, she thought as she took to her bed. After a few weeks, the fevers broke, and the swellings subsided, and everyone was glad to be up and out again.

"Aren't we lucky," they told each other, "nothing like 1918 or 2020. Just a little infection and now we are all well."

And life went on. Grass and gorse bushes grew along the edge of the mud plain, which was now a sea of dead earth. Every morning the sun rose and burned its way across the sky to set like fire at dusk. People talked about rain, but no rain fell, just a weak mist that occasionally hung over the countryside. It was hard to find vegetables in the markets and farm stands; prices rose to meet demand. To calm the townsfolk, the Mayor had a memorial built to The Lost, but soon it was covered with wild grape vines. Nobody cared. Then he and his wife held reading and arithmetic classes; he thought that would calm the townsfolk. Nobody came. They were becoming fearful of a world they didn't recognize.

One day June realized nobody was buying her soft baby sweaters and blankets anymore. The tiny pink and blue and yellow baby clothes were left untouched on their shelves, and then word went out that the virus, the chills and fevers and swollen glands had rendered the men sterile. At first, the furious men pounded their fists and shouted obscenities when told this had happened to them, but they finally gave up. They told each other no big deal and it was fun to have sex, anyway.

"So, what," they said, and they would shrug. Then it was whispered that in towns across the country, men had started stalking girls and trapping them, forcing themselves on them for sport.

"Why not," they said. "No consequences now, and it's our right."

Soon, no girl would go outside at night without a chaperone. June was shocked. Actually, she had to admit, she had already *almost* had sex because she had a boyfriend: a dairy farmer's son named Bobby. He had a slow smile June liked, and they would go up into the hayloft in the barn. They never undressed, that would be embarrassing, but he'd lie on top of her and move back and forth while the hay poked her in the bottom and she thought it felt fine.

However, June was glad she lived in an apartment above the shop because she certainly didn't want to be grabbed by some stranger while walking home at night. Before the sun went down, she would make sure the doors were locked tight and the windows closed and locked as well.

The little town where she lived was becoming a dangerous place and, sadly, there were no police officers to watch over it. The town tariffs only covered salaries for the Mayor and the Preacher and nothing more.

"No money," the Mayor had said years before, "and we really have no crime," so the police station was boarded up.

Now and again the National Police Force would arrive; but the townsfolk would scatter, hiding behind drawn curtains.

NPF agents drove black, solar-powered government vehicles that purred like kittens and had blacked out windows. They would creep silently up and down the side streets, watching and hoping to find a Non-Citizen to take away. There were rumors, but they were shared in whispers; nobody said a word out loud. "The *mines*," they whispered.

Sometimes NPF stopped for lunch in town at *The British Tea Shoppe* – big men in immaculate black uniforms and polished boots, their utility belts heavy with side arms and handcuffs. They had hard faces and cold eyes and never stopped scanning the streets and shops, looking for People Who Didn't Belong.

One of the two waitresses in the tea shop whispered that the men never talked and never even said Thank You. They would just shovel their food into their mouths, wipe their lips and drop their soiled napkins on the floor. Then they would get up and walk out.

"Shameful," she told a customer and shook her head in disgust. But two weeks later she was gone, disappeared without a trace, and nobody would say a thing. They were afraid.

June's mother had told her that years before when she was a little girl, there was no NPF, just a police force in every town and city and they were not cold or cruel. There were federal agents, too, who would apprehend undocumented immigrants, people from over the border who had committed crimes. They would pick them up and send them home, back to their countries. The agents had families of their own, she told June. They were just doing their job. They were called ICE. June thought that sounded cold, like the eyes of the NPF.

"But, things changed," her mother whispered and looked at her lap. "I remember. Little by little things changed, and soon everyone became angry and bitter. I married your Papa then because I was afraid. But pretty soon the Civil War came, and your Papa was gone."

June sat very still and listened, but she was frightened.

"After the war, we were ordered to carry Federal Identification Papers like wc have today," her mother whispered. "And then *they* came … the National Police Force," she paused a minute. "And the mines. The coal mines, they always need workers for the coal mines. They are so deep and dangerous now, but we need the coal." She glanced at June and changed the subject.

June thought about the cold eyes and cruel faces. It was hard to believe. What happened, she wondered, what are the mines? She frowned and there were no smiles that day.

She knew what documentation meant because she had it, but she didn't know what a *mine* was.

"What's a mine," she asked.

But her mother would say no more. She raised her finger to her lips, "Shhhhh!"

All Legal Citizens had a Federal Identification Form and June kept hers handy, just in case. It was an official document and held her full name and address, her family tree and, in the lower left-hand corner, her official photograph, which was now slightly out of date. Her hair was still long and light blond, but her heart-shaped face was a few years older now. Her chin was still soft, and her nose still tip-tilted, her lips full, but the young, cheerful expression on the photograph was gone.

Fortunately, all her ancestors were American Citizens, and a distinctive federal ID number had been stamped next to her name. So far NPF hadn't stopped her, but she tried to stay out of their way; she didn't like them. Once she had seen an NPF vehicle pull up next to a Wealthy Lady from across the River. The Agent stepped out and stopped her in the street, his hand grasping her arm.

The Lady drew herself up with her head held high and spoke sharp words, wrenching her arm free. June couldn't hear what she said, but the agent climbed back into his vehicle and kept on moving. June thought about what she had seen. I guess if you're wealthy NPF can't demand your Fed ID, she decided, and she remembered it.

Chapter 4

When June was growing up, Regular People didn't own televisions or radios, and they hadn't for many decades. They didn't even own cars. Many of them couldn't read so they didn't care about newspapers, and e-Cars were expensive.

The Post-War Government had seized all the newspapers and TV and radio stations and shut them down.

"Social Media is dangerous," they said and confiscated everyone's computers and phones, but nobody really cared because they were tired of war and, in fact, tired of upgrading their computer and phone systems all the time and it cost too much, anyway. Before long, the idea spread across the country and in every region, people turned in their computers and phones. "Enough," they said with an accent slow as honey in the Southern Region. "Yeah, enough with all the talk," they repeated with their broad accent in the Northern Region, and then it spread west until the cell towers were torn down and the World Wide Web turned dark across the country.

"Technology will ruin America," they all said, "it caused those school shootings," and that was the end of that!

The Regular People agreed it wasn't worth worrying about. TVs and radios used too much electricity. However, the Wealthy Ladies from across The River owned radios. They would chat while they shopped and June listened to their gossip. She learned that years before, something called Congress had all given up on the country; some called it very good and congratulated themselves for succeeding. Others had shouted and shaken their fists and called the others names. But they all agreed that Climate Change was real, and would be the ruin of them all. It was a mess!

Five years later, the American Civil War of 2045 had started – the war that had changed everything, and when it ended, all weapons were confiscated and destroyed. "Guns are dangerous," the government said. "Because of guns we had a war, so you must turn them in or go to jail." Across a newly divided country, the men ranted and raved about their Second Amendment Rights, so the government allowed them to carry knives, big sharp blades they kept in leather holsters on their belts.

However, the government was still a mess and Congress just lolled about the Capitol together, drinking scotch and Irish whiskey till the small hours and sleeping till noon.

The Wealthy Ladies would say "tut tut" and shake their heads.

"Bad," they said and rolled their eyes at June, "very bad. And not even an election now".

June knew the last election had been held before she was born, so she had never seen one, only read about it in an old American history book she found, hidden deep in her mother's closet. She spent hours poring over the old history and was amazed. It was like a make-believe world, a place that never existed. Maybe this is what Miss Lee means by "Before," June thought. She reflected on what she read and wondered why her mother had hidden the book away. By the time she got around to asking, her mother was gone.

A year after the Great Flood, life seemed to have returned to a new normal. People shopped, girls stayed home at night, and the National Police Force rolled through town. June began to think about making a little garden behind the shop. There were some fresh vegetables in the fruit stand on Main Street, but they were expensive. In March, she bought packets of carrot and cabbage seeds, turnip seeds and tomato seeds. She imagined red, ripe tomatoes and round cabbages out back in her own garden. She bought a gardening hoe at the hardware store and dug up the soil and readied it for planting. As soon as it was warm enough, she planted the seeds. Bobby came by and brought a cloth bag of dried cow dung for fertilizer.

"This is from my Ladies," he said. He called the cows his "Ladies."

"It's cow poop, and it smells," June said and wrinkled her nose.

Bobby smiled his slow smile. "But it makes the garden grow, and it's good for the environment. Plastic is bad." He untied the cloth bag, spread the cow dung along the rows and built a sturdy, wooden frame for the tomatoes. Then he took a break.

"I don't use plastic bags," Bobby said and stuffed the cloth bag in his back pocket. "I'll wash this when I get home."

June wrinkled her nose again. She didn't understand what he was talking about, but she brought two glasses of ice tea outside, and they worked on the garden together. She thought she might love him.

All summer June had fresh vegetables. The carrot tops looked like green feathers, and the tomato vines grew up around the wooden frame, the ripe tomatoes hanging like bright red ornaments. Soon there were enough carrots and tomatoes to share, and she carried a basketful to *The British Tea Shoppe.*

The basement under June's building was built of old stone, and it was cold in the winter. It was a scary, dark place with a dirt floor and cobwebs hanging from the ceiling, but she cleared out one corner and stored the turnips and cabbages there, wrapped in burlap.

That winter it turned bitter cold – colder than it had ever been in North Carolina, in fact, colder than it had ever been anywhere. Thick ice covered the River and the air was so dry a breath could turn to tiny ice crystals so sharp they could cut the inside of your nose. The townspeople gazed out of their windows and wondered when they would see snow; but day after day the sun would rise and hang in the sky, shrouded in an icy, gray mist. The trees and brush froze solid and looked like ice sculptures. June brought her root vegetables upstairs and stored them under the sink.

Only the Wealthy Ladies could afford enough electricity for heat, so the Regular People burned lumps of coal in small, open heaters. They bought the coal in the hardware store and brought it home in plastic bags, sneezing from the black dust. Their homes were filled with the ugly soot that hung in the air and covered their furniture. They hated the filth but prayed there would be enough fuel to last through winter. If not, they decided, they would have to break up some of their wooden furniture to burn.

It was too cold for the men to leave their warm home fires at night, so town girls felt free to visit friends after dark. They bundled up with layers of warm sweaters, and June's little shop was buzzing; she would knit late into the night to keep up. Now and again the black NPF vehicles would blow through town, their solar-powered engines wheezing in the frosty air, but they never stopped. People were cold, but they were also relieved.

Finally, spring arrived, and the ice in the river melted, flooding roads and fields with murky, dank-smelling water. The sun continued to hang in her misty veil but in early April little leaves appeared on the trees and in the gorse bushes. June was eager to plant her vegetable garden, and as soon as it was warm enough, she dressed in a loose dress and big hat, gathered her hoe and seeds and headed outside. The grass was still brown, and the earth she had carefully prepared in the fall was dry. It crunched and crumbled under her sandals. Puzzled, June squatted down and picked up a clump of dirt, but it turned to dust in her hand. She stuck her finger in the ground and pushed until finally she felt firm, healthy soil.

June sat back and thought about it and then she said, "huh," and planted her seeds by using her finger, crouching in the garden, pushing and planting, pushing and planting. By the end of the day, she had a garden. Her legs were cramped, and her back was sore, but she was proud of herself. Good job, she thought, and stood up, stretching her aching muscles.

A week later, tiny green shoots appeared and started to push through the dry soil, and she was happy. She would have her own fresh vegetables all summer, after all.

The sun emerged from her milky veil the second week of May and shone ruthlessly day after day. The new leaves on the trees wilted and turned brown, and June hauled pails of water morning and evening to keep her garden alive. But one day she saw it was too late. All the green shoots were dead. June put her hoe away and sat on the side of her bed and wept.

The next day Bobby came by and said they had lost all their crops, and he was worried about the dairy cattle.

"We may have to butcher all my Ladies," he said and his eyes filled with tears; June held him and let him cry, but she was confused. "What's happening," she whispered.

A heavy sepia cloud settled over the countryside, and the town became stifling. The sun was a copper coin that blinded people if they attempted to go outside during the day without dark sunglasses. The shop owners decided to open late in the day and close at midnight. Women began to wear light, cool dresses and they carried fans. Some carried umbrellas. Men stripped down to undershirts and light linen shorts. It was too hot to stalk girls, and by now they really didn't care.

"And it's still spring," they complained.

June put her knitting needles away. "No need for sweaters now," she said to herself.

On a whim, she took down the white gauzy curtains from the dining room and made herself two cool dresses, decorating the low necklines and short sleeves with colorful needlework: tiny stitches that her mother had taught her. The Wealthy Ladies from across the River admired the dresses, so they brought her material and paid her to make dresses for them. It was too hot to walk outside, and the sidewalks were beginning to melt, so June didn't mind sitting in her shadowy shop stitching dresses for the Wealthy Ladies. More dollar coupons for her savings, she thought, as sweat ran down her back and under her arms.

By the end of May there were no more fresh vegetables anywhere: none in the grocery store or on any of the farms. The sun had killed the gardens, and nothing had survived. There was no corn for the dairy cattle, and they were starving, too.

Soon their milk dried up. The farmers just shot them and sold the meat.

Down by the river, the magnolia petals turned brown and fell to the ground. Their sweet smell faded in the hot, still air. People made pitchers of weak ice tea to drink instead of milk. June bought canned vegetables, dried beans, and rice, and had a few cabbages and turnips left in the basement.

Bobby told her he was moving north, and they climbed into the hayloft one more time, but it was so hot they gave up. Before he left town, he gave her a container of milk as a good-bye gift, and she hugged him and pressed her face against his chest. Milk was something June had not tasted in months, and it was a thoughtful gift, but she was sad. "I guess you have to go if you think it's right," she said, but again she wondered what was happening.

Chapter 5

Over the next week, more and more people left town. The Wealthy Ladies from across the River disappeared, so June had no way of knowing what was happening. She knew it was burning hot and there were fewer cans and packages in the grocery store. The shelves were almost bare. Little by little the stores were shuttered up, doors locked and closed signs in the windows.

The sun was killing everything.

To make matters worse, there was only a trickle of water from the taps now, and it was murky and smelled terrible. Word went out from the Mayor that fresh water would be trucked in and finally a huge, silver tanker truck arrived in town. On each side of the silver tank was a green silhouette of a mountain and the words *Green Mountain Water*. June found a glass container in a kitchen cabinet and joined the rest of the townsfolk, filling it with fresh drinking water.

The driver was a friendly man. He was short and stout and had white hair and kind blue eyes. A pair of eyeglasses perched on the tip of his nose and June found that curious. He climbed down from the cab and opened the spigot so people could fill their containers. Sometimes he would laugh and talk to the townsfolk, but his words were hard to understand. June thought about the strange place called The Green Mountains. She wanted to ask the driver, but she was shy and wasn't sure she could grasp what he was saying, anyway.

At night June opened the windows and took her clothes off, trying to cool down while she slept. As she lay in her bed, she could see the moon through her bedroom window. Over the month, it grew from a tiny crescent to a full, silver globe, but it was faint and dull in the night sky. June sat on her bed in the dark and thought about leaving town, following her boyfriend north.

Maybe she could find the place called the Green Mountains. She wondered what it was like up there. June had grown up fearing the idea of The North. Her mother would never speak of it, and June knew her father had died somewhere up there. It had never entered her mind to actually go *Up There*. Up There, she'd think. What would happen if I went Up There? Would somebody kill me, too? Had they killed Bobby? But as the days went by, one day hotter than the next, June realized if she stayed where she was she would die of starvation, and finally one morning she decided to leave.

June was scared, but she knew she was competent. After all, she told herself raising her chin firmly, she *had* pulled herself together when her mother disappeared in the Great Flood. She had learned how to run the shop and how to budget the dollar coupons she earned.

I figured out how to make a garden and what seeds to buy, she thought, so now I have to figure out how to leave home and travel up to the North.

June remembered there was a map titled *The United States of America* in the old history book her mother had hidden in her closet. It was wedged in a brown envelope pasted to the back cover. She also knew from reading the history book that decades ago North Carolina had been part of a large country called America with many states, and that the North was also part of that country.

June pulled the old history book out and carefully spread the map on the floor. She could see North Carolina but couldn't see the name of her little town. It wasn't near the big water identified as *The Atlantic Ocean* and it wasn't in the mountains, either; so, she figured it had to be somewhere in the middle of the state.

She ran her finger up the map. Above North Carolina was a place called Virginia and maybe there would be food and water there. June found a pen and made a mark on Charlottesville. She liked the sound of Charlottesville. When she was a child, she had known a girl named Charlotte. Maybe she could live in Charlottesville.

June's eyes moved north. She could see Washington, D.C., but she crossed it out. I don't want to go there, she decided, but I can go around it if I must. She stopped for a minute and wondered if that was where the Wealthy Ladies had gone.

"Hmmm," June said out loud. "I wonder if Miss Archibald and the other ladies went to Washington, D.C., after all?" Then she closed the book, but she left the map on the floor.

June pulled out her knitting needles and some pink yarn and knit a money pouch to hide under her dress. She left an opening to slide in her saved dollar coupons and added a button to keep them secure. Nobody can steal them, she thought and stuffed the rest in her purse. June knew there were enough coupons to live on, but then she wondered if the people Up There would accept them. North Caroline printed and issued the vouchers, but it was her money, after all. If she had to, she'd knit scarves and mittens to barter, but she thought it would be very unfair.

She packed her clothes and her hairbrush in a backpack and then stuffed the old history book inside. While she traveled, she would read it from cover to cover to learn all she could about Up North. She filled a carry bag with packets of yarn until it bulged and then slid her knitting needles inside the wool.

When June was done, she stood up and looked around, took a deep breath and then walked from room to room looking one last time at the home she loved and where she had always lived.

She stood at the kitchen door and gazed at the pans arranged on hooks on the wall, just the way her mother had organized them, the cheerful wallpaper and the curtains with the blue, Dutch design.

She longed to sit at the little kitchen table drawn up by the back wall, the table where June and her mother ate their meals, its fresh white cloth draped just so, the blue glass salt and pepper shakers centered the way her mother had always placed them, but she kept on.

She walked through the dining room and ran her hand along the mahogany dining room table, its dark glossy finish silky under her fingers. This was her mother's pride and joy and was only used for Christmas, set with the best dishes and silverware and the crystal glasses, all kept in the matching mahogany china cabinet with the glass doors.

Finally, June walked through the living room with its soft couch and bright pillows, the side table with the brass lamp and ebony statue of David. She stood for a moment and looked out the front windows at Main Street: its tall trees – proud trees that were dying in the relentless heat.

June dreaded going upstairs to her bedroom. She was afraid she would give up, crawl into bed and forget what she had to do, but she climbed the stairs and stepped inside, looked around and quickly slipped a picture of her mother into her backpack.

And then, with a lump in her throat, June peeked inside her mother's room. It was neat as a pin, cleaned and dusted but otherwise untouched since her mother had disappeared in the Great Flood. She stood for a moment and then turned away. "Goodbye, Mama," she said and headed down the stairs in tears. When June was done, she found a pencil and made a small sign for the shop window. She attached it with some tape she had found in one of the kitchen drawers among the rolls of string and ribbons.

June knew she had to leave to catch the bus but stood and looked at it for a minute. She felt as if her heart was breaking. The sign said CLOSED and it seemed to her that *closed* was just how *she* felt.

Chapter 6

On the Road

June locked the shop door and headed across Main Street to the bus stop, the same trip her mother had made two years before. She felt sick with fear and almost threw up behind the little structure. She didn't want to look back, but when the old electric bus hissed to a stop, she finally turned and looked at her home once more before she climbed inside.

It was dim, and June blinked until her eyes adjusted. She had never been on a bus before, had never even left her little town, but she gave the driver the dollar coupons he wanted and found a window seat. I wonder if this is where Mama sat, June thought and felt her eyes fill with tears. She watched out the window as the bus headed down Main Street and her stomach hurt.

There was *The British Tea Shoppe* with its foxhunt print, the hardware store and grocery store, the faded white church. And yes, the boarded-up police station covered in twiggy undergrowth. She was afraid it would be the last time she would see the little town she loved and had called home all her life: a town that was dying.

The bus crossed the bridge and passed the houses where the Wealthy Ladies lived: beautiful Southern mansions, with wide verandas and tall columns, stately homes on a lovely tree-lined street. Spacious lawns swept down to the River Road and tall trees spread their branches overhead, but the trees were dropping dry leaves that blew across the neighborhood in the hot breezes. The grass was turning brown and the river was just a stream, dwindling down more and more each day.

June had never ventured over the bridge. She had stood on her side of the river and looked, but she had never crossed to the other side. She gazed out the window as they passed, curious but filled with dread.

They look dead, she thought. The windows are dirty, and they look blank, like the blind man who used to come to the shops with his dog. The Wealthy Ladies have left their homes, and they're letting them die! It was almost unbelievable, and June looked away.

The burning sun was setting as the bus turned onto the main road and it painted everything with an angry red glow, making the town look like it was on fire. June leaned her head against the glass and closed her eyes. I'll never call anyone by their name again, she decided. If I know someone's name, if I call them by their name, then I will lose them, and with this odd thought, she drifted off.

Someone said something behind her and June realized she had been sleeping. Two people were quarreling about having sex, and she thought she was dreaming. She looked out the window, but it was dark, and all she could see was her reflection staring back. The same blond hair and a familiar face, but it seemed like a stranger: frightened and lost. The bus was swaying gently as it headed north and the lights inside had been dimmed further. It was quiet behind her, and she wondered how the quarrel had ended but didn't really want to know. Some passengers were moving around nervously, and she heard someone weeping, but nobody talked to anyone else. Finally, she leaned her head against the cool glass again and closed her eyes, drifting away to the sound of the purring bus engine, falling into deep pools of exhaustion.

June woke with the sun, and for a minute she didn't know where she was; then she sat up, frightened.

"We are now approaching the Virginia border," the driver announced, "but NPF agents have stopped us."

June could hear people murmuring around her and looked out the window. A black government vehicle had pulled in front of the bus, and two agents were standing on either side of the bus door, faces hard and hands on their weapons. Passengers fumbled around in their bags, their pale faces white with dread.

A woman crouched in her seat and covered her face with her hands, but the others ignored her and started getting out of their seats.

"Help me!" the woman begged. Can somebody, please help me out!"

"I don't know what to do," June said, "I don't know what to do."

"You can do nothing," the woman whispered, and pushed herself to her feet. "Just remember me!"

June slipped her Fed ID out of the history book and shoved her backpack under the seat in front of her. A few of the passengers were already heading timidly down the aisle and June joined them, still worried about the crouching woman. She hopped down and stood with the others in a shifting, nervous group. She remembered the Wealthy Lady at home and how she had acted with NPF, so when it was her turn, June straightened her back and lifted her chin. The agent stepped in front of her and looked her up and down, his mouth twisted in a smirk. He had short red hair in tight curls and cold blue eyes, and he wasn't impressed.

"ID papers," he said and held his hand out, palm up.

June passed him her ID and stared back at him as he scanned the page. He studied her face, then handed it back and turned his back on her, bearing down on the Quarreling Couple who were clinging together by the side of the road. June climbed back on the bus and found her seat; she tucked her ID back in her backpack and looked out the window. "Rude," she said.

As the bus finally moved away, she saw the NPF agents pushing and shoving three frightened people into the back of their vehicle, and the crouching woman was one of them. The sight horrified June and then angered her. How dare they, she thought and stared out of the window, her face frozen with shock.

As the bus crossed into Virginia, some of the passengers clapped and cheered, but June noticed the sunburnt landscape and brown grass. She realized there would be no new home in Charlottesville. Mile after mile of leafless trees and scorched land rolled past the window, and the burning sun rose in a cloudless sky.

During the morning, the bus turned towards the west to avoid Washington, D. C., and the driver told them they would be passing through a place called West Virginia.

"Where you get your coal," he said. "Not much left," he added.

At noon, he turned east onto a secondary road and stopped at a small country store for refreshment and electricity for the bus. June waited in her seat until the others climbed down, yawning and stretching, then she followed, squinting in the bright sun. The little store clung to the side of the road in the hot, still air. A sign affirming, '*North Carolina Dollar Coupons are Accepted*' was leaning against the window. There were a few bushes and scraggly brush and a field of dried corn stalks. Four clay flowerpots lined the path to the store, but they were empty except for a discarded cigarette package. The wooden steps were split, and the old porch swayed dangerously.

The others were clamoring for food and June crept carefully across the crumbling porch and joined them inside. Sliced loaves of dark bread and a giant wheel of hard cheese were arranged on a wooden shelf along with a few oatmeal cookies, crumbling in their packs; cases upon cases of cola were stacked up by the door, but that was all.

June managed to buy a slice of bread, one package of cookies and a cola before everything was gone and she slipped behind the store to eat. The Quarreling Couple was hidden in the few bushes out back, and June watched as the dried leaves shook and shuddered. Pretty soon they crawled out and brushed dirt and dried grass off their clothing. June wondered if this would take care of their harsh words in the night, but she looked away.

There was no public bathroom in the store, so everyone headed into the trees to relieve themselves. June dusted crumbs off her lap and crawled into the bushes where the Couple had been thrashing around. It was full of brambles and dried leaves, and the grass had been crushed flat, but it was private, and June squatted down and lifted her dress. You do what you have to do, she told herself as the others tramped by on their way back to the bus with their empty soda bottles.

The secondary road they were now traveling was crumbling, and grass was growing in gaping holes. The bus bumped and lurched, groaning and shaking as they headed out. The driver said they'd be on a major highway soon and manhandled his way east.

Every now and then he would pull over and stop so one or another of the carsick passengers could walk around or throw up in the dried grass. There were no other buses on the road, but June saw people with backpacks or carts drifting along the burning pavement.

She spotted a water tanker truck in the distance, and the people hurried to the side of the road and knelt down, tapping their cups and containers on the broken asphalt until the truck lurched over and stopped. The bus pulled in behind, and everyone climbed down with their empty soda bottles.

"Who are those people," June asked the bus driver. He glanced up at her with weary disinterest. "Travelers," he said. "Just Travelers."

June thought about the walking people, the Travelers, tapping their cups on the road. We may die of thirst, she thought. We might all just die of thirst, but she joined the others in the line with her empty soda bottle.

By nightfall, the bus driver stopped and handed out bread and hard cheese that he'd purchased at the little store. "We will be heading north now," he said.

June pinched off tiny pieces of her cheese and tried to make it last. The bread she stored in her backpack and then she leaned her head against the window. North, June thought. All she could see was a dim, treeless landscape and a faded moon. She thought about her mother and how they knit and talked in the evening, surrounded by the soft colors of the yarn. Every night there would be a good meal and a glass of fresh milk. Yet, here she was, on a bus heading Up There to the North, eating a piece of hard cheese and drinking water from a used soda bottle. "Why," she whispered. "What is happening to us?" Her last thought before she drifted off was – Who did this?

Chapter 7

June was jolted awake, and it was still early. The bus was hissing and shaking, as the driver pulled over to the side of the road. It lurched once again and then sank into silence.

"I'm sorry," the bus driver shouted. "The bus has died. Y'all have to get off and find another way." He cleared his throat nervously, "Just so you know, during the night we crossed West Virginia and into Pennsylvania, the Northern Region. You may find some relief here. There are other Travelers on the road" he added, "you won't be alone."

June yawned and looked out the window.

"Travelers," she said softly, "just Travelers." The sun was rising, and there was soft mist covering the ground. She was in the North now, and it scared her, but she wanted to walk around and drink in the moisture. The other passengers were shuffling down the aisle, complaining and frightened, nudging each other and hauling their luggage. June made a face and slung her backpack over her shoulder, pulled her carry bag down from the overhead space above her seat and joined them. The bus hissed and started to shake, and everyone pushed and shoved to get down, whimpering with fear and relieved when they all landed on the pavement.

"Maybe the bus is going to explode," a woman cried out and threw her skirt over her face.

Oh, for heaven's sake, June thought.

Everyone moved away and stood nervously by the road, looking around. It was an aging highway, broken and ruined, but bushes lined the sides and June could see some green among the twigs. Nobody knew where to go and little by little they wandered away.

June stood there thinking. In the distance, she could see hills, gray-green in the morning light, and that was where she headed:

one foot after another. People were drifting along the highway, Travelers pulling wagons filled with belongings, but she hardly noticed; she was too busy watching the broken asphalt and holes in front of her. For hours, she kept her pace without stopping, occasionally glancing at the hills in the distance. Green Hills, she thought. You keep moving away.

A child was sobbing, and June became aware of her fellow travelers. A woman passed her with the tearful child. Her belongings were wrapped in a sheet and balanced on her head. The little one was pulling and fussing, and the mother started to sing softly. June stopped and looked at the hills, but they looked as far away as they'd been two hours before and she sighed. I'm a Traveler now, she thought. Just another Traveler.

A man pushed himself past her on a flat wooden cart with wheels. His legs were shriveled and bent, but his arms and chest bulged with muscles. He wore a black cap with two stars and the words Civil War embroidered in gold and white. His skin shone with sweat as he pushed himself by and after a while, he was almost lost in the distance.

June sat down on some grass by the side of the road and rested as two men strolled by. They were covered with dirt and grime from their travels, but they were holding hands, their heads close, talking to each other in soft, loving voices. June was puzzled but she thought it was nice they were happy. They have each other, she thought.

Finally, she pulled herself together and headed onward towards the gray-green hills.

Now and again, a water truck trundled by, and June was able to fill her soda bottle. By noon the asphalt started to burn through her sandals, her light dress was drenched and moisture slid down her back. Even in Pennsylvania, the midday sun burned like fire.

"It's time to get out of the heat," someone shouted.

The Travelers started heading into the forest along the side of the road and June followed them, finding a spot under a tree. She sat down and gazed up at the branches above her head, glad to be out of the sun. There were a few green leaves, and a small bird twittered its way into the sky. She dug the piece of hard bread out of her backpack and, sitting cross-legged under the tree, June ate the stale bread and began to feel hopeful for the first time. When she was done, she curled up on her side, resting her face on her hands. Far away she heard the sound of running water, but she knew she was dreaming and there were many long days to come. I'll stay right here, she thought and settled down.

The next morning June set out as the sun rose and she felt refreshed. People glanced at her as she climbed up the bank and shook the twigs and dried leaves off her dress. But they said nothing and kept on walking: men, women, and children carrying what they could on their backs or piled in small wagons. Now and then something would drop off one of the carts as they walked along and they would come back to retrieve it. June wondered why. Why are the wagons so small?

A water truck heading south pulled up by the side of the road, and June joined the line. When her turn came, she recognized the driver: the man with the mane of white hair and kind blue eyes, and yes, the glasses!

"How far are you going?" June asked him. "How far south?"

"Just as far as Virginia," he said. "There is nobody left farther south. Everything is burned up, and the ocean tides are coming in." His eyes were filled with sorrow. "I remember you, young lady," he said and shook his head. "It's all gone now. Soon it will all be under the sea."

June was shocked. Her home? The dining room with its mahogany table, the bright kitchen and cozy bedrooms? *The Knitting Shop* and *The British Tea Shoppe* with its fox hunt print, all gone? She could almost see the river with its sloping green banks, the tall trees and the weeping willows with their graceful branches sweeping towards the water. She felt her lower lip tremble and her eyes burn with tears, but she thanked the driver and joined the Travelers heading north. June felt faint with disappointment because now she knew she'd never see her home again, but she sniffed and straightened her shoulders.

Maybe when she reached the hills, she could find a place to live, food to eat and water to drink. She remembered a line from the Bible her mother taught her and sang as she walked:

"I will lift up mine eyes unto the hills, from whence cometh my help."

She sang it softly to herself, and it made her feel much better and not so alone.

It was late the next day when June heard the high, shrill whistle for the first time. It was faint and far behind them, then closer and then repeated – again and again until it reached her. The people around June scattered and hurried into the woods, the men hoisting the small wagons onto their shoulders, stumbling through the trees, twigs cracking and snapping as they ran.

"What's happening?" June shouted.

"NPF," someone called out, and June froze, the memory of the crouching woman still fresh. She joined the others and tumbled down the bank into some underbrush, curled into a tight ball and pushed herself as far as she could into the bank. For a few minutes, there was nothing, just a bird rustling around in the underbrush, then the sound of a vehicle purring along the road above her head and June recognized NPF. She heard them slow down and stop, the doors hiss open, and then the agents were standing on the bank, almost on top of her, so close she could see how the dust rose up and dirtied their shiny, black boots. They talked in low voices for a few minutes and June pressed her face into the bank. The bird flew up and they stopped talking, and June held her breath, afraid she would sneeze. Then they turned away and walked up the road, and she heard nothing more. She lay there, terrified, and then she fell asleep with her face in the dust.

Chapter 8

One sweltering day turned into another, but by now June was used to the pace: walking during the morning hours and sleeping during the heat of the day then heading out again after dark. Occasionally she would see a small store by the highway and stop for bread and cheese. Thankfully they would accept her dollar coupons. Once she was able to buy an apple, and she sat on an old wooden fence by the side of the road holding it for a long time before she bit into it, tasting the fresh fruit for the first time in two years.

If a water truck stopped, she lined up with the others to fill her soda bottle. She considered herself one of the Travelers now, but no one talked to her. It was a grim pilgrimage they all were on, and June was getting lonely.

Whenever she heard the warning whistle behind her she would hurry into the woods before NPF arrived, but as she traveled further into Pennsylvania, it happened less often, and she was relieved. Every day the gray-green hills were closer, and it kept June going: mile after mile, day after day. "I lift up mine eyes ...," she'd sing, but she longed for companionship.

The sun rose, and the sun set, and it seemed to June that weeks and months had passed, but there was always something new on the road. One day she saw an old man with long white hair and a tangled white beard wrapped in an American flag. She glanced back at him as she walked by and saw he was weeping as he stumbled along. She thought about the old man as she continued on and wondered where he was from and why his face was covered with tears. Finally, she decided to go back and help him, but he was gone. She asked the other Travelers but they just shook their heads and looked away, and that made June unhappy. She wondered about him as she traveled towards the gray-green hills, and for some reason, she missed him.

The sun didn't burn her now, and it was more comfortable to walk. There were more green leaves, and the grass by the side of the highway was thriving. Sometimes a little breeze lifted the leaves and would cool her face. In the early morning, the soft mist hung over the countryside and June would open her mouth and try to drink it in. She didn't know how many days had passed since the bus had broken down, but she knew she was getting close to the hills. June's heart lifted as she kept walking. So many people, she thought. So many interesting people.

A large wagon trundled by. It was red with gold trim and pulled by two scrawny brown mules with feathered headpieces. A thin, pale man was perched on the seat driving the poor beasts. The wagon's red paint was faded, and the gold was peeling off in long strips. CIRCUS was painted on the side, but the letters were so faint they were hard to read. The wagon was filled with ladies dressed in colorful gowns. They had feathers and baubles in their hair and were laughing and singing. When the wagon passed the men, the ladies would lean over the side and show their breasts or lift their skirts above their lacy underclothes.

"We take dollar coupons," they called and jiggled their naked breasts. "Come out of the heat and play house." Some of the men chased the wagon and soon they all disappeared around a bend in the road.

June thought it was funny. She knew what the ladies were doing was a sin, but the sight cheered her up and made her laugh. She wondered what they would do if NPF came along. Maybe the NPF agents would get in the wagon and play house, too.

Days went by, and the hills were always a little closer. Every day there was something new, something that excited her or made her sad, things she had never seen before.

One afternoon, June saw a young man by the side of the highway. He was juggling red and blue rubber balls, and there was a ferret on a leash, small and sleek, at his feet. Some people were stopping to watch, and they would drop dollar coupons in a hat on the ground. June stopped and then drew closer. The juggler was young and the color of her mother's polished mahogany dining room table. His only clothing was a pair of shorts that hung low on his hips. His body was smooth and muscled and reminded June of her mother's little statue of David. He had short black curls and dark eyes, his nose was broad and his lips full, and he was quite beautiful. June had never seen anyone like him before and wished she could touch him. She moved closer and took out a dollar coupon to put in his hat. He turned and looked at her and flashed white teeth in a broad smile, his eyes smoldering. Then he shook his head "no" and motioned to the woods behind him.

"Follow me," he said, softly, and his voice was mellow as honey.

June backed up and turned away. She heard him laugh behind her and she wondered what would have happened if she had followed him into the woods. For a few minutes, she wished she had, and it made her shiver.

Two young women walked by holding parasols over their heads. They wore long, colorful dresses and had wrapped sashes around their tiny waists. June thought they looked like flowers. They turned back to watch the beautiful juggler and twittered behind their hands, fluffing their long blond hair and smiling with wet, red lips. June wondered if they would go into the woods, but she didn't want to know, so she hurried away.

During the afternoons, when the sun was at its hottest, June would find a place to sleep. There were more leaves on the trees now, and the bushes were full of berries, fat and sweet. Every day she found some shade and then she opened the history book. It was full of text and hard to read, but before she slept, June would cover a few pages. It had pictures, and she learned about the Founding Fathers. They wore funny clothes, but they seemed like smart men, and they made things work. She was reading about war. It was called the Revolutionary War, and it was about The Birth of America. It made her sad.

"Did America die?" she wondered one hot afternoon as she drifted off to sleep. It was something she never really understood.

"Wake up," someone said. The voice was low and gentle.

At first, June thought she was dreaming. A woman was squatting next to her gently poking her arm. Her hair was black and pinned up on top of her head. Her eyes were dark and her voice was soft, her words like music. She was lighter than the beautiful juggler, but June had never seen anyone like her, either. In North Carolina, everyone was pale with blond hair and blue eyes just like her. June blinked, she felt as though she had awakened in some strange upside-down world: where up was down, and down was up.

The woman nudged her. "Come, it's afternoon, and we can go to the stream to bathe."

June hugged her backpack and tried to focus her sleepy eyes on the woman, and yes, she was still there.

"Stream?" The idea of running water made her ache all over, and she could almost feel it flowing over her body.

"Hide your things under the bushes and follow me," the woman said. "The men bathe later, so we need to go right away." She looked down at June and shook her head. "It is not right that you should be alone, a young girl like you."

June sat very still. The woman was a stranger, but oh how June wanted to go to the stream. Finally, she slipped her money pouch into her backpack, shoved everything deep into the bushes and stumbled to her feet.

They hurried through the forest to the top of a hill and there, down below, clear water tumbled over rocks and fell into a small, deep pool. It was just what June had longed for as she trudged mile after mile in the dust: cool water on her body, cleaning off the days and nights of filth, and a waterfall to wash the dry leaves from her hair. She followed the woman down the hill, wide awake and eager. "Thank you, thank you," she whispered.

Grass and rocks surrounded the pool and here and there rays of sun touched the water like sparks.

The woman pulled her dress over her head and dropped it on the ground. Her body was solid and her breasts heavy. June was embarrassed, but the woman didn't seem to care.

"You can wash your hair in the little waterfall." She said and let her own hair fall down over her shoulders: dark, heavy hair that June had never seen before. Then she was gone, her body as sleek as a seal as she swam across the pool.

June took off her dress and underclothes and hung them carefully on a bush. She looked around shyly and then slid down the bank and stuck her toe in the water. It was cold, but it was clear, and she could see leaves covering the bottom of the pool. When it was up to her waist, she took a deep breath and then sank in over her head, feeling the rush of the water as it moved past her. She could hear the thrum of the little waterfall and swam towards it, catching her breath as she came up. Oh yes, she thought and let the waterfall cascade down over her head and body, washing the dust away. Oh, yes!

The woman joined her and nodded at the rocks behind June. "This is where you hide if NPF comes," she said, and her voice was almost as low as a whisper. "Behind the waterfall. Remember that." She touched June's arm and then she laughed. "We always camp near clear water so we can wash away the road we have traveled. Not the memories, just the dust" She wound her wet hair up and pinned it on top of her head. "Shhh! Listen, the men are coming now, so, we have to leave."

June paddled back to the bank and wrapped her dress around her wet body. She ran her fingers through her hair and then followed the woman back through the brush and dropped down by her tree. All around them, the forest was filled with small sounds, and for the first time June was aware of her surroundings.

The woman squatted on the ground, her skirt full around her feet. "We are running from NPF," she said. "My son and daughter and me. We have done nothing wrong, but we are illegal immigrants, so NPF wants us. They have been searching for us for months, so we're running for the Northern Border."

June wondered about the Northern Border. She thought about illegal immigrants. Was it the Southern Border *they'd* come over? Should she go over the Northern Border, too? But she thought it might be rude to ask.

"A few other illegal families are camping here by the stream, just to rest," the woman said, "but we go our own way, and you can join us if you wish. So, it's dangerous to be a young girl alone. No Mama? You have no Mama?"

June shook her head but didn't say a word. She didn't want to think about her mother.

"But," the woman warned and her face was serious, again, "if NPF finds us, they may take you, too. We have food, and we know how to travel. We sleep during the heat of the day and head out in the evening." She leaned forward and looked June over carefully. "You look like a citizen so you can go into the shops for us. We have dollar coupons."

"I am a Citizen," June said, her voice firm. "I have my citizenship papers."

The woman reached out and stroked June's wet hair, and she laughed. "My son will favor you, but you must tell him to stay away if you want to travel with us. He cannot take a pale wife like you. She must be one of us." She touched June's hair, again. "Ah, yes," she said softly and shook her head, again. "I'll come back for you later, and then tell me if you want to join us. No young girl should be traveling alone." Then the stranger disappeared into the trees.

Chapter 9

June put on her other dress and combed out her hair. She hung her wet clothing on the brush and sat and thought about joining the Illegals. Her Fed ID was in her backpack tucked into the history book. She couldn't believe NPF would take her; after all, she was an American Citizen with papers. She considered herself too young to marry, but she was tired of being alone. She thought about the pool and little waterfall and how it felt to sink into the water, to feel it flow past her body. "Water," she said out loud.

By the end of the day, June had decided to travel with the woman and her family. It's evident, she thought, they are smarter than NPF so we won't be caught. She lay down under the tree and dozed until she heard footsteps on the leaves. From now on, I will think of her as the Woman, June decided.

"Come now," the Woman said and paused. "If you want to travel with us."

June picked up her belongings and followed her deep into the forest, stumbling over logs and branches. Her legs ached and her feet were sore, it felt as if they had walked for hours, but she kept following.

The Woman finally stopped. "Here's our camp," she said, and she pushed through the thick underbrush.

Leaves and bushes were cleared away, and tall trees hung low over the Illegals' camp; a wagon, painted dark green and black, sat to one side almost invisible in the underbrush. It looked like a little house on wheels and June stared at it, fascinated. A gray mule grazing nearby lifted his head for a moment. The forest was thick, and the highway was far away. It was a safe place. A young man and a girl were sitting by a small fire eating something with their fingers. The Woman nudged June into the camp, and the others looked up.

The young people were dark, and both were beautiful, with dusky skin, black hair and big, dark eyes like their mother. The girl had long, thick hair and she let it hang over her back and shoulders. She was younger than June but had a ripe, full body and small waist. She looked at June and smiled shyly.

"That's my daughter," the Woman said softly, and she was proud.

The young man was slender with dark good looks. His hair was a curly mass, and he had piercing eyes that looked at June hungrily. He stood up and came over. "Gold," he said and ran a strand of her hair through his fingers, his breath warm on her cheek. "I love gold."

His touch made her shiver.

"This is my son," the Woman said. "Don't forget, you tell him to stay away. Now, go on to the caravan. You can find a corner for your bag."

June headed to the wagon and didn't look back. He's just a boy, she thought. She stood for a minute and gazed at the little house on wheels. "*Caravan*," she said, "this is a caravan." It sat on tall wheels, and the paint was fresh. When she looked closely, she could see gold designs traced lightly across the paint: leaves and curly-ques, hearts, flowers and birds, even a horse. Copper pots and pans hung from a wooden overhang, and when June climbed inside, she looked around charmed. Long red drapes hung over the two windows, and the walls were decorated with the same gold tracings. At the back of the caravan, a bed was made up with a colorful quilt and a mound of bright pillows. A delicate, spicy odor hung in the air. It was faint, but June breathed it in. It was the most magical room she had ever seen.

That night June joined the Illegals, but she never knew their given names. She remembered her promise, had closed her ears and refused to listen.

The family remained in the camp for days and June lost count, but she was happy. She helped gather wood for the fire and learned to peel vegetables with a hunting knife. Now and again, dark-skinned strangers stopped by and talked to the Woman, and they'd look at June with fear. The Woman would shake her head and talk to them in a strange, musical language and then the strangers smiled and nodded their heads.

"Why are the people afraid of me?' June asked.

"You are not one of us," the Woman said. "But you are a friend."

Every afternoon, June went to the stream with the Woman and the Daughter. She would rinse her dress and underclothes in the running water and hang them on the bushes while she paddled in the pool. She'd wash her hair under the waterfall and dry it in the sun. Now and then June glimpsed the Son standing in the trees watching, and she'd hide under the water until he went away. Sometimes, back in the camp, he touched her, just softly, or tried to take her hand. He couldn't keep his hands off her hair and would lift a lock and let it run through his fingers. His dark eyes would glow as if a fire burned inside him, and when he was near her, he moved as if listening to music that only he could hear.

"Gold," he'd say. "Oro."

"Stay away," she told him and she would shiver. But she started to feel a flutter in her belly and an ache in her heart.

"Go away, or I'll tell your mother."

On the highway near the camp, there was a small store where June shopped for groceries every evening. It was neat and well stocked and a fat coffee machine hummed to itself on the counter. June would buy beans and rice, vegetables and fruit and bars of cold-water soap. She would pay with the dollar coupons the Woman gave her and sometimes she used her own. She was happy and relieved that Pennsylvania accepted them.

A young woman owned the store – just a wisp of a girl. She was June's age with curly light brown hair and large violet eyes. She had a pretty smile and June liked her. The girl told June her name was January because that was the month of her birth and she insisted June use it.

"You are my friend," she said. "My best friend." But it made June uneasy.

January would smile and laugh when she saw June. Sometimes June would hear her singing.

"June and January," she'd sing. "January and June."

June looked forward to her trips to the little store, and soon she realized that for the first time in her life she had a friend. There *was* Charlotte, she thought, but we were just babies. This is different. We are grown-up best friends!

January loved to listen to the stories June told as she wove amazing tales of her days on the road and the people she had seen: the old soldier who was weeping, the circus wagon, the ladies who looked like flowers. She told her about the beautiful juggler, her head close to January's, her voice low, and they giggled like children.

"You are my best friend," June said, and January agreed.

A heavy wooden table and four chairs were placed in the middle of the room. June would buy herself a cup of coffee, and the two girls lingered there like two old ladies gossiping, but June never told her about the camp or the caravan with the gold tracings. She said she was a Citizen traveling to the North. January said she was a Citizen, too.

"Many generations have owned this store, and now it's mine," she said proudly. "It's my heritage." Then she looked troubled and shuddered. June wondered why but didn't ask. She knew it would be rude.

Then she found out.

One evening, while June was shopping, she heard the familiar whistle, and it was close. Very close.

"NPF," she said and was filled with dread. There was no time to run, and she was holding a string bag of groceries.

January had been laughing and singing, but she stopped.

"Take your purchases and hide in the broom closet by the counter," she whispered. "And do *not* come out. No matter what you hear."

June clutched the little string bag and squeezed through the closet door, pulling it after her. She crouched on the floor with the mops and brooms just as the NPF vehicle hummed to a stop in front of the store. June tugged on the door again, but it wouldn't close all the way. Then she heard the heavy boots tramping up the steps and across the porch. Frantic, she crawled behind a bucket and, holding her breath, she peered through the crack. The screen door creaked open, and she saw the black uniform, the shiny black boots, and the utility belt.

But why was there was only one agent? June didn't know what to make of it, the NPF always traveled in pairs. Shocked, she saw the tight red curls and cold blue eyes, and she remembered him; he had asked for her papers when NPF stopped the bus in North Carolina, the agent who had sneered at her and turned his back rudely.

"Is anyone else here?" his eyes scanned the store, his face hard and his voice husky.

January shook her head and looked at the floor.

The agent locked the front door behind him and turned over the *Closed* sign. Then he turned back. His eyes were narrowed, and he ran his tongue across his lips. His breath quickened as he strode over to January and grabbed her arms, lifted her up and threw her onto the table. June heard her head hit and froze. She saw him tear her dress and when January cried out, he slapped her hard across the mouth.

"Quiet," he hissed. "You be quiet! You know better! You shut up!"

June couldn't believe it. January was a Citizen; NPF should not be hitting her. It was the *law* – NPF could not *touch* a Citizen, certainly not strike them like that. And then she saw what he was going to do and felt sick.

January never made another sound; she just stared at the ceiling, but June shut her eyes tight and put her hands over her ears to shut out the ugly sounds he was making. Her body felt tight with an unfamiliar emotion. "I hate him," she whispered. "I hate him, I hate him, I hate him!'

When the NPF vehicle finally purred away, June crept out of the closet. January was sitting upright on the edge of the table, crying, both hands tight against her lap. Her dress and underclothes were torn and hanging off. There was blood on her lips, and her arms were covered with faint bruises. June wet some cloth and washed the blood away. She found some pins and pinned January's dress together. Then she made hot coffee and held a cup up to the broken lips. "I'm so sorry," she kept saying. "I'm so sorry."

January grabbed June's hand, her violet eyes as big as pansies. "Don't ever let an NPF agent touch you," she said, her voice firm. "Because then they own you and they keep coming back." She shuddered, "and they do *this!*"

"Come with me," June begged, "You're my best friend."

January shook her head. "I can't leave," she whispered. "This store is my heritage." She pressed her legs together and looked at her lap, and her tears fell down.

June left the groceries behind and fled through the woods. She stopped once and threw up in the bushes, holding her stomach until there was nothing left; then she kept running. The Woman saw her coming, and June fell at her feet, weeping, telling her what she had seen.

That night the Illegals packed up. The Son hitched the gray mule to the caravan, climbed onto the seat and they headed out onto the highway, the women walking together. As they passed the little store, June saw it was closed, no lights in any of the windows – dark like it had never been open and she was filled with shame.

"Oh January," she whispered and looked away. "I'm so sorry, and now I've lost you, too."

Chapter 10

They traveled until dawn lightened the eastern sky and sometime during the night, June climbed into the caravan and fell into a fretful sleep, her head resting on one of the big pillows from the bed. She dreamed of the narrowed eyes and wet lips, and she'd moan and shiver.

In the darkness, the Woman would leave her bed and come and sit by her side. "It's only a dream," she'd say and once she sang a lullaby in her strange, musical language. She woke June when the sun was rising, and June sat up, frightened.

"Eat," the Woman said and handed her a thick piece of black bread smothered with sweet, crushed berries. "Eat! You are safe, and soon you'll forget the bad man."

They had left the highway and were traveling on a back road far away from the little store. June climbed out and sat on the seat beside the Son, the pots and pans ringing softly over her head. She ate the bread and couldn't seem to get enough into her mouth; the berries stained her lips, and she realized how hungry she had been. Now and again the Son would glance over at her. He didn't try to touch her, but his dark eyes asked, "what happened?"

An hour passed and she sat quietly and watched the mule's head bobbing in front of her. Then they turned onto a dirt road, and June knew she had reached the hills. She could hear the sound of rushing water and saw it glinting like silver through the trees.

"I lift my eyes unto the hills..." she sang softly, and the Son looked over and smiled.

After a while, she hopped down and started walking with the Woman, and her heart felt lighter.

"When we camp, it will be near the river," the Woman said. "We can travel on the forest road until the sun is overhead, and then we'll stop."

The Daughter drew close. "Look, look at the forest around us!" She almost sang the words and her steps were as light as a dance.

June fell into step next to her and let her mind drift. When she thought of January, she would make fists with her hands and try to think of something else, but her mind kept coming back to her friend's warning: "Don't let NPF touch you." June looked at the pretty young woman by her side and felt a sudden chill. What would they do to *her?* With a sick feeling in the pit or her stomach, she realized that even with her Fed ID, she was not safe either, and she was angry. How *dare* they, she thought, incensed. I should have hit him with the mop! I should have hit him when his pants were down around his boots, hit him until he was *dead!*

She glared at her feet as she plodded along and was glad she was traveling deep in the woods with the Illegals. The trees overhead shielded them with their green leaves and sun made pools of light here and there. It was quiet except for the occasional strumming of an insect, but they were safe. She walked, eyes on the ground and her mind miles away.

At a turn in the road, they came upon a clearing and June saw a large Victorian house almost as large as the Wealthy Ladies' homes back in North Carolina. It was tall with a handsome peaked roof and an ornate metal veranda that circled the first floor. But the paint had flaked down to the gray boards, and the railings were red with rust and covered with wild vines. Broken flower pots and junk littered the front yard, and an old car balanced on bricks rested forlornly by the side of the house. An overgrown driveway wound down an embankment and stopped at the car.

On the veranda, a hugely fat lady was sitting in a rocking chair, creaking back and forth slowly. Her dress was the size of a tent, and her hair hung down in long, greasy curls like a child's.

"You," she called. "You! Gypsies!" She stopped rocking and leaned forward.

The Son slowed the mule, and his mother spat out a string of vindictive words in her language. The lady on the veranda laughed, her massive body shaking with the effort.

"Come," she said and started rocking again. "I won't hurt you. You can pick vegetables from my garden if you bring some to me. Look!" she flung one massive arm out towards a small garden by the side of the House. "Vegetables and herbs! Take what you want for your travels, just bring some to me!"

"Go," the Woman said and handed June a basket. "You and my daughter, see what you can find." She gave them a shove, and they glanced at each other and set off.

"Hey you!" The lady on the veranda stopped rocking and pointed at June. "Blond girl, come here."

June sidled closer, and now she could see the lady's face was covered in heavy pancake makeup, eyeliner, and red lipstick melting in the heat. She fluttered false eyelashes as she spoke and June was horrified.

"You'd make a fine wife for my son." Her voice softened until she was almost crooning. "Come closer!" Then she nodded her head and June saw a man standing in the shadows staring at her. He was as thin as a stick, with a broad face, deep-set eyes and oddly thick, rubbery lips. His hands hung limply by his side as he moved into the light, but his fingers were busy working at the fabric of his trousers.

"Wife," he said, and a string of drool slipped down his chin.

June dropped the basket and fled back to the caravan, with the Daughter not far behind. They scrambled up the bank and onto the road without looking back. The Son snapped the reins, and the caravan headed down the trail.

"You!" the lady on the veranda started rocking again as June and the Illegals disappeared around a corner. "Come pick vegetables, just leave some for me." Then she laughed, her huge body shaking with the effort.

June and the Daughter hung onto each other as they hiked along, and when they looked at each other they started to laugh.

The road rolled out in front of them, and they traveled through vast fields that spread out on either side. A fence lay broken and discarded, the cattle long gone. Soon after they left the lady's house, the sound of the river faded, and it was hot in the sun, but they kept moving until June lost track of time. She just watched her feet as they plodded along.

The Woman said something in her own language and June glanced up. A stranger was walking towards them, his image almost lost in the sun's glare. June was frightened. She didn't understand what the Woman was saying, and the stranger was walking directly towards them. He was dark and had a long braid hanging over one shoulder. A red scarf was wound around his head, and his bearing was dignified, almost majestic. As he drew close, June saw his almond-shaped eyes and high cheekbones. He's an Indian she thought, just like in my history book: the native people.

"Ola," he said, and the Woman pulled the pins out of her hair, letting it fall over her shoulders. June turned and stared at her. She looks like a young girl, she thought, a beautiful young girl! The Daughter took June's hand and giggled.

"Don't be afraid, he is a friend," the Woman said, and her eyes were shining. "He makes me happy, very happy. He is a Traveler, too. He will show us where we can camp." She looked back at the man and smiled. "And he will stay with us!" she whispered.

The Man touched the Woman's face with his fingers and then swung up onto the seat beside the Son.

"Who?" he asked and nodded at June. He wasn't scared of her, just curious. "Pretty," he said, and the Son scowled.

The Woman stopped smiling and spit out another stream of words and her voice was angry. Then she added in English, "She is a Traveler, but she is not one of us. She is not to be touched." She turned her face away and marched ahead.

"Okay," the Man laughed softly, but he still glanced at June before he turned his attention to the road. He talked in a low tone and pointed at a turn up ahead as the Son sulked in his seat. The Daughter laughed, and June ignored them.

Heavy brush lined both sides of the road with dense green leaves; June couldn't see the river, but now she could hear it again. At the turn the Man jumped down and pushed a cluster of bushes aside, allowing the caravan to turn onto a trail into the forest. The path led down a hill to the bank of a wide river that tumbled and rushed downstream, and from the top of the hill, June could see the trail on the opposite side as it headed deeper into the trees.

"We can cross here, the Man said in English, "it isn't too deep, and we'll camp further on."

The mule snorted in alarm and braced his feet as they started down the hill, twitching his ears and trembling. The Man held his head and spoke softly, coaxing him forward until mule and caravan were safely on the river bank.

The river bubbled over broken tree branches and stones as it swept along and there were pools in the rocks, water whirling around in small eddies. June thought about the pool they had left behind. Would they really bathe in this wild river with it currents and whirlpools? It looked cold and dangerous.

The frightened mule snorted and balked on the riverbank, his big ears twitching back and forth and his nostrils flaring, but the Man whispered into his ear again and led him into the water, one foot at a time. The current was strong, and the caravan swayed and lurched, pots and pans swinging and clanging overhead. The Son twisted the reins around a post by his seat and jumped down to push from behind.

The Man had to shout over the sound of the river. "It moves fast, so the water is safe to drink," he said in English. "You can come back later to fill containers." He looked at June and raised his eyebrows.

June was embarrassed and at a loss for words but she followed the others into the river, finding her way over the smooth stones. She stumbled once and held her dress up when the water reached her waist. It wasn't as cold as it looked, but it was pushing at her, almost pulling her off her feet and soaking her to the skin. The Son laughed, his dark eyes dancing, and she ignored him. On the other side, she could see the forest: the trees reaching up to the sky, their green leaves like a canopy, beautiful and serene, so she kept on, letting the river have its way.

Once they reached the opposite bank, they dried off and then set off into the trees heading away from the rushing water. The forest was dark, and it was difficult to see through the underbrush that covered the trail, but they pushed on, the mule's hooves beating softly against the dirt. Here and there, ferns grew in abundance. Pretty, June thought, like green lace. Dust motes danced in the sunbeams and shadows moved across the trail. They were deep in the forest now, and she was far away from the man with the red hair. I'm happy, she thought, and it was a strange feeling.

At midday, they broke through the thick bushes and came upon a glade enclosed by trees that were old and grand, their trunks bent and twisted. Sun spilled through the leaves high above, but it was a cool and quiet space surrounded by deep forest.

"Here," the Man said. "Here we are safe and can make camp."

Chapter 11

June loved it. "This is a safe place," she said, and she felt like singing as she looked around. She could hear the sound of the wind sighing in the trees, and it comforted her.

The Man and the Son cut branches with their hunting knives, slicing them into firewood and piling them by the caravan. June helped the Woman and her daughter sweep away the leaves and twigs from the glade, clearing a large space. When they were done, they hiked back to the river and collected rocks and hauled them back in their skirts. The Woman built a small, stone fire pit in the middle of the camp and filled it with some of the wood the men had cut. "Go on back and fetch a cooking pot," she said, and June hurried to the caravan and unhitched one of the pots that had swung over her head for so many miles. The Woman drove metal stakes into the ground and hung the pot over the wood. When she was done, she smiled with satisfaction and motioned to her daughter and June.

"It's the women's time to bathe," she called and then she laughed, her eyes bright as they headed to the river.

Upriver from the wild currents, they found a deep pool in the rocks, dropped their clothes on the bank and slipped in, ducking under the water and washing away the dust and grime from their travel. The Woman and the Daughter splashed each other like children and June floated on her back, dreamily gazing at the sky. She could see how blue it was and realized for the first time in two years that it was beautiful.

"Blue sky," she sang. "Blue, blue sky..."

She found a tiny whirlpool and let it carry her around and around until it was time to go back to the camp.

"Blue, blue sky,"

The men had caught a rabbit, and it was skinned and gutted, cooking on a spit over the fire when they returned. The smell of cooking meat made June shiver. She hadn't tasted meat in months, and she felt her mouth water. She helped peel the last of the potatoes and broke up a cabbage that she'd bought in the little store. June felt sad when she tore the cabbage apart. January, she thought, I'm so sorry. She wondered if she would ever forget what she'd seen.

While the men bathed in the river the big pot bubbled over the fire. The Woman added some of the juice from the meat as it sizzled over the fire, stirring the soup with a big spoon.

It was dusk when the men returned, and they all shared the meal together, eating tiny bits of meat with their fingers and drinking the potato and cabbage soup from brown earthen jars.

Darkness fell, and the fire danced in the shadows. It made June sleepy; the shock of the brutal rape and the memory of the fat lady and her strange son left her limp with exhaustion. She excused herself and curled up under one of the old trees. The sound of the Illegals' musical language as they bantered back and forth lulled her and the leaves made a soft bed. The Daughter came and sat by her side. She sang softly and patted June on the arm. After a while, June found herself relaxing and she began to drift off.

The Man and the Woman stood up and headed to the caravan together, but June was too drowsy to notice. Her eyes closed and she slept. She dreamed of the waterfall and how it felt to stand under the cascading water. June dreamed she was floating in the rock pool, the water was caressing her: her legs, her arms, her body, and she dreamed a warm breeze was moving across the pool and touching her face. It seemed to whisper in her ear, and she opened her eyes. The Son was lying next to her, his face close to hers, his breath soft on her face. His eyes were hungry, and his other hand was under her dress, his fingers lightly touching her body. He leaned over, and his breath was warm on her cheek.

"The man is making my mother happy now," he whispered. "Why don't you let me make you happy." His lips brushed her lips, and his fingers touched her breast.

June pushed his hands away and jumped to her feet. "Stay away," she whispered. "Don't you dare touch me like that! Your mother will send me away."

She turned and stormed back to sit by the fire, but she ached, and her body felt bruised. She *wanted* the Son to make her happy, wanted to know what it was *really* like, not the frightening attack on January or her boyfriend's fumbling around in the barn, but the happiness the Woman had talked about.

The Son called to her, but June never looked back. She was afraid his mother would force her to leave the family. She turned her back and wrapped her arms around her knees, and when the Man and the Woman returned to the fire. June was asleep, curled up close to the Daughter.

The Woman looked around and then sang softly to herself as she squatted down and shook dirt over the burning coals, her anxious heart at peace. The Man smiled down at her, and then disappeared into the surrounding woods.

Chapter 12

They stayed in the campsite for a week, and now and again the Man would disappear. He told them that he scouted the area and crept through the brush at night, taking eggs or honey from farms that were located far from the river. Then he laughed and slapped his knee. "They don't need them," he said and laughed again.

June thought about the eggs she had eaten and the honey they spread on their black bread. She'd never wondered where they had come from before. It had never entered her mind. Silly girl, she thought, you silly girl!

One evening the Man crouched down next to her as she sat by the fire. He stared at the flames for a minute and then told her about a food shop he had seen up the road.

"We need supplies," he said and pulled out a handful of dollar coupons. "You go, you're a Citizen. Leave early and walk with the sun in your face. It's in a shopping mall about half a mile away. Here are coupons and a list."

The Man scared June with his shrewd eyes and hard jaw, but she took the money and stuffed it into her pocket. She was afraid to ask him what a mall was. What in the world would I do if he laughed at me, she wondered.

"I'll go tomorrow morning," she said and turned away.

June worried about leaving the camp and traveling to a mall alone, a place she had never seen before, but she didn't say anything to the others. The uneasiness hung over her like a cloud, and that night she dreamed of demons, the ones the Preacher had warned her about back home: creatures with horns and tails that waited for her on the road. She finally fell into a deep sleep and woke at dawn. Her first thought was, I'll be fine!

June slipped on a clean dress and hung the kettle over the smoldering coals, made herself hot tea with milk and sugar, and sipped it as the shadows faded away. Finally, she slung her backpack over her shoulder and set out. It was still early, and a low mist hung over the forest, giving it an eerie beauty. Here and there a few birds fluttered through the trees, chirping, and whistling in the green leaves.

Early birds, June thought and chirped back. The morning trip was making her happy.

She found a ridge of rocks downstream from their crossing and skipped across the river without getting wet. Ha! She thought, June discovered this crossing ... not the Man. It made her feel proud, and she sang:

"River, river, rocks and river ..."

When June reached the road, it was empty and still, the sun just touching the pavement. Her thoughts turned to the Man as she wandered along. He was kind to her and helped the Illegal family, but he was secretive, even intimidating in a way. When he was angry he used a bad word in English and once he'd spit out a stream of them that shocked June and made the Daughter turn red. She wondered if he was an Illegal, too. Were American Natives illegal now? He looked different than the Family: taller and darker with wise eyes that saw right through you. She thought about how he took the Woman into the caravan at night and trembled. She knew what the Son meant; he was making her happy with sex. She contemplated that for a while as she walked. June wondered if she loved the Son now; loved him the way the Woman loved this stranger. Maybe, but what could she do? The Woman would turn her away.

The food shop was in a cluster of buildings with a hardware store, a bank and a small cafe. There was a freshly painted sign by the road that read *River Road Mall*. June had never seen a mall before, just the shops on Main Street in North Carolina and the small country stores along the road. She stopped and looked around. So, this is a mall, she thought and wasn't impressed.

An almost empty parking lot was surrounded by tall pine trees and a red solar van was the only vehicle parked there. Birds twittered in the pines, but there was a stillness about the place, like a held breath. Maybe it's too early, she thought uneasily, but a small light over the door was turned on, and a dim glow shone through the food shop window.

June walked across the empty parking lot and pushed open the door tentatively. A bell rang deep inside, and it made her jump. She missed the familiar shops at home, little places where she knew everyone, where they said 'hello Honey' and 'howdy do." This food shop was large with endless shelves, some filled with items she'd never seen before. She heard rustling sounds, and somebody coughed, but she could see no one.

June was intimidated, but she was fascinated, too. So many things to choose from and she reached out to touch a bottle of cold-water shampoo. She wanted to pick it up and inspect it but knew she'd better ask if they accepted dollar coupons before she handled anything.

She followed the rustling sound and found the clerk standing behind a back counter with a newspaper spread out in front of him and a mug of coffee in his hand. He was a tall man with light balding hair and cold blue eyes that watched her suspiciously as she walked up.

June felt ashamed of her wrinkled cotton dress and pale hair, loose and hanging over her shoulders. She knew that as soon as she opened her mouth and the soft drawl spilled out, he would know she was a Traveler from the Southern Region and that frightened her. He was a Northerner! One of those people she was raised to fear. But, she told herself, *she* was a Citizen with Rights, and it was her duty to buy the supplies, and she would do it!

"Do you accept dollar coupons?" she asked, her chin in the air.

"What?" he asked rudely. "I didn't understand you."

"Do you accept dollar coupons?" she asked again, slowly, and took out one of the bills.

"You're a Traveler, aren't you?" He shook his head, puzzled, "So many people traveling now. Someday we may all be on the road." He nodded his head at the shelves, "go ahead, Southern Girl, take what you need. I'll accept the coupons. I guess I have to, now *you* people are shopping in here."

"Travelers," he muttered, "Climate Refugees," and he spit.

"I don't like you, either," June said under her breath.

She didn't waste time with her selections, and was relieved to be back on the road to the campsite, carrying her string bag of supplies, hurrying away from the *River Road Mall* and the cold-eyed store clerk as quickly as possible.

"How rude and nasty," she fumed, "He held my dollar coupons up to the light as if he thought I had printed them, myself. Nasty man!" June missed January, the bright smile and their easy companionship. She missed the small neat store that had everything she needed. My best friend, she thought, my only friend, and she felt a lump in her throat. She thought of a word the Man used but knew it was bad. "Damn," she said instead, and it shocked her. But then she started to laugh out loud.

The sun was up now, and there were Travelers with their wagons and belongings drifting by: silent and grim as they marched along. They looked neither left nor right, but they made June feel better. She was fortunate to have a family and a camp. She sniffed and wiped her eyes on her sleeve. Even the American Native Man was part of the family now, someone who would keep them safe and show them the way to the Border.

June's thoughts turned to the Son with his dark, hungry eyes and how she felt about him, how his touch made her shiver, but she quickly put him out of her mind and started watching her feet as she hiked along, counting the steps to the turnoff.

The sun was hot on the open road, and the asphalt was steaming. June was daydreaming and close to the wooded path when she heard the familiar whistle in the distance: *Danger!* It jolted her back to reality, and she joined the others as they pushed through the underbrush and into the forest, scattering leaves as they fled. June crouched in the bushes as the black NPF vehicle purred by, headed in the direction she had just traveled, and she knew they were headed to the store. She could almost see it: They would park in the big empty parking lot next to the red van and push open the door to the food shop. The little bell would ring, and the clerk would welcome them. Would he tell them about the girl with the pale hair who paid with dollar coupons – the girl from the South? Of course, they will stop there, she thought, and she knew the clerk would talk about her, sending the agents back the way they had come.

June crawled behind a tree and sat still, her mind busy. Her first urge was to dash across the river and run to the camp, but she was afraid the NPF agents might already be on their way back. She might lead them right into the middle of the Illegals' campsite. She made up her mind and pushed the bags aside. Frantically June created a shallow hole in the leaves, dug into the forest's floor and dragged fallen branches to cover it, then rubbed dirt on her face and crept into the refuge, curling her body around her backpack and the string bag.

The shelter was hot, and her body was soon moist with sweat. Her fingernails were broken from digging in the dirt, and her fingers hurt, but she didn't move. The other Travelers pushed back to the road, but June didn't make a sound. She knew in her heart that the NPF would come back and they would be looking for her. A fly buzzed around her face and made her blink, but still, June didn't move. She lay still and forced herself to daydream. She dreamed of a safe place, a place where she could settle down, grow a garden, and be happy. "Happy," she whispered fiercely. "I want to be happy!"

Before long June's daydreams were cut short when the Travelers came crashing back into the underbrush; she heard the NPF agents' boots as they tramped on the forest floor and she knew they were searching with their cold eyes, grabbing anyone but looking for *her*, the Southern Girl. She heard their harsh voices as they seized people and dragged them back to the road; men cursed, and women and children screamed.

"Where is she?" the agents shouted back and forth as they tramped through the brush. "Where is that Southern Girl with the long blond hair?"

June squeezed her eyes shut. She remembered the terrified woman on the bus, and she remembered what January had told her. Never! She thought, and she held her breath. She felt sick to her stomach, but she knew they would never find her; *she* was traveling with the Illegals and the Illegals were smarter than they were.

The agents finally gave up, and the NPF vehicle headed back the way it had come. Here and there, Travelers picked themselves up and continued their silent, lonely march. Only then did June dust herself off and scramble towards the river, hauling the string bag with her. She would *never* use that road again and would *never* shop in that food shop again. The clerk had told the NPF agents about her, and they were searching for her. How *dare* they, she thought and called them the bad words she had heard the Man use, "Damn them!"

When June came to the river, she followed it upstream until she came to the rock crossing and dashed across, splashing water on her dress and underclothes. She knew she was filthy with dirt and sweat, but she didn't stop. All she wanted was to see the camp, to find the family and tell them what had happened. She circled around and backtracked through the woods as an extra measure of caution, stumbling over rocks and pushing through dense underbrush. Nasty man, she thought, nasty, *bastard* man!

June was exhausted by the time she saw the familiar green and black caravan hidden in the trees. "Help me," she called out and sat down hard.

The others hurried to help, calling out in their musical language. The Son took the string bag and brushed the dirt off her clothes, helping her back to her feet. "Okay," he told her, "You're okay now. You're safe."

"What in Hell happened to you?" the Man asked. "You're covered with dirt and dried leaves? What happened?"

"NPF," she whispered and started to cry. "The man in the food shop told them about me, and they came looking for me. I hid and, *look*, I didn't drop the supplies, but I'm scared they'll come back."

The Daughter was distressed and put her arms around June. "Don't cry, Please, don't cry!"

The Woman brought her water to drink and brushed the filthy hair out of her face. She pulled her close and led her back to the campsite. "Tell us everything," she said gently.

And June did.

Chapter 13

That afternoon the Man headed back to the road to observe. He had stoically inspected June for a few minutes as she sobbed between words, frowned at her dirty face and stained dress, then taken her seriously and told them it might be time to move on.

"I'll check it out," he said. "It could be dangerous to stay if NPF is nosing around. While I'm gone, clean up the camp. We shouldn't leave a single piece of paper behind. Nothing to lead NPF to us!" His face was serious as he looked around the campsite. He stripped off his white t-shirt, and his body was tan and muscled. "I'll hide in the trees."

"Come," he said to the Woman and took her aside. He spoke to her in their own language; June couldn't understand him, but she was sure he was talking about her. He glanced at June, but the Woman shook her head and turned away until he left.

"No," she called after him. "No!" And June watched him go.

The Man slipped through the trees, his footsteps so light the only sound was the breeze as it tossed the leaves overhead. When he was gone, the Woman turned back and glared at the others.

"Come," she said.

They rolled the stones away from the fire pit and stamped on the blackened wood until it was tramped into dust. The Woman took a branch and brushed it over the space until there was no trace of the pit. She covered it with dead leaves, and they all danced on the leaves, too. Then they added more.

The Daughter took the string bag and searched through the brush for the slightest thing that could lead NPR to them; June helped the Son pack everything back into the caravan. He touched her hair, and she pulled away.

"No," she said. "I don't want to be left behind."

"Now we eat," the Woman said when they were done, and she tore apart a loaf of thick, black bread that she'd kept aside. They sat in a circle and ate, but nobody had anything to say.

June picked out tiny pieces of bread and put them on her tongue. She felt sad and guilty. She loved the campsite, and she knew it was her fault NPF was now a threat to them all. Overhead, the breeze moved the leaves and birds fluttered from tree to tree. This was a safe place, she thought, a good place.

"When my man comes back we will go to the river, and you can clean off the dirt." the Woman told June. "Now it's time to rest. We have a long trip ahead of us."

June curled up under the caravan, and she fell asleep as soon as her head touched the ground. She dreamed of a garden and honey bees, and she smiled in her sleep. "I'm afraid of bees," she murmured. The Daughter crept under the caravan and lay down next to her. She touched her gently with her fingertips and whispered softly in her halting English, "My sister, my beautiful sister."

When the Man returned it was already dark, but a full moon filled the campsite with light. June woke when she heard his voice and almost rolled over on top of the Daughter.

"Come," she ordered and shook her awake. They crawled from under the caravan and stumbled to where the Man and the Woman were talking. June was still frightened, but she wanted to find out what he had seen.

"Come here and listen to me," he said in English, and then he laughed. "I climbed a tall tree to watch the road. See how strong I am?" He flexed his muscles, and his body gleamed in the moonlight. The daughter took June's hand and shivered, and the Son scowled. June looked away.

"The NPF agents were still traveling up and down the road," the Man told them. "Sometimes they'd stop that black vehicle and hike as far as the riverbank, but they didn't want to get wet." He laughed again. "They walked right under me and never looked up. Very strange men but very persistent," he shook his head. "Now, we should wait here and rest tonight, but we leave at first light."

"Yes," the Woman said, and her eyes were fixed on his face.

"Look, I will show you how we will travel." He squatted down, and they all gathered around him. He picked up a twig and brushed some leaves away. "We will have no fire tonight, but the moon is bright. I will draw in the dust." he drew a line. "Always travel towards the rising sun." He drew a round circle.

"After one day's travel, we will find a safe place to camp and rest for as long as you want. In two days, we will come to many tall pine trees. Then, after one day more, an open meadow. It is long and open, and there is a little brook that runs through it and ends in a shallow pool. It is very pretty."

Then he drew a larger circle on the ground. "On the other side of the meadow, two big roads come together. Then we must turn and travel with the rising sun over our right shoulders," he leaned over and touched the Woman's right shoulder and then pulled her close. "The other road goes east with the sun to the Garden State." He sat back on his heels and looked at the Woman, then cleared the circles in the dust and spread leaves over the spot.

The Woman nodded and stood up, "We are going to bathe now; we have scoured the camp and packed the caravan. Now it's your turn. You can carry the rocks away."

"Son," she said, "You can help and bathe later."

She led the way back to the pool in the rocks. It was dark under the trees, but the moon spilled a silver light over the water; the river currents made little sparkles as it moved. They felt their way with small, careful footsteps along the rocks. June could see the shadows of the others ahead of her, and when she heard them splash in, she followed and dropped her clothes on the bank.

She rinsed her dress and hung it on a branch that hung over the pool and then dove in. She scrubbed the dirt off her body and washed the twigs out of her hair, then floated on her back and looked up at the sky. It was vast and black. It reminded her of the velvet cape her mother had once owned. She could see stars high above the treetops and was amazed. June couldn't remember the last time she'd seen stars. At home, they had faded with the burning sun. The full moon was almost hidden by the trees, but it was as bright as if it had been wiped clean with a soft cloth. She swam to the whirlpool and let the eddies spin her around while the stars spun in the darkness overhead.

By the time they returned to the camp the moon had disappeared, and June and the Daughter crawled under the caravan. She thought about the Garden State; she loved the sound: Garden State. She rolled the words around on her tongue and daydreamed. June dreamed of the Garden State and then she dreamed of the Green Mountains. Places where things were growing, not dying.

The Woman followed the Man deep into the forest, but June was asleep when they returned.

The next morning, he was gone.

Chapter 14

When June woke up, the morning mist was burning off and the sun was just rising. The Woman knelt down next to her and gave her a piece of black bread with honey. Her face was sad, and she wouldn't look at June.

"My man is gone," she said. "He left sometime in the night. It makes me sad. My heart, it is broken." Without another word she got up and walked away.

June ate her bread, but now she was sad, too; she had believed the Man was part of the family. Then she was angry. How dare he go away after he had been with the Woman for so many days? He had made her happy, had taken her body and then he had gone away and made her sad. She stuffed the rest of the bread into her mouth and chewed angrily. Her boyfriend had left her, too. He had left her and gone to The North without a thought, just gave her some milk. The more she thought about it, the angrier she became.

The Son was fitting a harness on the mule when June stormed up and confronted him.

"The Man made your mother sad," she snapped. "First, he made her happy … you know what I mean, and now he's gone! So, she's sad, and her heart is broken. You told me you'd make me happy, but now look what he did, the Man broke her heart." June's face was almost white with outrage. "What do you have to say about that? Was it all a lie?"

The Son kept working. "He will come back someday because he loves her," he said. "He always finds us." He fastened the harness and turned around. "Yes, I want to make you happy because I love you!" He reached out and touched June's hand, and his dark eyes were pleading. "But I didn't lie. I would *never* leave you."

"No," June whispered and snatched her hand away.

"Come," the Woman ordered. She had seen her son's face and was troubled, but there was no time to waste. "We need to head into the sun, and we must hurry before NPF decides to cross the river."

The Woman had been distracted, but now she realized her son wanted the outsider, the Citizen with the pale hair, and she would have to do something soon. "That just can't happen. I, myself, understand what he is feeling, but I can't let it happen! God willing, maybe someday he will forget her and love one of his own." She felt a moment of despair and looked away.

The Son swung onto the caravan seat and headed out, the mule finding his way carefully along the track and the women walking behind, single file.

They traveled towards the east, and after a while, the Woman started to sing: strange musical words that sounded forlorn and then sounded happy. They followed the pathway as it meandered through the trees and dense brush, and then June started to sing:

"I will lift up mine eyes unto the hills," she sang, "from whence cometh my help."

The Woman looked at her and smiled. She seemed to be at peace, to have left the memory of the man behind her and worry about her son's future for another day.

Now and then the Son stopped the mule and climbed down to cut away the underbrush with a large curved knife. He would glance at June, but she ignored him.

When the sun was high, the forest seemed to close in around them, and it became stifling. Sweat ran down June's back and under her arms. She wanted to lie down and was afraid she would fall asleep on her feet.

"Please," she called, but the Woman kept on walking, never stopping and never looking back.

June lost track of time and keep trudging along, the Daughter close at her side. Every now and then they would glance at each other and smile. She's like a sister, June thought, and it made her wistful.

They came to a small brook and an open, grassy glade. "We stop here," the Woman said. "These are wetlands, and there are cattails, see them?" She looked at June and her daughter. "We rest until dusk, and then we find some stones and gather wood for a fire. We need nourishment and sleep. I can make soup from the cattails. Son," she ordered, "you can catch fish from the brook."

June was tired and her legs ached, but she wanted to see the wetlands and walked on. Clumps of swamp grass swayed in the breeze and water pooled where the cattails grew. It reminded her of home, of a place they called the Marshes. Cattails had grown there, too, but nobody ate them. She thought about the Great Flood, about how the Marshes were consumed by the River until there were no more cattails.

I have run so far from home and for so long, she thought, but will there be a great flood here, too?

"Learn to swim," her mother had told her." "You never know..." Was that what she meant? The idea frightened her, and she trembled.

"Come, rest," the Woman said gently, and June realized she had been standing behind her. Wearily she followed the Woman back to the caravan and fell asleep under the trees. She dreamed of the NPF agents, and then dreamed the brook was overflowing its banks, water spilling across the campsite and drowning them. She moaned and gasped and the Woman came and stroked her cheek.

"Dreaming," she said. "Shhh, we are safe here." And then June relaxed and slept without dreams.

Early in the evening they collected stones and built a fire pit. The Son gathered dried reeds and logs and lit a fire. The Woman took June with her to collect cattails and told her to tuck her dress up to her waist and take off her shoes.

"We go barefoot," she said. "No snakes, just mud," and she kicked off her sandals.

They trudged through the wetlands, their feet sinking in the wet earth and making sucking sounds. June liked the feel of the warm mud as it squished up between her toes and wondered what it would be like to roll around in it, just lie down here and roll around. I bet people take mud baths, she thought, and it made her laugh.

"Mud bath," she said.

The Woman laughed, too, but she kept moving.

"Wait," June stopped short, her heart beating hard against her ribs. "What is that?"

A slender, brown creature had come out of the woods to the brook for water, but it raised its head, big ears twitching, and then turned and was gone.

"A deer," the Woman said. "She will not hurt you."

"It's beautiful," June said, and she was happy. Other than the mule, it had been a long time since she'd seen an animal. All the dairy cattle had been slaughtered; the big lumbering creatures Bobby had called his Ladies were gone. This lovely brown creature was magical. "It's magical!" she said out loud.

The Woman smiled at her, "Come help me cut these cattails. Don't worry, the deer will come back. This is her watering hole."

The Daughter had set the pot to boil, and when they returned the Woman cleaned and cut the cattails, tossing the heads into the fire. She dropped the rest in the boiling water and added some rice. June was hungry, but she was hesitant about cattail soup; she leaned over the pot and sniffed. Not awful, she thought, and found a place by the fire to sit down.

"I saw a deer," she said. "It was beautiful, and when we came, it just floated into the woods, just like magic."

"They *are* magic," the Daughter said and sat down next to June. "They are lost souls in animal bodies."

"It certainly would be good meat," the Son added and June glared at him, outraged.

'Shush," the Woman said, and dropped the flesh of a large trout into the pot; soon the smell of a hearty stew hung over the camp.

"We can stay here for a few days," the Woman said. "We have enough provisions, and there are fish in the brook." She looked around. Shadows filled the camp as they ate and made the trees seem taller and the forest deeper. "Yes, we are safe, now. Tomorrow we can finish setting up camp.

That night, June sat and watched the fire as it flickered in the dark and she thought about what the Man had said: *The Garden State.* More and more she was thinking about The Garden State. Maybe it would be wise to head East when they arrived at the two roads.

June knew the Son wanted her, he had even said he loved her, but she remembered what his mother had said, and the memory of the Man's leaving still haunted her. She didn't know if she wanted to be married, but June believed she did love the Son now, and more and more she was tempted to slip into the woods with him. She could almost see how his eyes glowed when he looked at her and his dark hair curled over his neck. The thought made her shiver with longing and her breath catch in her throat.

So, she thought, maybe I should be the one to leave. Maybe it's time for me to go. She thought about her home. The Preacher would say I was a bad girl for these thoughts ... a sinner. She smiled to herself. "Well, I guess he would think I had already *been* a bad girl back home, playing around in the hayloft with Bobby." Briefly, June wondered what had happened to Bobby, but now she didn't care; she thought about the Preacher. Did he leave town? Maybe he was just another Traveler on the road North. She remembered the circus wagon with the fancy ladies and wondered if the Preacher had seen them, too. Maybe he had given up and joined them. "It would do him good," she said and laughed out loud.

The Son sat down beside June and touched her hair. "I love you," he said. He stroked her cheek, and his thumb brushed her lips. "I would never leave you. How could I?"

"I am not right for you," she said and moved away. "Not one of your own people." But it hurt her inside.

The Son dropped his hand, and they sat side-by-side watching the fire for a while. "It doesn't matter," he said. "Can't you see?"

"Please," June whispered, "don't ever kill the deer. You would be killing *magic*." Then she got up and went to join the Daughter under the caravan and left him sitting by the fire alone.

Chapter 15

Just before dawn, June woke to the sound of thunder. It was far away, but every now and then the sky shimmered with lightning. The leaves started to rustle, and then there was the soft tapping of raindrops hitting the wagon like fingers. It's raining, June thought, clean rain, then the sky opened, and the rain came down. The leaves heaved and quivered but June wasn't afraid. She rolled over and lay on her back under the caravan and listened to the storm as it raged and decided she loved the sound. Then as she fell asleep, she wondered about the deer.

The storm blew away in the night, and they finished setting up camp at dawn. The Woman found wild onions to add to the stew and red, tart berries that she crushed with the last of the sugar. The Son caught fish that were as bright as rainbows, but then turned dull as they lay by the fire. There were provisions in the caravan: rice and beans, loaves of thick black bread and large containers of drinking water, enough food for many days.

In the evening June sat quietly by the brook and waited for the deer. It was her mystical animal: sleek and graceful, its tail flipping up and down like a little flag as she drank. The third day she brought a baby, a miniature version of herself, with white spots across its back. The tiny creature bent its front legs to drink, and June was thrilled.

"That's a fawn," the Woman said behind her. "It's her baby."

At the sound of the Woman's voice, the deer flipped her tail up and bounded away, the fawn close behind.

"She had a baby," June said. She thought about all the baby clothes she had knitted: pink and blue and yellow, still sitting on the shelves at home, and it made her sad.

"Someday, there will be more animals than people," she said.

Nearby the woman had found some mushrooms, but she glanced up at June, then shook her head and went back to digging by the trees.

Every night June sat by the fire, and every night the Son sat next to her. He would touch her hair or stroke her cheek, and every night June pushed him away. He would beg her to go into the woods and once he kissed her on the lips, hard and urgent, but she always said *no*, and joined the Daughter under the caravan, sometimes tossing and turning in her sleep.

The Woman noticed and decided it was time to move on. Once they reached the two roads, she would tell June to leave them. Her son had to marry one of his own, and while this pale stranger was traveling with them, he would never want anyone else. She had not realized how much he would desire this stranger and she was frightened.

Chapter 16

June looked back at the wetlands as they headed towards the woods. She wanted so much to see the deer and her fawn again, but the Woman was firm: They would move on with the rising sun.

On the other side of the glade, the path opened up into a pine forest, and the trees reached high over their heads. There was thick underbrush but after a while, it fell away, and the ground was covered with ferns that swept over the forest floor like a green ocean.

"It looks like the picture of that cathedral I saw in my history book," June said and squatted down to see what the ferns felt like. The Daughter sat down close to her, and the group rested for a while. A breeze rushed through the forest and made strange sighing sounds in the trees.

"I'd love to live here," June said. "Build a little house in this forest and live here forever."

"Me, too," the Daughter said. She gazed at June and leaned against her arm. "You're like my sister," she said. "Like a pale me."

June was surprised and moved. She rested her head against the Daughter's dark hair and felt a lump in her throat. A sister, she thought, she really is like my sister.

They spent the heat of the day in the pine forest, and the Woman passed out black bread with crushed, tart berries. She knew when they reached the two roads June would have to go her own way, but she was shaken. She felt as if she were losing a daughter and, distressed, looked away.

After they ate, June lay on her back and looked at the tops of the pine trees. The ferns covered her like a blanket, hidden and safe, and the ground was soft with fallen pine needles. She had finally decided to leave the Illegals when they reached the two roads, but June felt as if she would be losing her mother all over again. The Woman had been kind to her, but June knew she was doing the right thing. She would go to the Garden State and would tell the Woman the next day.

June could see the sky through the tops of the trees, high above and as blue as the picture of the cathedral. "Blue sky," she sang softly, "Blue, blue sky …." and when she fell asleep, she dreamed of home.

The Woman decided they should stay the night under the trees, and she sent June and the Daughter to look for water to bathe in. A short way from the track they found an old wooden bridge and a small brook that wandered through a dip in the forest floor. The bridge was rotten and falling apart; pieces of wood with rusted nails lay in the water, so they moved downstream to splash around. June looked at the bridge and frowned.

"Why is there a bridge in the forest?" she asked. "It doesn't go anywhere."

"It's magic," the Daughter told her. "Old houses are magic, so an old bridge would be magic, too. Little people live there." She looked dreamily upstream. "Faeries live there with butterfly wings and long flowing hair. The Faerie Princess has a crown made of flowers." She smiled at June. "And Elves live there, too. They play flutes and dance in the moonlight. It's what my Mama told me."

That night, June thought about the bridge as she curled up under the caravan. Beside her, the Daughter mumbled a little in her sleep, and June touched her hand softly. Like a sister, she thought. The forest was quiet and dark, and a breeze drifted through the trees; it sighed and murmured like voices. "Maybe the Little People," June said and fell asleep.

The voices grew loud and angry, and June woke up with a start. She could hear the Woman, and the Woman was angry, flinging strange words that struck like blows. There was a second voice: defiant and stubborn, then pleading and filled with grief. The Daughter woke up and started to cry.

"My Mama and my brother," she whispered. "Something bad is happening."

June put her arms around the girl and held her, and finally, the voices faded away, but June had a difficult time falling asleep again. The Daughter clung to her, and June remembered what the NPF agent had done to January. She stiffened, and a chill ran up her spine. No matter what happens, she thought, this family must cross the Border. There can be no argument and no hard feelings.

Just as the sun rose, the Woman called softly to June and led her back to the wooden bridge. They sat side-by-side on the bank, and the Woman gave her a piece of dark bread with herbs and mushrooms. Except for a lone Thrush's sweet song somewhere nearby, it was quiet.

"You must leave us," she said at last. We will cross the big field and come to the two roads today. Tomorrow we will go North to the Border, but you must go the other way." She pulled June close and held her, and June felt her sorrow.

"My man told me to send you away when NPF came looking for you at the river, but I said I would not do that. You are like my very own daughter." The Woman leaned her head against June's. "But my son must choose one of his own and have babies that look like me and mine."

June thought about the Son and some stranger, being together, having babies. "Nobody has babies," she said. "Nobody has babies now because of the sickness." She pulled away and looked at the Woman.

"We didn't have the sickness," the Woman said. "We are Illegals, and we were hiding. We never caught that sickness so, God willing, yes, my son can have babies."

June envisioned the Son and a Woman Who Didn't Exist Yet and she was filled with jealousy, but she knew what the Woman said was true. She realized the two had argued about her in the night and she felt guilty – guilty because she had already decided to leave them and travel to the Garden State, but she had an empty feeling in her stomach and an ache in her throat.

"I'll go to the Garden State," she said finally. "When we reach the two roads, I'll turn into the sun. Thank you," she added softly. "You have been good to me and kept me safe. I'll never forget you." Then her eyes filled with tears that rolled down her cheeks.

The Woman wiped June's tears away with her fingers. "We will leave when the sun rises," she said." By noon we should be near the open field and will stay there until the new day. Please," she begged, "do not tell the others. My daughter will be heartbroken, and my son will be angry."

The Woman held her for another few minutes, then she got up and headed back to the camp. June sat and looked at the magic bridge for a long time and wept.

Chapter 17

They headed out with the rising sun, and the Daughter stayed close to June, glancing at her now and again, but June just stared straight ahead. After three hours the ferns thinned out and, again, underbrush filled the forest floor. The track climbed a hill, and at the top, they stopped to rest. Below them, a large field was spread out, long and wide. A brook led to a small pool of water sparkling in the sun, just as the Man had said.

"We stop now," the Woman said and turned to the others. "We will set up our camp within the pine trees on the edge of the field below."

The Son jumped down and took the mule's bridle as they headed down the hill. The poor animal balked, and his footsteps sent up little clouds of dust as he made his way down.

They settled at the forest edge and June built the fire pit as they set up camp. She worked alone and kept her feelings hidden as she fitted the stones next to one another. At least I know how to build a fire pit, she thought, and carefully set the last stone in place.

During the heat of the day, the group rested in the shadows of the pines. June found a grassy spot surrounded by small pines and underbrush and lay on her back gazing at the sky. I wonder how many more days I'll be looking up at the sky, she thought. Will it look different when I finally find a place to settle down? She knew the two roads were on the other side of the field, but not how far it would be to the Garden State, and it occurred to her that she would again be traveling alone. June felt a sense of deep sorrow, but she pushed it away. Her last thought before she fell asleep was: what will I do when I get there?

It was afternoon when June woke up. She had rolled over in her sleep, and her face was pressed into a small mound of grass.

The Woman was sitting quietly beside her and June sat up and spit out a blade of dried grass.

"Please," the Woman said, "go to the pool with my daughter. I have some cooking I want to do, but you two will be able to bathe in the water." She sighed deeply, and her breast rose and fell with her breath. "Tomorrow we will travel to the two roads and go our separate ways, but the time is short." She gazed at June, and her face was solemn. "I'd like you to spend a little of what time is left with her. She will miss you." And the Woman stood up and pushed through the underbrush and was gone.

When June arrived at the camp, she found the Daughter waiting by the path, hopping from one foot to the other.

"Come on, come on," she called, and June grabbed her backpack and followed her along the track to the open field. When they stepped out of the trees, the both stopped short and stared. The meadow was filled with sunshine; flowers were growing wild. Bright yellow, deep blue, red, white, and purple blooms grew in the long grass. "Oh," June whispered, "it looks like a wonderland."

The Daughter danced on her toes and pointed, "Look at that, a butterfly. It looks like a faerie princess, see the wings? And just look at the clouds in the sky!"

June took a deep breath of the sweet air and looked around. This field, she thought, this beautiful meadow, it's as far away from the burning days back home as it could ever be. The sun was warm, but it was not hot, and the grass was green. She had not seen flowers in years and, yes, there were clouds in the sky. How long has it been, she thought? Oh, why couldn't it have stayed like this in North Carolina? The thought upset her, and she quickly pushed it away. Enough, June, she told herself, this is a day to enjoy and to remember!

The pool was in a hollow, and the water was waist deep and clean. June and the Daughter dropped their clothes in the grass and jumped in, splashing water on each other and dipping out of sight, playing like children. Overhead the clouds drifted by and a small breeze tossed the long grass. Later, they shook out their hair and lay on the grass looking up at the clouds as the sun dried their wet bodies.

"What does that cloud look like?" June asked.

"A rabbit," the Daughter said and laughed. "And I see a cow."

June sat up and brushed her hair dry in the sun. It fell down over her face, and the Daughter reached out and touched it.

"Gold," she said, "My brother loves your golden hair. He loves you," she added and sat up. "If you marry him then you really *will* be my sister." Her face became animated and filled with joy. "We will always be together!"

June turned away for a minute and then ran her fingers through the Daughter's long dark hair. "Let me brush your hair now," she said and swallowed the lump in her throat.

The Daughter changed her position, and June brushed her hair until it fell in long, dark waves over the girl's shoulders and down her back. She picked some of the bright yellow and purple wildflowers and wove a crown, knitting the stems together. Her fingers were nimble with memory.

"You are a Faerie Princess," June said and put the crown on the shiny dark hair, "and nothing can hurt you now."

She picked more flowers, white, red, and deep blue, and wove one for herself, pressing it down on her head.

The Daughter jumped to her feet. "We are both Faerie Princesses now," she shouted and danced around June in a circle, singing in her strange musical language. June lay back on the grass and let the sun warm her. Nearby, a butterfly fluttered around the flowers and settled on her hand then disappeared over the grass.

When they returned to the camp, both girls were still wearing their faerie crowns, and the Woman smiled, her eyes soft.

"Here is food for you," she said and handed them brown earthen bowls of vegetable stew.

June sat for a long time in front of the fire. The Son sat down next to her, but he didn't touch her, and he didn't say a word. After a while, June leaned against him, and the Son pulled her close as they sat and watched the flames burn down to embers. He sighed and stroked her pale hair, running a lock through his fingers over and over. And then they both got up and went their separate ways.

June found it hard to sleep, drifting in and out of dreams: dreams of waterfalls and rivers – always dreams of water. When the sky began to lighten, she sat up and looked at the Daughter curled up next to her breathing softly with one hand under her cheek; her dark hair was tousled, and the flowers were falling apart in her curls. June pulled one of the brightest red blossoms out of her own crown and carefully placed it next to the sleeping girl, then she crawled out from under the caravan and looked around.

The night before she had stored her backpack with the carry bag where the Woman slept, and now she looked at the caravan in frustration. "Why in the world didn't I keep them with me?" She scolded herself. "What was I thinking?"

She crept through the open doorway to the caravan, careful not to wake the Woman, but there was the sound of deep, even breaths coming from a heap on the bed. She collected her belongings and looked back at the Woman, wanting to say something, maybe goodbye or thank you, but she climbed down instead and carried her bags to the track and leaned them against a tree.

The Son always slept near the mule, and she found him sprawled on his back, one arm slung over his head. He was snoring softly, and his eyelashes were shadows on his cheeks. June stood looking at him for a few minutes. "You are beautiful," she whispered, and then she thought about him with the Woman Who Didn't Exist Yet, holding her and making babies with her and she felt tight with jealousy. I'm going to the Garden State, she told herself firmly, and then she stooped and placed her faerie crown next to him in the grass.

"I love you," she said softly and turned away.

The Woman was waiting for June, squatting next to her belongings, the skirt of her long nightgown spread out around her. Her dark hair hung loose down and her face was sad.

"I was awake," she said. "Oh, I heard you when you came in, but I didn't want to disturb you. You were trying so hard not to waken me."

They walked down the track and into the field together. Dawn was just breaking, and it was already warm; a light breeze moved across the tall grass, but neither of them talked and neither smiled. When they reached the pond, the Woman stopped and took June's hand, turning her around to face her.

"Goodbye, Most Beloved of my Heart," she said. "Be careful in your travels, and my prayers will always be with you. Someday you will find love with one of your own." She handed June a cloth package, made up from a colorful headscarf.

"You will need food," she said. "I made rice cakes for you while you were with my daughter yesterday. They're in this packet with some bread and cheese."

Then she turned and walked away, her body rigid and her eyes looking neither left nor right.

June paused by the pool and thought about the Daughter. She thought about the faeries and little people the girl had talked about and felt an overwhelming loss. She wanted to turn and call to the Woman, but instead, started out across the field and headed into the woods. The backpack and carry bag seemed even heavier than before she'd met the Illegals.

"I'm going to the Garden State," she said out loud. "I am *going* to the Garden State!" But she didn't want to think about finding love with *one of her own*. "Never," she said out loud. "Never!"

In her heart, she hid her longing for the young man with the dark eyes and the mass of black curls. "Never," she whispered.

The breeze moved through the pine trees, and to June it sounded like the voices of the little people.

Chapter 18

When June reached the two roads, the sun had just tipped over the horizon. The way to the north led through more open fields and disappeared into the forest, again. She looked back one more time and then headed east on another endless highway surrounded by tall trees and dense undergrowth. There were Travelers, but they looked like shadows drifting along, quiet and grim. Nobody noticed her. She was just another Traveler, another Climate Refugee.

June crossed the road and hugged the shoulder, uneasy after so many days on the wooded trail. After a few minutes, she started to sing the lullaby her mother had sung to her when she was a little girl:

"You show me the path of life, Lord
In your presence, there is fullness of joy ..."

The Travelers heard her singing, but they never look her way. They just kept on walking, watching their feet as they trudged by.

Before long June fell into the rhythm that had kept her going for so many days – the long hot days before the Woman had found her. She kept her eyes on the roadway ahead, and by the time the sun was high, she was miles away. The road was dusty, no homes or buildings, just trees, but the pavement was smooth with no ruts or potholes, and she found it easy to keep walking, passing the other Travelers as they slowly marched along.

It was afternoon when June came upon a burned-out house set back in the trees. The only thing left standing was a charred chimney; a ruined truck was parked and abandoned in an overgrown yard. By the roadside stood an unusual structure – a small, wooden house with an arch that spanned the motorway. The odd building looked deserted, its white paint chipping off in places, but it was untouched by the fire. A placard attached to the arch was a faded pink and might have been a sign in some distant past.

"Huh," June said and paused at a metal marker next to the road, its words almost lost in rust. *"Dingman's Ferry Bridge,"* she read out loud. *"The Last Privately-Owned Toll Bridge on the Delaware River.* Well, I wonder who Mr. Dingman was ... maybe a wealthy mayor or a preacher."

Farther on, the bridge crossed a wide river, and she stepped onto what appeared to be old wooden boards, weathered by wind and rain. Halfway across she leaned on the railing and looked down.

"The Delaware River," she said out loud and leaned over.

Below the water rushed along, and she could see a man in a small boat. The boat looked like a toy as he headed downriver. Thick forest climbed steep hills on either side of the river and clouds drifted high above the trees. June stepped back and let her body relax, letting her eyes rest on the sight. Green, she thought, everything is so green. Now and again, Travelers passed her, but she ignored them and wandered on.

On the other side of the bridge, a road sign with big black letters spelled out *Welcome to the Garden State*, and June stopped and gazed at the words with excitement.

"I'm in the Garden State," she shouted and skipped past the sign and up the roadway. "Garden State," she sang, "Garden State, *Garden* State."

She was singing and searching the woods for a place to rest when she heard the familiar whistle as it passed from Traveler to Traveler.

"NPF," someone shouted, his voice high and frightened. As the others scattered, June plunged down the bank and into the trees, and she didn't stop running until she was deep in the forest. Her backpack snagged a branch, and her dress was drenched with sweat when she finally dropped down in the underbrush. Terrified and exhausted, June curled up under a bush and closed her eyes.

"Please, Sir," she prayed, "please keep me safe."

She finally fell asleep with her head on her backpack, and the sound of birdsong in her dreams.

June woke with a start. The sun was low in the west and she lay quietly and watched the birds fluttering from tree to tree. As early shadows fell across the woods, they fluffed their feathers and twittered among themselves. It was a safe place, far from the main road and the cold eyes of the NPF, and she sat up and looked around. Thick vines, heavy with greenery and white blossoms, grew helter-skelter; dark green foliage filled the branches of stunted trees.

Through the leaves, June saw the ruins of an old stone arch smothered with the same thick vines. She yawned loudly, climbed out of the underbrush and pushed through the bushes. In front of her, an ancient brick path led to the arch. She followed it, skipping over the missing bricks. The structure was built of primitive gray stone, and June stared. She had never seen anything as ancient as this. Ferns and a bank of wild yellow lilies grew along the base, and here and there stones had fallen to the ground, leaving moss filled holes in the wall.

June followed the path through the archway and into a flagstone courtyard. More bricks had been laid out around and around like a snail shell, ending at a broken tile in the middle. The enclosure was overgrown with grass and surrounded by trees; rays of sun streamed through the leaves. A small brook bubbled in the underbrush nearby, and June decided to stay in the strange, deserted ruin until she was ready to travel again. She was still exhausted and filled with fear, and this was a quiet place to stay.

I can read and daydream, she thought, maybe find my way now that I'm finally in the Garden State. It had been many days since she had read even one page in her history book or given a thought to what she wanted when she got where she was going. Wherever that is, she thought and then she began to sing, her voice soft and filled with sorrow.

"You show me the path of life, Lord
In your presence, there is fullness of joy ..."
She sang it loudly, sitting cross-legged in the empty courtyard by the stone arch, surrounded by trees and white forest blossoms.

"Show me the path," she sang, "*Please,* Sir, show me the path," and then she started to cry.

Chapter 19

June stayed by the arch for three days. At night, she could hear rustling in the underbrush, and sometimes little eyes shone like lamps in the dark, yet she felt safe. Somehow, she knew this place was special, even magical. "I know something is watching over me," June told herself.

Her first night alone, she found a place under a tree, soft with leaves. The Daughter would love it here, she thought, and a sudden wave of nostalgia washed over her. I lost my mother, and I keep losing my friends, she thought. I'm lonely. I'm lonely, and I miss my mama. Why am I here in this place instead of *The Knitting Shop* with her? She whispered the bad words the Man had used and went to sleep with a frown on her face.

The next morning, it was cool, and the sun was just rising when June opened her history book and dutifully started reading. She tried to understand what was happening, but it gave her a headache. Who were these people, she wondered, what were they even thinking? How did we get *here* from *there*?

When she was tired of reading and wondering, June closed the book and decided to explore the area around the arch. She had enough food for three or four more days. The brook was fast and clean to drink from, so now she wanted to see her surroundings in the daylight.

On the other side of the water, the forest reached forever, trees and underbrush blocking any view, but June knew that was the direction she would have to travel, away from the main road. She stood still and thought about setting off into that dark wilderness and then turned walked and away.

The second day she discovered something fascinating; when the noonday sun touched the tile in the middle of the patio, it would glow with a light of its own. She knelt down and rubbed the dirt off and found the image of the sun, its rays reaching out like fingers. June thought about this for a while and then jumped up and skipped around the brick snail shell design, closer and closer to the center tile. As she followed the old bricks around the patio floor, she felt a sense of tranquility, and when she came to the sun tile, June took a deep, cleansing breath, then returned the way she had come, almost dancing around the design. That's nice, she thought, and it made her happy.

The noon sun slid off the tile, and June sat down cross-legged and pulled the map out of her history book. Maybe I can find out where I am, she thought and opened the brown envelope on the back cover. The map caught, and when it slipped out it was attached to a piece of paper folded into a neat little square. Carefully she opened the creased paper and found a poem written in her mother's hand. It was titled *America the Beautiful* and was filled with odd but lovely words that made her eyes well up with tears.

"What is this, Mama?" June said aloud and read the poem twice. She liked the words, and she particularly liked the part about the pilgrims in the wilderness. She had learned about pilgrims in her history book and firmly believed that she was now a 21st Century pilgrim. June read it again and then made up a tune and sang softly:

"O beautiful for pilgrim feet
Whose stern impassioned stress
A thoroughfare of freedom beat
Across the wilderness ... "

She didn't know what impassioned meant, but she figured it had something to do with passion and she certainly knew what passion was.

"A thoroughfare of freedom," she told herself. "A roadway like the track through the woods with the Illegals, far away from NPF." She nodded. "This is me," she whispered, "in the wilderness." And she sang it again.

June memorized the words and folded the old paper back into the little square and slipped it into her purse.

"Close to my heart," she said and sang her new song once more.

Later that afternoon, there was a sudden rainstorm. June stood in the middle of the courtyard with her face turned up and let the rain drench her hair and wash her dress clean.

The storm passed, and the sun came, out filling the patio with a soft light. June took her dress and underclothes off and hung them on a tree to dry. She liked the feeling of being undressed, loved feeling naked and close to nature. She hummed a tune and then danced around the sun tile, tossing her hair in the sun, and waving her arms above her head.

"I am the great Goddess Diana," she sang and danced until a movement caught her eye: a shadow and a whisper of something nearby.

Next to the arch, the bushes moved, and June stopped singing; goosebumps rose on the back of her neck, and her heart began to race. She crouched down and covered her naked body with her hands, her eyes on the bushes. "Who's there?" she shouted.

A small, rust-red animal crept out and stood near the patio, its pointed nose testing the air, black feet shifting. The small creature moved under the arch and watched June with bright eyes.

"Oh my," June said and stared. "You're a fox. You look like the little animal in the foxhunt painting," and she was filled with wonder. "You're real, and you're so beautiful. Who would want to hurt you?"

She sat down on the warm bricks and looked back. "Hello, Fox," she said, "have you been watching me? Do those glowing eyes in the dark belong to you?"

The fox also sat down and stared back at June. He opened his mouth, tongue lolling out, and his bushy tail wrapped around his body.

"You're smiling," June said and laughed. "You know me, don't you? Oh, Fox, I'd so love to stroke your red fur and bury my face in your soft white ruff, but you wouldn't stay, would you?" June sat quietly, almost holding her breath; if she moved, she knew he would disappear. He was a wild animal like the deer back in the water meadow.

June and the fox sat and gazed at each other for a while and then he twitched his tail and trotted back into the brush. For some reason, June didn't feel as lonely, anymore. Fox is watching over me, she told herself. Something from home.

That night the fox brought a small, smooth stone and dropped it carefully by her side as she slept. June woke as he crept away and picked up his gift. As she held the stone in her open palm, the moon turned it to silver.

"Thank you, Fox," she said sleepily, "I'll always keep your gift," and she fell asleep with it held tightly in her hand. The next day June stored it in her backpack, and that's where it safely stayed.

The third day, June knew she had to leave her safe hiding place. She loved the arch and hated the thought of leaving Fox behind. The early morning sun was warm, and a light breeze tossed her hair. The birds were flitting from tree to tree, and the courtyard was a sanctuary of peace and safety.

I wish I could stay here, she thought, but she only had enough food for another day or two. Reluctantly, June changed into her clean, dry dress and underclothes. She picked up her history book and thumbed through a few pages, then shoved it angrily into her backpack.

June had been reading things that troubled her: people who looked like the beautiful juggler being enslaved by people who looked like her and some old Civil War; *The Brothers' War* the book called it. It wasn't the war her father had died in; this was an old one in the 1860s, for heaven's sake, but it was the same thing – North and South. In the old war, they even had different flags and different names: The Confederate States and The United States. She thought that was ridiculous and sad. What is wrong with us, she wondered. You'd really think we would learn. It was difficult for June to read about things she never knew existed, things that made her feel ignorant and ask questions. It gave her a headache.

"Is that why you hid the book in your closet, Mama?" she asked. But the only sound was the sighing of the wind in the trees.

June thought about the Illegals and her friend, January, how kind they were and how good. She thought about the friendly water truck driver from the Green Mountains and all the warm, generous people in her town. Then she thought about the sarcastic store clerk in the mall and the NPF agents. With a chill, June remembered what had happened to January and she shivered. There is evil in this world, she thought and war in my history book. She looked around at the arch and the flower-filled greenery, and she wanted to hit something.

"Something is *wrong*," June shouted. The birds flew up from the trees, and she was ashamed.

"It's time for me to go," she said sadly. "I'm sorry I scared you, birds, but I don't understand this crap! Ha!" she said, and then she said "crap" again – because it made her feel better.

June put one of her rice cakes under the arch as a parting gift and hoped that Fox would like it. Do foxes eat rice cakes, she wondered, and laughed softly. Do they even have rice up here in the Northern Region?

"Bobby was right, you really are silly, June," she said out loud.

She hoisted her backpack onto her back, picked up the carry bag and headed into the morning sun without looking back, but when she stopped at the brook to fill her plastic bottle, she saw Fox. He appeared on the other side of the brook and stood with his tongue hanging out and his bushy tail twitching. He stared at her for a minute and then turned and headed into the woods, stopped after a few steps and looked back. After a minute, June realized he was waiting for her. She crossed the brook and the animal continued with June close behind. Every now and then he would look back at her as she puffed along.

All morning, the fox padded along ahead of her through the forest, but when the sun was high, and the heat hung over the woods, he stopped, looked back once more, and disappeared into the underbrush.

June gazed at the spot where Fox had vanished. He lives in the arch, she thought. He's going home, but already she missed him. Other than Travelers, the little animal was the only living thing she had seen since leaving the Illegals. Now he was gone, and she was alone again. She whispered the Man's bad word out loud, but it didn't help.

Exhausted and discouraged, June dumped her backpack on the ground and sat down. Her back ached, and moisture soaked her dress. After she rested a minute, she dug out her water bottle and let the cold water run down her throat.

The forest sloped upward, and the ground was covered with brush and ferns. Here and there large, moss-covered rocks broke through the earth like huge marbles someone had tossed down the hill. This is a mountain, June thought and was amazed. She looked back down the wooded trail. "Huh," she said, "No wonder I'm pooped."

It would be a hard hike, but she decided it was unwise to go back to the main road. Travelers and the roving NPF, she thought, even if I could find my way, again. I'll stay here tonight and travel into the rising sun in the morning. No matter what, I'll be fine, she added, moved under a tree and pulled out her history book.

June ate some bread and read a few more pages, but it was so disturbing she packed it away. So many dead men, she thought, right here in the Garden State. There on these pages are old photographs of bodies in the snow, so it isn't fake. Those poor dead soldiers look so sad and alone I really don't want to know any more about it.

June lay down and looked up at the treetops. Through the leaves, she could see blue sky and wisps of clouds drifting by, and it made her drowsy. All around her the leaves moved like a river, murmuring as the breeze touched them. She remembered when her home had been beautiful, too. She thought about Fox, and about *the British Tea Shoppe* with its foxhunt print hanging on the wall. Fox is safe living in the arch, June thought, he's not being chased by dogs and hunters on horses. She rolled over and found the little stone in her backpack, the gift he'd given her, and held it in her hand. As she drifted off, she knew she'd never forget him, she had the smooth, white stone as a memory.

Chapter 20

June had never climbed a mountain, she had never even *seen* a mountain, and this one was jutting up or sloping down, and overgrown with brush. In her North Carolina, the land had been gently rolling, with green lawns, tall shade trees and the lazy river that rolled through town. Bobby lived on a farm with a large cornfield and a grassy meadow that sloped down to the very same river. Maybe that was like a small mountain, she thought.

She stood at the bottom of the overgrown incline, shifted her backpack and looked up. In a way, it reminded June of Bobby's farm. She remembered helping him drive the cows into the meadow: the large, slow black and white creatures with soft eyes, long eyelashes, and pink noses. His *Ladies*.

She had told him she wished she had eyelashes like his ladies. "Just look," she'd said, "their eyelashes are so long and pretty."

"You're a silly girl," Bobby had scoffed. But he still wanted to be with her, so she believed it was love. That was before I knew what love really was, she thought, the confusion and the heat in my body. She felt a painful moment of longing that brought a lump to her throat.

June ate one of the rice cakes and drank some more water, then hoisted her backpack up onto her back again and headed into the sun. She fought her way through the underbrush, breaking branches and tearing a leafy twig out of her hair that clung like a limpet.

The sun was at its highest and June was becoming discouraged when she broke through a patch of thick bramble bushes and discovered a small dirt trail that wandered upward and curved out of sight. Trees hung over the path and underbrush almost covered it; here and there rocks or tree roots had broken through the hard-packed earth, but it was a path, and it was heading in the right direction.

"It's a trail and trails go somewhere," she said and started hiking up the mountain, stopping now and then take a sip out of her water bottle. The forest floor fell away on her left, and she could see the tops of trees and a glint of water far below. The sight made her dizzy, but she kept on, hugging the side of the mountain as she hiked along. Around a bend, she noticed a pile of rocks stacked neatly, one on top the other. They were just off the path on the sloping side of the mountain, but she crept closer to look. Well, this is odd, she thought. It looks like somebody made this thing. What is it? … a monument way out in the woods. I wonder why?

Clumps of dirt and stones broke loose and tumbled down the steep hillside and June jumped back, then quickly left the rock pile behind. The path seemed to go on forever, but finally, it made a right turn around a bank and headed into the woods and away from the gorge. She stood for a minute and looked out over the countryside below: green trees and flat landscape as far as her eye could see. Here and there houses, the size of a doll's house, sprung up on the farmland. I'm so far away, she thought, and so far away from home; then she shifted her backpack and turned away.

A little further on, there was a cutoff, and June stopped to think, two paths, which way to go? The cutoff seemed to head back down in the direction she had come from so she kept trudging up the mountain. The forest was vast, and except for the birds and a chorus of insects that kept up a constant low whirring sound, it seemed to hold its breath. Insects, June thought. It's been so long since I heard the sound of insects.

"Oh, beautiful for Pilgrims feet …" she sang as she climbed.

She shifted her backpack, again, and kept on as the path curved left and right, and she found herself in a clearing – the kind of place the Illegals would choose for a campsite. Tall trees surrounded the area and sunlight chased shadows across the ground as the leaves moved high above. She stood still and looked around: curious and puzzled. The path ended at a massive rock cliff; brush and small, dying pine trees grew along the base.

"How can a path lead to a clearing and then just stop?" she wondered and turned around, and then turned around again.

Something caught June's eye as she examined the clearing, and she gazed back. At first, she didn't know what she was missing – something out of place. She closed her eyes and visualized the clearing. And then she realized what it was. The thick pine trees at the base of the cliff were not growing there, they were pine branches, and they had been stacked against the cliff in a pile.

June dropped her backpack and went to take a closer look. The brush wasn't tossed haphazardly by the wind, it was stacked neatly against the face of the cliff, obviously put there by human hands.

"Is something hidden here?" she wondered aloud, "somebody's belongings or maybe some dollar coupons? Maybe a treasure."

She pulled the branches away from the cliff and stood back and stared. A crude doorway had been hacked from a crevice in the side of the rock, and it made an opening into the cliff. It's a cave, she thought, out here on the top of this mountain. She listened intently but there was no sound from the cave, no rustling or growling, and it was cool inside.

This is where I'm going to stay, June decided. She held her breath and crawled into the cave, listening for the slightest sound. Inside, she stood up carefully and looked around. It was dim, but the walls rose up around her. High above, she could see daylight streaming through an opening that was hacked through the rock. The sides of the cave were rough, but a firepit had been built in the middle of the floor.

June looked at the firepit and then up at the opening above. "Well, look at that. It's a chimney. The fire pit is built right under the hole. Someone lived here."

The cave was swept clean except for some old rags piled up against one of the walls. June contemplated the rags for a minute and then went to inspect them. They look mighty old, she thought, but they look clean and soft. I bet I can sleep on them. She touched the rags with her foot and leaned over and sniffed. "Clean," she added.

And the pile of rags moved!

Chapter 21

"Who are you?" Eyes peered out at June, and the pile of rags rose up and hugged the wall.

June jumped back and crouched on the floor, her heart pounding. She tried to scream, but all that came out was a tiny rush of air, a harsh squawk.

A hand came out of the rags and pointed at June. "Who sent you?" The voice was an angry rasp like the sound of a saw. June kept crouching on the floor, terrified. She couldn't find her voice, and her eyes were wide with shock, adrenalin pumping through her veins, yet she knew her legs wouldn't hold her if she tried to run.

Then the rags settled, and an old man appeared. He was as thin and frail as a stick with hair that fell over his shoulders and a long grey beard that reached his waist. He smelled of sweat and dirt, but his ragged clothes were clean. His wrinkled face was filled with fear, and his body trembled. June realized this strange person was more afraid of her than she was of him, and the shock subsided.

"My name is June," she said, "and I'm a Traveler." She spoke softly, hoping it would calm him, and after days without speaking her words spilled out as slow as honey. "Nobody has sent me. I'm traveling to the Garden State because my home is burning."

"Your voice," he said, and the fear and anger were gone. "Your words. You sound like home." The fear was replaced with sorrow. "A Traveler? Are you running from them, too?" He grew angry, again. "It has come to this … young women now!" The old man slumped down on the pile of rags and covered his face with his hands.

"Who?" June asked. "Who are we running from?" She drew closer and sat down next to him.

"The Loyalists," he took his hands away and looked at her from the corner of his eye. "The Northern Loyalists, of course. Everyone else died, but *I* got away and have hidden from them right here, ever since. He looked directly at June. "*They* have never found me."

He was proud, and he held his head high, long hair straggling over his shoulders. "Oh, I would hear them outside, yes missy, talking and laughing, but not now, not for a long time now. They gave up, missy, just gave up and went away!" He sat up straight and tossed his hair back over his shoulders. "When the War is over, then I'll go home." His voice had grown stronger, and now June heard the familiar sweet, mellow drawl she had grown up with.

Slowly she understood what this strange old man was talking about, and she was stunned. My God, she thought, he thinks we're still at war! Oh, poor old soul.

"There is no war," she said gently. "The American War ended when I was a baby, but I had to leave the Southern Region because my home is dying and there is no food."

"Bombs," he said. "Drones with bombs! And missiles!" He put his hands over his face. "Oh, no! Now they be down home!"

"No bombs, no missiles: the war is *over*," June said. "But there is no rain and the sun has killed every living thing. You won't be able to go there, it's all gone, under the sea."

"What? What in tarnation does *that* mean?" His voice rose. "The War has ended, but now I can't go home because of the *weather*?" His face twisted with confusion and then tears welled up in his eyes. "But, I don't understand." He raised one hand to his face, again. "If the War is over, I will go home and find my family and now … now, nobody can stop me."

June took his hand in hers; the fingers were bent, and she could feel how fragile the bones were. "No, no," she said. "Not now, listen."

She told him what home had been like when she was growing up, how beautiful her town was with the tall trees and the gentle people; then she told him about the Great Flood that had taken her mama. She told him about the icy cold winter and the burning days that killed all the crops and how the farmers slaughtered their cattle; how the Green Mountain Water truck came with fresh, untainted water to drink because all the water was brown and polluted. Then she told him how everybody left town and how she locked up her mother's knitting shop in North Carolina and traveled all these many miles to find a safe place to live.

"And," she paused, "the National Police." June lowered her voice and looked around as if NPF were in the cave with them. "They are dangerous and cruel." She told him how they had searched for her in the woods and how she had hidden in the brush. It made her angry all over again. "And," she continued. "You have no FedID. They will arrest you and take you away like that poor woman who was on my bus!"

The more she talked, the more June wanted to talk, and it spilled out – all the sorrow and fear she had lived with for more weeks than she could count. She paused, but decided not to tell the old soldier about the Illegals; she knew he'd never understand. She had to admit to herself that *she* never would have understood, either … before. She tried to tell him about January but couldn't find the right words. The memories welled up, and June sobbed and rubbed the tears from her eyes like a baby.

The old man sat quietly and then took her hand, but he didn't say anything.

"Come with me," June said, and finally the tears dried on her cheeks. The old man reminded her of the soldier wrapped in the flag and how he was gone when she went back to find him. "Travel with me," she begged. "We can find a safe place with food and clean water, and I'm very good at hiding."

"No, I will stay here," the old man patted her hand. "I trust you because you have the voice of home, but truly I find it hard to believe the War is over and that weather thing you told me about." He sat and thought for a minute, "I still don't trust them folks up here, but now this is my home. I'm old and sick, but I'm still a soldier. I can trap, and there be water below the mountain."

He nodded towards the path that meandered down the mountain and tapped his nose slyly. "Sometimes I slip down to the farms in the night and pick vegetables from the gardens." He patted her hand again. "I have lived here since I escaped into the woods and so this is where I'll live out my life, Missy June." He cocked his head and raised one eyebrow, "Since you was a baby, you say? Huh! That long?" And he shook his head in disbelief and stared into the distance, his rheumy old eyes half closed.

Chapter 22

June stayed with the old soldier that night. She thought about it for a long while, but she was not afraid of him. He was a frail, sick old man and a Southern Gentleman, and she knew he would never touch her. Anyway, she decided, for him, those days are gone forever, and this cave is comfortable and safe.

That evening he left the cave, and when it was dark, he brought back a rabbit that he skinned and gutted. June gathered wood and brush and set a fire like the Illegals had taught her. She hung the rabbit on the spit, and when it was done, she dug around and found the bread in her backpack and shared it. As they sat by the fire and ate, June asked the old man about "His war."

"My Daddy died in the War," she said. "But my Mama never talked about it, and there is nothing in my history book about *this* War, only the old one in the 1860s, The Civil War and all those other, "Why? Why so many wars?"

"People are greedy," the old man said, "Ah, but the War of Northern Aggression, the *old* Civil War." He thought for a moment. "Yes! Well, none of us ever forgot it, but my Great Grampa, yeah, he fought for the United States of America in a World War and my Daddy fought in another one, too, someplace in China or something, but then one day they took our flags and knocked down our Confederate statues because times had changed and people were hurt by that history. But we did not forget, no Missy, we didn't forget." The old man's eyes were filled with memories, and June visualized the Memorial for the Lost the mayor had built in her town. There is nobody left to remember them, she thought, and it made her eyes burn again. I just keep crying, she thought, and it made it worse.

"When the American Civil War started … my war," he began, "I was a farming man in Mississippi, forty odd years old I was, with a wife and family, but we came from all the towns and out of all the hamlets to join the Cause."

June was filled with relief and realized it had crossed her mind this frail, dirty old man might be her own father. Then what would I do? she thought.

"Young and old," the old man continued, "we believed we should be free and not beholden to any Government but our own state … and there was so many other people coming into our country, different people." He frowned. "They wasn't bad people, oh, not at all, they was nice folks, but they was taking our place, making our country foreign-like. So, we went to War."

"We did things that wasn't Christian, but then we took Virginia and Washington D.C. in 2046, and the President hid under his desk. The rest all ran like rabbits," he stopped and laughed. "Just ran away, oh yes, they ran … except the ones who joined us. Those silly clowns came out begging to be part of our Cause, and so we let them join. They was fancy folks, politicians, but we let them join. They said they'd build our statues for us again."

The old soldier sat in silence for a minute and then shook his head.

"Fools!" he said. "We had what we wanted, but then the Generals wanted more. 'Y'all go up North and take Pennsylvania,' they ordered. 'They'll just lay down like the rest of them folks.' And so, we went up to Pennsylvania, but they was ready! Yeah, we had guns, big assault weapons, but they came swarm'n down to Pennsylvania from New Jersey and even as far as some place called New Hampshire, and they had armed drones, big drones with missiles and they just wiped us out!" He paused and his face twisted. "And then, oh yes, then the Generals with their big orders, they just went silent. My unit escaped into the forest and the mountains, and we planned to find our way home, travel at night, you know. But some of them fellas died from their wounds, cry'n for their mamas, and others fell down the cliff back there. Just fell over and disappeared in the trees." He gazed at June, his shaggy eyebrows raised. "So, then it was just me." He looked away for a minute, "did you see the monument I built for them?"

June nodded. "Yes, I wondered."

"I visit it," he said. "Over these many years, I still visit it. Maybe they just be stones, but I don't feel so alone." His voice was low, but then he brightened, "but I escaped and I been here ever since, waiting for the war to end." He made a fist with his thin, broken hand. "We had what we wanted!" he said bitterly and shook his fist.

"But you did it!" June told him. "I lived in the Southern Region and our own town decides everything, the state even prints our money." She pulled out a dollar coupon and handed it to the old soldier. "Well, at least they did," she added.

"Well, just lookee here," he said and held it up. "Right there on this bill, General Robert E. Lee on his Tennessee Walking Horse." He shook his head in amazement. "How about that?"

"I never noticed," June said. "But you can keep it. And, here," she fumbled in her backpack, "This is a gift for your hospitality." She handed him one of her last bars of cold-water soap, the soap she had purchased in January's store. "It's nice," she added, fearing he would be insulted.

But he laughed, took a sniff and thanked her. "Very nice, missy. I thank ye kindly."

June let the old man talk, and she pictured her father leaving home to fight for the Cause, leaving her Mama and his baby girl at home. Did this Cause drive him to go to War? Were the Illegals these "folks" the old man had spoken about? She relaxed against the stone wall of the cave with the soothing sound of his voice in her ears as he told her about his home in Mississippi, his family, about the friends he had lost and the little monument he'd built back on the trail.

June awoke at dawn when it was still dim inside the cave. It took her a minute to remember where she was. The rough rock behind her was cool and the dirt floor hard, and she reached out and touched it. She was lying on her side, and her head was resting on something soft. June yawned and then sat up. All the memories of the night before flooded in and she found the old soldier relaxing against the wall across from her, his faded eyes half closed.

"That's my flag," he said. "I put it under your head in the night. It's soft. You needed something soft to sleep on."

June turned around and picked up the material she had been sleeping on.

"But ... it's an *American* flag," she said and turned back. "Wasn't your flag different?"

"I am an American, we was *all* Americans," the old soldier said indignantly. "Not Confederates. That's all ancient history."

Again, June thought about the old man on the road with the flag wrapped around him. She remembered the crippled man on his flat wooden cart, his cap embroidered with the stars, and she realized they had been soldiers, too, just like this old man.

"Well, I have to wonder if we are all *still* Americans like in my book," she snapped and pulled the book out of her backpack. "It's a history book. I can read some of it to you if you want, but it's all old fashioned."

The old man laughed. "I went to school, and I can still read," he held his hand out. "My eyes may be old, but they can still see a rabbit in the brush before it jumps away. Look, I brewed some lemon balm tea if you want. You can use my tin cup and have some while I take a lookee here."

June carefully folded up the flag and then poured some of the hot, odd smelling brew into an old tin cup and tasted it. It was strong, but it was hot and oddly delicious. She broke a rice cake in two and handed one piece to the old man.

"I want to leave before the sun is high," she said and popped a piece of cake into her mouth. "I need to find a safe place to live." She chewed thoughtfully. "You can come with me if you want."

The old man slipped the dollar coupon between two pages to keep his place and then closed the book carefully. He tasted the rice cake. "This is where I'll stay," he said. "I don't want to leave my friends."

His eyes blurred and June thought he would cry. "I don't want them to be forgotten." He looked down at the book. "Please wait till I have finished the part about the 1860s," he pleaded. "It reminds me of the Cause and makes me wanna add a few more stones to the monument!"

June nodded and leaned back against the stone wall and daydreamed. She'd meet the Illegals again, maybe where it was safe, and perhaps the Son would still love her. It filled her with longing. This time she would never leave him no matter what his mother said. She made designs on the dirt floor with her finger and watched the old man read. His eyes were straining in the dim light, but now and again he whispered a comment or chuckled out loud.

When the sun was high, the old man got up. He had been deep in the history book all morning, but now he handed it back to June. "Nothing in this book about the Cause. Nothing about *our* War, and I even skipped to the last chapter." He scratched his head. "It's strange. It ends at the year two thousand and twenty-something! Like everything just ended before it even began."

June thought about that and frowned. She packed the book, and they pushed through the dried pine branches into the sunshine. The old man pointed at the path that June had hiked up.

"Go the way you came," he told her. "When you come to the cutoff, take that path. It will take you to the waterfalls and then on to the main roadway."

June lifted her backpack onto her shoulders and picked up her carry bag. "Thank you," she said and then paused. "Wait! I don't even know your name, Sir! What is it? I should know your name, it's only proper!"

The old man thought for a minute, his face twisted in a frown of concentration. "Bo John," he finally said, one thin finger in the air, "I think it's *Bo John*!"

"Bo John," she whispered, "it doesn't matter that I speak your name, because I have to leave you behind anyway."

"Goodbye, Mr. Bo John," June dipped one knee and bobbed her head the way she had been taught.

She heard his raspy laugh as she started back down the trail and it made her smile, but she was wondering why the history book ended when it did.

Chapter 23

June retraced her steps to the cut off and took the track that led away from the ridge. The path led downhill and passed piles of brush and rocks where the old man had cleared the way. Birds were rustling in the trees and chattering to each other, but otherwise, the forest was as still and peaceful as the river that flowed through her town. Halfway down the track, she found a faded, green arrow nailed to a tree and stopped to take a look. The nails were rusted, and the lettering was faint, but she could make out the words: *Butternut Falls.*

Butternut Falls, June thought. Water where I can bathe and wash my hair. It reminded her of the first time she had met the Woman and the little waterfall where they had bathed. So many days and weeks had passed, but she remembered how wonderful the water had felt as it cascaded over her body.

"This is where you hide from the NPF," the Woman had told her. "Behind the waterfall."

Back then June had no idea what she meant, but she certainly did now, and the memory made her cringe. "January," she said out loud. "I will never forget you."

June adjusted her backpack. It was hot now, but she didn't care, all she cared about was Butternut Falls and letting the water wash away the dirt and leaves from her trip through the brush and the dust from the old soldier's cave.

"And, of course, this path leads to the main roadway!" she said out loud. "Maybe it will lead me to a place where I can live my life in peace." The birds quieted for a moment and then started their twittering again.

She thought about the old man with the lonely eyes and how he had found peace and security deep in the forest. So many years hiding in a cave, she thought, and not even knowing the war was over. How sad, but that's his life now, and he really doesn't want to leave, doesn't want to leave the memory of his friends. The Daughter would say they were his spirit brothers, she thought, and it made her smile.

The path wandered down and around, and now June had to step over rocks and roots. The birds kept up their songs, and it kept her spirits up. Every now and then, some little creature would appear and then disappear in the brush, chattering in alarm.

She stopped and checked what was left of her bread and rice cakes, then picked off a piece of bread and stuffed it in her mouth. The Woman had taught her what wild berries, greens and roots were good to eat, so she didn't worry about food, but she wanted to conserve the bread and cakes for as long as possible.

The path twisted and curved around a group of large rocks and there it was – the waterfall! It slid and tumbled down a rock face and ended in a pool where the water was as smooth as glass. On the other side of the water, the path continued through the forest and headed to the east. She could see the sun through the leaves and stood at the top and looked down. She knew this was where she wanted to camp.

There was no path, just some broken down wooden steps that looked dangerous, so June picked her way over fallen trees and moss-covered rocks. She hung onto low-hanging branches and slipped down a pine needle-covered slope on her bottom, finally landing at the shaded clearing by the pool. The water was not deep, but it was clear; a few leaves floated on top. The waterfall fell in a long, bright wash of water and the clearing was tucked into the rocks: safe and secure.

June found a spot under some stunted pine trees that was soft with pine needles and dropped her belongings under a gnarled root. It was peaceful by the pool, and she pulled off her dress and underclothes and slipped into the water with a sigh. She wondered how long the old soldier would be able to find his way to the waterfall, and *then* where could he get water to drink? Her mind was full of his stories, and she understood why he had chosen to stay in the cave and live out his life in the woods. It was where his friends were and his dreams of home: Southern Pride deep in the forest of the Northern Region.

June spent two days resting at the falls. She washed her dress and underclothes and hung them on the stunted trees then ducked under the waterfall and let the water cascade over her, washing her hair with the last bar of cold-water soap. She read her history book and knitted a new money belt for her savings, chewing off the end of the yarn when she was finished. At night, small creatures moved through the underbrush, and the wind whispered in the pine trees, but June never knew, because she was curled up with her head on her backpack, dreaming of home.

Chapter 24

The third day, June realized she had to find the main road and, eventually, a store. There was only one rice cake and a small piece of bread left in her backpack, and she had eaten her fill of roots and berries.

"Yuck, I'm skinny," she shouted. "I'm skinny, and I'm lonely!" But there was nobody to hear and not even an echo.

At sunrise, June left the waterfall and followed the path on the other side of the bank and then down the mountain. The trail twisted, and sometimes it even turned back on itself. Here and there, she had to hang onto overhanging branches to keep from falling. One turn brought her to a sheer cliff where she could see over the tall pine trees and into the valley below. Rocks and shale broke loose and bounced down into the trees as she passed. Another cliff, she thought, but this time she wasn't afraid, and she kept on walking.

The sun was well over the horizon when June stumbled down the final turn and into a long valley surrounded by trees. The sky was bright blue overhead, and across the sweep of land, she could see a road, and it headed into the sun.

"Oh, how amazing," June said and set off. The field was green with soft grasses and wildflowers, and she stopped now and again to breathe it in. She picked a daisy and stuck it in her hair, wedged behind her ear. It reminded her of the Daughter and the faerie crowns she had made. The memory hurt her heart.

Where are they now, she wondered. She thought about the NPF chasing them and prayed out loud:

"Please, Sir, keep them safe. Please help them reach the Border!" But she kept her eyes on the road ahead and kept on walking

On the other side of a copse of trees, June climbed up a bank and looked around. The road was smooth and well kept, the grass on either side tall and filled with white, lacy flowers. There were no potholes or broken asphalt here, just this open roadway heading into the morning sun. A few Travelers, out early, glanced at her as she dusted herself off and joined them.

A woman was pushing a baby carriage, and she smiled at June and stopped. June smiled back and peeked into the baby carriage then stepped back, shocked. There was no baby in the carriage, just an elderly dog, its muzzle gray and its eyes dim with age. The woman stopped smiling, grunted, and headed up the road again.

"Is there a store?" June called after her. "I'm hungry. Please, I need some food."

"Up ahead," the woman shouted, but she kept on going without looking back.

June followed her receding back and ignored the other Travelers. She thought about the dog in the carriage. That woman loved her old dog so much, she couldn't leave him behind, June thought, and has pushed him in a baby carriage, all these many miles. I don't understand. Her stomach rumbled loudly, and she knew she needed to eat as soon as possible or she'd be sick.

The store stood a little way off the roadway. It wasn't as big as the food shop in the mall, but it wasn't falling apart like the country store where the bus had stopped, either. A picnic table sat in a grove of trees. Some Travelers were seated at the table, but they ate their food in silence. June crossed the porch and pushed open the screen door. The store was small but well stocked.

A young man was making sandwiches behind a counter. Next to him was a large, glass case with bread and rolls piled in baskets on top. Behind the case, a young woman grilled hamburgers and June's stomach rumbled again. People stood in line at the counter, but they were silent, staring ahead. June looked in the case and her mouth watered. Through the glass she could see meat and cheese, fish salad and hardboiled eggs; there was fruit salad in a big silver bowl and a mound of potato salad on a big white platter.

"Do they take dollar coupons," she called, and the people in the line looked over at her. Someone said, "yes," and then they all looked away.

She was the last one in line, and soon the others disappeared through the front door and trudged off the porch.

The young man looked at her and smiled. He had a kind face and a white cap perched on his head. His eyes were blue, and his cheeks crinkled when he smiled.

"Do you know you have a wilted daisy stuck in your hair?" he said and gently removed it. "You look like a forest nymph."

June nodded her head and smiled shyly.

"So, where do you come from?" he asked and leaned on the counter.

"North Carolina," June told him. "The Southern Region. I have been on the road for many days, sir. Will you accept my dollar coupons?

"Of course!" The young man pushed his cap back and nodded. "And you traveled all this way?"

"I wanted to come to the Garden State," June said. "I had a garden back home … before the sun, you know? I liked the sound of the Garden State."

"Barb," he called over his shoulder, "come and fix a tray for this young Climate Refugee and take her out back to eat. Stay with her, please. I'll pack up a lunch for her to take with her."

The young man turned back to June, "NPF is due very soon. They always stop here for lunch, but you will be safe out back. They never go into our backyard; they're not allowed."

June drew herself up and lifted her chin. "I'm a Citizen," she said firmly. "I have my documents. They won't take me."

"You are young, and you're pretty," he said. "It doesn't matter anymore." His mouth twisted as if he'd tasted something bad

The young woman pushed the hamburgers to one side and slid one onto a bun, added potato salad and a bowl of fruit. She poured a mug of hot tea and added milk and sugar and then led June through the back of the store and out onto a small porch where the air was sweet with the scent of flowers. A table with two chairs sat on the porch, and flowering vines climbed along the railings. Steps led to a walled-in garden deep in shadow.

"My name is Barb," she said. "My husband is Bob and this is our store."

June's hands shook as she ate her food. Tears filled her eyes and ran down her cheeks. "Thank you, Miss Barb," she said.

"So, you like to garden?" Barb's voice was soft, and she pretended not to notice the tears. "It's been a dry summer, and our flowers aren't as pretty this year."

June nodded. "I had a garden at home with fresh vegetables. Then the burning days came, and it killed everything. We had no food, so all of us had to leave." She nibbled a piece of fruit. "I took a bus, but it broke down when we were in Virginia, or maybe Pennsylvania. So, I had to walk the rest of the way."

Barb frowned, "Alone?"

"Oh, yes," June paused, "Most of the way. But, there are others."

"You're a brave girl. I don't know if I could be as strong as you."

June shook her head. "It can't happen here," she said firmly, "this is the Garden State."

"You're very innocent," Barb said quietly. "Very sweet. You know what?" She pressed a finger against her lips and nodded. "There's an organic farm up the road. They used to have students working for them, but not anymore. I think they would love to hire someone to help them if you want to, and they would give you a place to live and some money to spend. You'd be safe there."

June nodded her head enthusiastically. She mumbled thank you through a mouth full of food.

"It's a few miles or so up the road," Barb continued. "Watch for a big red barn and a white house. There are two sheep in the pasture, big gardens, and a wheat field. It's nice."

June tasted her tea and sighed. "You're both so nice," she said, "Thank you, Ma'am."

Northerners aren't all nasty, she thought. Not like the man in the mall or the one who killed my father. She was sure Bob and Barb would be kind to the old soldier in the cave. The war was long over, and they were nice, but she didn't mention his name. I will never tell anyone, Bo John, she vowed.

When she had finished, June followed Barb back inside. Bob had put a cold meat sandwich and some potato chips into a paper bag, and he asked for a twenty-dollar coupon.

"NPF has been and gone," he said. "You'll be safe now. Just don't let them see you."

This reminded June of what January had said, and she burned with anger, but she handed him the coupon.

"Thank you, Mister Bob," she said and smiled stiffly.

"Wait," he said as she turned away and handed her some paper bills and round silvers disks.

June looked at them. "What are these?" she asked.

"It's money," he said. "It's your change: three American dollars and thirty cents. This will be the money you use here in the Northern Region. The bank in the Village will change your coupons for you."

June stared at the dollar bills and then back at Bob. "That's George Washington," she said in amazement.

"Well, I guess it is," he said and raised his eyebrows. "I never even noticed. It looks like we've kept all the old-fashioned money up here."

June kept the silver coins in her hand as she joined the Travelers on the road. Now and again she would stop and look at them or roll them around in her hand. Change, she thought. There was no change at home. Everything was even: a five-dollar coupon or ten-dollar coupon. The coins amused her and made her happy.

"American money," she sang to herself. "American change!" She was beginning to feel better about this place called the Northern Region.

The Travelers never looked her way. They just kept marching along, their eyes fixed on some distant horizon.

Chapter 25

The sun was behind her now, and she was tired and dusty. The road rolled out into the distance, and more Travelers had joined the march. After a few minutes, she slipped the coins in her little purse and headed off the road and into the woods. Tomorrow I'll go to the farm and ask for work, she decided. I'll be a farmhand. The idea was exotic!

"I used to knit sweaters," she said out loud. "I ran a shop. Farmhands work on farms. They worked on Bobby's farm, mucking about in the cow dung." The idea made her laugh out loud. "June, the Farmhand," she sang as she trudged along.

She pushed through a patch of brambles and saw a ray of sun flash off what looked like water through the trees. Water, she thought, beautiful water.

A sign was posted nearby: DANGER, QUARRY. The words were printed in large black letters and demanded attention.

June glanced at the sign but kept going, ignoring the warning.

The quarry was wide and deep: a wound in the forest floor. The terrain sloped gently up to an embankment, and June stood on the bank and looked down. Dark ripples moved across the water and shimmered in the light. Three rough rock sides rose up, but the fourth was almost level with the surface and looked as if someone had chiseled steps into the stone.

She had never seen a quarry before, but the idea of plunging into that dark, watery hole in the ground and washing off the day's dust was irresistible. She dropped her bags and pulled off her clothes, hanging them on a bush, then picked her way down the steps. The stone was rough on her feet and the rocky wall hard, but she lowered herself onto the edge of the last step, and dangled her feet. The water was cold, colder than she expected and it was dark, almost black: dark water in a hole in the forest. June pushed herself to the edge of the step and plunged in.

It was rumored the quarry was bottomless. It was an old gravel mine, abandoned a century before. Over time it had filled with water, so deep it would suck a person down with the weight of it. Years before, high school boys had used hammers and chisels to carve out the steps. Swimming in the quarry was the "Big Guy" thing to do until one of them sank out of sight and was never seen again. The quarry had taken him, and that was the end of the swimming. The sign had been posted two days later.

June sank deeper and deeper, the water pulling her down. Her eyes stared into the darkness, then squeezed shut, and she felt her body begin to wilt in the cold until she had no breath left. I'm dying, she thought, drowning out here in the woods alone.

Memories flashed through her mind. She remembered the beautiful juggler, and now she wished she had gone into the woods with him. She thought about the Son, how he wanted to "make her happy," and she wanted to weep with regret. I'm going to die before I've ever lived, she thought. Then she thought about her boyfriend's leaving town, and that made her angry. She thought the bad words the Man had said, and pushed her arms hard against the water, kicking her feet like she had in the River currents at home – up and up until she broke the surface a few feet away from the stone shelf.

Icy water spilled down over her face and hair as she paddled towards safety. She gasped for breath and then pulled herself onto the shelf, leaning against the quarry wall shaking with cold. Somewhere, she heard her mother's voice, "Just in case …!" But the only thing she could think was, I want to be happy!

June spent the night in the woods near the quarry. She took her clean dress out of her backpack and hung it on a tree branch. Then she slept with her head on her carry bag. Sometime during the night, she dreamed she was sinking into the dark water. Someone was standing on the stone shelf shouting, "You should have sex, you silly girl!" And all she could do was swim through the dark.

The next morning, June woke with the memory of the dream hanging over her. "How funny," she said, and it made her laugh, but it scared her, too.

"I'm ALIVE!" she shouted, and the birds flew out of the trees. She refused to think of the quarry again, or of the black water that had almost ended her life.

She brushed her hair and put on her clean dress, ate the takeout lunch she'd bought the day before and then headed out of the woods. It was already warm, and a few Travelers were on the road, but as usual, they didn't talk, just marched along with grim faces.

The sun was high when she spotted the farm. It stood on a gentle rise in the distance, just as Miss Barb had told her, the red barn and white house, fields of wheat and vegetable plots, the place where she would become a farmhand.

The Garden State, she thought, and her spirits lifted. I want to settle down here and be happy.

Off the road to her left was a pasture with a grove of leafy trees, and June decided to rest during the heat of the day. I'll visit the farmers later, she thought.

A split rail fence surrounded the pasture, but June wasn't afraid of fences, she and Bobby had climbed plenty of them in North Carolina. She left the hot pavement and headed down the bank without looking back. A few Travelers stopped to watch, but she didn't notice. June threw her backpack and carry bag over the fence, hitched her dress over her hips and climbed over. The Travelers turned back and started walking again.

Chapter 26

The pasture was rough with grass and weeds, and she stumbled over some loose rocks, but she trudged on. Just past the grove of trees, she spotted the sheep and stopped, uncertain. June had never seen sheep before, but they looked like gentle creatures. They reminded her of Bobby's Ladies. The two animals watched her for a while and then went back to grazing. June waited a few more minutes and then continued across the rough ground and into the trees.

It was quiet and secluded, and to her delight, the trees surrounded a pond, small ripples breaking its surface. June lay down on the rocky ground near the pond and gazed at the sky. Dark clouds covered the sun for a few minutes, and she heard thunder in the distance. Against her will, she thought of the quarry, the deep water grabbing her and sucking her down, and she shivered in the heat. I'll never go there again, she vowed. She forced herself to think about the sheep with their gentle faces and strange eyes. Do they go into the barn at night like Bobby's Ladies, she wondered? The Bible stories she'd read told of the shepherds with their sheep. They were always in the hills, not in barns like cows.

June had just started to doze when she felt a presence nearby. A shadow fell over her face, and she opened her eyes. One of the sheep was standing next to her, gazing down with curious, golden eyes. It continued to chew, jaws moving back and forth, tail twitching. June sat up and looked back at it. The sheep had a short white coat and a black muzzle, and June realized it had been shorn. Of course, she thought, and the wool is on its way to market.

"Wool," June informed the sheep. "This is where we get our knitting yarn." She reached out and touched the animal. The coat wasn't smooth like cowhide, it felt spongy; the black nose was soft.

"Nice sheep," she said.

The sheep dipped its head and dragged off another tuft of grass, and its jaws continued to move back and forth. It seemed comfortable with June's presence, and after a few more minutes it ambled away.

"Nice sheep," she called after it, pulled out he history book and settled back to read.

Later in the afternoon, June heaved her backpack onto her shoulders, picked up her carry bag, and headed through the meadow, stepping over rocks and trampled weeds. The sheep lifted their heads and watched her for a while and then headed into the trees.

During the afternoon, the storm had moved off over the hills, and the sky was blue, a few clouds drifting away from the sun. Insects buzzed and clicked as she walked and she remembered what Miss Barb had said, "It's been a dry summer." June felt the sun on her back and had a moment of unease.

"No," she said out loud, "this is the Garden State."

A man and woman were standing by the pasture gate, watching as she trudged up. The woman was tall and wore blue overalls over a yellow t-shirt. Her light brown hair was in little girl pigtails, but there was gray in the brown hair and a few laugh lines by her eyes.

The man was taller, but dressed in the same manner, with blue overalls and a white t-shirt. His gray hair was pulled back in a ponytail, and his eyes were as blue as the sky. June had never seen a man with long hair before, and she tried not to stare.

"Barb said you would come," the woman said and laughed, a high, sweet sound in the still air. "I just didn't think you would arrive by the pasture gate." She had kind eyes and June liked her at once, but she felt shy. "I like to garden," she said, at last, struggling for words.

The woman opened the gate. "Then welcome to Natural World Farm. You are a God Send. We have no help now, it's just us folks."

June didn't know what the woman meant about God sending her, but it sounded nice and reminded her of home.

"My name is Eve," the woman said, "and this is my husband, Adam. He's the farmer. Very biblical, isn't it?" she continued, and laughed again.

June thought it was biblical, too, but didn't know why that would be funny. She turned to the man, bent her knee and bobbed her head the way she'd been taught. The woman's eyebrows flew up like bird's wings, and the husband smiled.

"You curtsied," the woman said.

"Yes, Ma'am," June said shyly. "It's proper."

Oh my, the woman thought, this little gal is from another time and place for sure, but she didn't comment again and turned and nodded at the house.

"I have a small apartment in the basement of our house, and you can live there. It's not much, but it has all you'll need, you know, a bed, stove, refrigerator, bathroom with a shower. We live upstairs." She turned and headed towards the house, and June followed. Again, she didn't know what to say and felt like crying.

"I have dollar coupons," she offered. "My savings are from North Carolina. Will you accept them?"

"Oh no," the woman said. "We'll pay *you* to work in the gardens with us. We can change your coupons at the Chase Bank in the Village. That's your money."

June trailed along behind, trying to find the words, at least something that would show how much she appreciated the woman's kindness.

"Thank you, Ma'am," she said and that was all she could think of to show the woman how grateful she was.

The house was tall and white. Clean, June thought, as fancy as the houses the Ladies from the other side of the River owned. The ground sloped, and there was the basement with two high windows, one on either side of a bright red door.

"This is the apartment," the woman said, and June followed her inside.

The basement was a large room with stone walls painted a clean white. Colorful curtains hung on the two high windows, and a table and two chairs were drawn up under one of them. A sagging brown couch hugged the wall under the other window. A big, comfortable bed took up one of the back corners by a side window. An enclosed bath took up the other corner. The rest of the wall was taken up by a locked basement door, a stove, sink, and a refrigerator.

June searched for words, again. Finally, she looked at the woman and just nodded. She walked around the apartment touching things, then stopped and patted the bed and looked back.

"It's soft," she said, and then she started to cry.

"All those people, all those people," she said through her tears. "The poor old man wrapped in the flag, why didn't I go back?" She snuffled and wiped her nose on her arm. "January, my friend, January. Why didn't I help her? And the Son! Oh, I miss him so much. It hurts me in my heart!" She patted her chest softly.

This started another bout of tears, and the woman put her arm around her and let her cry.

What a beautiful, lost soul, she thought and looked down at the bowed head with its long pale hair. Over the phone, Barb had told her what the young woman had told her, that she was a Traveler from the Southern Region and she liked to garden. But this was still just a girl, a young girl who had been on the road for months. What had happened to her? What happened to her friend, January, and who is the son? She found a tissue in her overall pocket and handed it to June. It's the least I can do, she thought. But, she added, I hope someday she will tell me what happened.

~ ~ ~ ~

June stayed at Natural World Farm for close to two years and worked side by side with Adam and Eve. At first, she thought of them as the People Upstairs – or the Farmer and the Wife – never Adam nor Eve. The Farmer owned a big black and white Shepard dog named Sherpa. Sherpa wagged his way around the farm and teased the sheep, and June called him by his name. He was a *dog*, after all, but he was a good dog, not at all like the wealthy lady's snappy little dog with the shoe-button eyes. June felt safe with him watching the house.

After a few months, she began to feel at home in her little basement apartment. Every morning when she woke up, she would gaze at the big window by the bed. Its shade was warm with the sun, and June would feel pleased. She loved working in the gardens, getting her hands dirty in the brown earth; tending the vegetables was her favorite chore. The tomatoes tasted as sweet as sugar, and June loved the green beans and carrots. The tender corn with its thin stalks and floating tassels was so unlike the sticky field corn she ate at home. The Wife told her she could take whatever she wanted, and in the fall, June wrapped turnips and cabbages in burlap and stored them in a cold space behind the kitchen cupboard she'd discovered while she was scrubbing the floor. The perfect place for winter vegetables, cold and roomy.

There were bees in hives behind the barn, buzzing and busy, but she was afraid to go near them. That chore she left up to the Farmer.

When the winter winds blew snow against the windows, she'd pull out the burlap sack and make turnip or cabbage soup with potatoes or rice that made a hardy supper.

The first spring after she arrived, June learned to drive the Ion tractor across the garden and wheat field. She sat high up on the seat with her big sun hat perched on her head, feeling proud. This is what it's like being a farmhand, she told herself.

She loved the sheep and helped the Farmer shear them, gathering armloads of the oily fleece and stuffing them into baskets for the Wife to spin during the winter. The chickens charmed her as they clucked their way around the barnyard.

June learned to feel comfortable in the Village, too, with its fancy stores and different people – contented people who lived side by side – but she always watched for the NPF. She was ready to run at the sight of their black vehicle with the dark tinted windows.

The People Upstairs were good to June, and she liked them but she never thought of them as her family, that honor belonged to her Mama. During the lonely, quiet hours at night, she'd think of the Illegals she had traveled with for so many weeks, and no matter how many months passed or no matter who she met, June could not forget the Son with his black curls and hungry eyes. She carried his memory with her every single day, like a dull pain in her heart.

Chapter 27

The Garden State

June found the apartment fully stocked with food and necessities. There was dishwashing liquid, plates, and silverware, bedclothes, and towels; there was even shampoo in the tiny bathroom and toilet tissue. The big bed was made up with sheets and a blue blanket, and June lay down and looked up at the ceiling. She felt overwhelmed and thankful at the same time.

Months had passed since she had slept in a bed, but the first three nights at the farm, June decided to sleep on the grass outside the basement door. The bed was lovely, but it was too big and soft, and it was indoors. She wanted to see the stars and feel the breeze on her face. In the starlight, she could see the open fields and the barnyard. Then things changed.

In the middle of the third night, June was startled awake by a loud crack of thunder. Rain poured out of the sky in a torrent, and soon the fields and gardens were nowhere in sight. Now and again, lightning flashed far away, lighting up the dark, oppressive clouds that had descended on the countryside.

The lights in the house blazed on, Sherpa barked, and doors slammed; then the Wife and the Farmer ran outside, laughing and dancing in the rain.

"Look, look ... June has come out, too!" The Wife twirled around the grass, her wet nightgown flapping around her feet. "Woohoo, rain," she called out, "the drought has ended."

June sat on the bank with her face turned up and let the rain drum down on her body, soaking her hair and nightdress. It brought back memories of stormy days in North Carolina, and she was filled with longing, but, as she sat quietly by herself, her tears were washed away by the rain. It poured the rest of the night and throughout the next day, with heavy clouds hiding the field, but there was a sense of celebration in the household upstairs.

June stayed inside and sat at the table reading her history book. She had come to a chapter she liked – the ladies in their long skirts who marched around with signs that insisted on their "right to vote". They were called Suffragettes, but June thought of them as the Brave Ladies and returned to those pages over and over. I wonder if ladies can vote up here in the Garden State, she thought. I wonder if *anyone* can vote up here. And she vowed to ask the Wife one day.

She read about another war called World War One, and a terrible illness called the Spanish Flu that fell over the world like the Black Plague. She learned about young soldiers in their American Army uniforms dying in faraway places, and things called 'trenches' – long passages the poor souls had dug into the ground. Passages that were dirty and dangerous.

Oh, poor America, she thought. Why did you do this? Then she closed the book and looked out the window, watching the rain as it soaked the world outside.

Later, the Wife came down to see if she needed anything, sloshing through the puddles in her big boots and a rain hat.

June told her she was sick of war and sadness. "Look at this," she said and handed the Wife her history book.

"You must keep reading this book," the Wife turned a few pages, and her voice was firm. "It's American history and very important for you to know all about our country ... the good *and* the bad!" She gave the book back to June. "I'll bring you something nice to read as well. It's a book of poetry by a poet named Rumi. He lived many centuries ago." She smiled softly. "It's beautiful, and it will make you happy. Here," she added, "I brought you some honey," and she pulled a glass bottle out of her pocket and put it on the table, patted June's shoulder and disappeared into the rain, again.

On Saturday, the sun was shining again, and the Wife took June to the Village in an elderly electric truck, a red pickup with a dented front fender. June sat silently in her seat and looked out the window. The road was lined with trees, heavy with leaves. Daisies and bright yellow lilies were growing wild, and June thought it looked like heaven.

"What is that?" she asked, and pointed to a field that shone in the sun. It looked like a glass meadow and rolled out as far as her eye could see. Row after row of glass panels were lined up facing the sun. June had never seen anything like it.

"That's the Solar Farm," the Wife said, "and those are solar panels. It's the way we produce electricity here. You can see those panels on top of the roof of our house, too. It's clean energy."

The rest of the trip, the Wife chatted away about solar panels and clean energy, but June sat quietly and thought about the Solar Farm. There were so many things she didn't know, it was almost overwhelming. "The Glass Meadow," she whispered, "to me, it's the Glass Meadow."

Their first stop in the Village was the Chase Bank, and the Wife introduced June to Mr. Scott, the bank manager. June bent her knee and bobbed her head politely, but gazed at him in amazement. Mr. Scott was as dark as the beautiful juggler – dark skin, dark eyes and black curly hair. He helped her fill out a form, and she stole glances at him, and when he took her coupon dollar savings behind the counter, she couldn't help but stare.

When they left the bank, June had a brown envelope filled with crisp dollar bills, and a small savings book with *Chase Bank* in gold letters printed on a green cover. Her new bills had pictures of different American presidents on them, and even a picture of a kindly looking woman, but she was too filled with curiosity to look at them all and glanced at the Wife.

"Who was that man?" She asked. "The manager, I mean."

"Mr. Scott?" the Wife glanced at June. "What do you mean, who *was* he? He's the bank manager, but he's an important man in the Village, too. Mr. Scott is the treasurer on the Board of Directors."

June thought about that and was puzzled. She didn't know what a *treasurer* was but it certainly sounded important. She had never seen anything like that at home, but she said nothing more.

She followed the Wife into a clothing store called *The Farm Bureau* and used some of her new American money for the first time. The Wife helped her pick out two pairs of overalls – blue denim like the Wife's – some white t-Shirts, red rubber boots and a hat with a wide brim. This was the first time June had ever worn pants, and when she saw herself in the full-length mirror, she blushed.

"I'm a farmhand," she said shyly, but again she didn't smile.

"Yes, you are," the Wife said, "so now we're going to celebrate," and she took June to a small coffee shop for lunch.

Inside, June glanced around and felt a wave of homesickness. It looked like the coffee shop at home. There were the same tables and chairs, the same bright table cloths, the look-alike counter with its round stools and the same big, silver coffee machine that was making humming noises, but the painting on the wall was a seascape.

"There was a coffee shop in my town," she said. "It was called *The British Tea Shoppe*, but everyone drank coffee."

"Hmm hmmm," the Wife said and chose a table by the window with a view of the main street.

June slid into a chair across from the Wife and nodded at a family seated by the wall. The father was laughing, his head thrown back and his face animated.

"Are those Scotts, too?"

The Wife looked confused. "No, that's the Peterson family. Why do you think they're the Scotts?"

June looked embarrassed. "I guess because they're the same color. There's nobody like that at home. Everyone looks like me." Her face brightened, "but I did see a young man like that on the road. He was a juggler, and he was beautiful." Then she blushed again and changed the subject.

Wow, the Wife thought. But she didn't press June, she just felt sad that the Southern Region was so different; it was almost like a foreign country.

Everything has changed from when Granny was alive, she thought. The whole world has changed, and she wouldn't even recognize it.

Chapter 28

June learned how to feed the chickens, and it made her surprisingly cheerful. They were round feathered creatures that murmured and clucked in a comforting way. The chickens lived in a henhouse with straw on the floor, but the Wife told June they could roam the farmyard just like the few hens had at Bobby's farm.

"These are free range chickens," she told June. "We let them run around outside, and we mix our own chicken feed."

June wondered why Bobby had never mentioned that. He was always interested in all the nature and outdoor things.

Inside the henhouse, there were wire-covered windows with shutters that could be closed in cold weather, and the Wife showed June how to lower and secure them. She taught her how to collect the eggs from the straw-filled nesting boxes that lined one wall, and how to toss the feed around.

"Sometimes the eggs are fertilized, but that's okay, we eat them, anyway," she said, and June tried to understand but didn't want to ask. Maybe she'd think I was uneducated, she thought and nodded her head in agreement.

So, tending to the chickens became part of June's job. During the day, she would work in the gardens among the cauliflower and cabbages, peppers and brussels sprouts, but morning and evening the chickens were her responsibility, and she loved them. As shadows filled the farmyard, she would climb up onto a beam inside the henhouse and watch as they pecked around, their little heads bobbing up and down, yellow feet scratching as they looked for food. It was a peaceful place, and she could sit and daydream as the chickens rustled around down below.

There was a rooster, too – an elegant bird with feathers the color of jewels and a tail that arched up and over his back like a waterfall. He would strut around the hens, often causing a racket of clucks, and he'd wake June up every morning with his raucous crowing.

The first few days, she was afraid of him. He would fluff his feathers and spread out his tail and look at her with his head cocked to one side, and it made June nervous. There had been a rooster at Bobby's farm, too, a big bird with dusty red feathers and a mean streak. One day, he'd chased her into a doorway and beat her with his wings, scaring her so much she had screamed and cowered, ripping her dress on a nail. Bobby had laughed, but she didn't think it was funny at all and refused to come to the farm if the rooster was loose. And here was another rooster, but she soon discovered he was as nervous around her as she was around him. "Shoo," she'd say and wave her hands, and he'd hustle away. So, after a while they made peace with each other, and life went on.

Now and again, the Wife would join June in the henhouse. "Luckily, we don't have to worry about any bears or coyotes," she told her one evening. "And there are no foxes either. They've all become extinct. It's sad, but at least the chickens are safe."

June didn't know what extinct meant, but she thought it implied there were no more foxes, and she knew that was wrong.

"No," she said firmly, "foxes are not extinct! I saw one when I was resting at the old arch. He was beautiful, with a red coat and black feet. He lives in the arch, but he showed me the way to a path in the woods."

The Wife knew that foxes had disappeared decades ago, she remembered how sad that had seemed at the time, but she saw the look on June's face and decided not to argue. Maybe she'd seen a stray dog, she thought. It was lucky it hadn't attacked her. And, by the way, where is this old arch? The Wife shook her head. Just another mystery this young woman carried with her.

June was curious about the sheep, too, and one day, when the Wife brought her clean towels, she asked her.

"Do the sheep stay outside all winter? How do they eat if there's snow on the ground?"

"The sheep are named Maud and Ella," the Wife told her, "and they live outside all year. They like it that way. We have a wooden shelter behind the barn, and in the winter, Adam hauls hay out there and gives them alfalfa and grain every day, so they stay pretty close to the barn." She piled the towels on the sofa and rested her hands on her hips. "Their wool is thick and keeps them warm and dry all winter. I've even seen them outside the shelter with snow piled up on their backs, and they looked happy as clams."

June almost smiled at the thought of happy clams, and the Wife noticed.

"In the spring, we shear their woolen fleece so they won't overheat in the summer, and we process the wool here inside the barn. That's the old fashion way, but Natural World Farm is a green farm, not a factory farm." The Wife smiled with pride. "During the winter months, I spin the wool, myself, and sell the yarn all summer long."

June was excited. She didn't know what the Wife meant by a Green Farm, but she certainly knew about yarn, and she jumped up and went to find her carry bag.

"Look," she said. "My yarn. I brought it all the way from North Carolina and here are my knitting needles." She pulled the needles out and laid them on the table. The colorful yarn spilled out of the bag, and the sight made June happy. Here was something from home, something beautiful that reminded her of her mother.

"I'll knit you a sweater instead of reading about war," she said, and the Wife saw her smile for the first time.

Chapter 29

Within a few months, June knew every crack and cranny of her new home. However, there was one place she was not allowed to go. The People Upstairs ran a big farm stand by the road in front of the house. Every spring, the Farmer would slap on a new coat of green paint, and when June arrived, it was already open for business. Now, eggs and vegetables were on sale, but the Wife never allowed June to work with her there.

"I can help," June told her. "I learned my sums and managed my own yarn shop back home."

But the Wife shook her head. "You can help bring fresh vegetables from the garden, but it's the National Police Force I worry about. They come by off and on, and I really fear them. If they see you … well, then I don't know how we can protect you. I don't want them here, anyway. They're very rude."

June drew herself up. "I am a Citizen," she said with her chin in the air. "I have my papers!"

But the Wife frowned and repeated the words the counterman had said, "It doesn't matter, anymore. You are young and pretty, and they just take what they want now. It's one thing when they stop and take bags of fruit, but not you! No, you're different. They shall *not* take you!" She patted June on the arm. "Look, when I see them, I'll ring this little bell, and you know you have to stay out of sight behind the house."

June was afraid of the NPF and didn't argue. It made her angry all over again. She couldn't forget what the agent had done to January, grabbing her like she belonged to him, and hadn't forgotten how she, June, had hidden under the hot underbrush, as the NPF searched for her. No, those things she would never forget!

How dare they, she thought, how dare they? But when she heard the bell ring, she always stayed hidden behind the farmhouse. It reminded her of her traveling, and the whistle that was repeated up and down the highway – Danger, NPF.

The days became hotter, and June asked the Wife about the pond in the pasture. She remembered the hidden place where she had rested the day she arrived at the farm. The shower in her bathroom was beautiful, but the water fell out on top of her head, and June missed being *in* it.

"I miss the water," she said, "and that pond is not deep like that old Quarry was."

"My God!" the Wife stared at June in shock. "Don't tell me you went swimming in the Quarry!"

"Well, I was hot, and I jumped in." June was embarrassed. Maybe she had done something bad, like a sin. "It was pretty deep."

"Well, don't ever swim in the Quarry," the Wife said. "It's very dangerous, and people die in there. I don't even know if it has a bottom." She told June about the schoolboy who had disappeared years before, "And he was never found!" she added for effect. "Of course, you can swim in the watering hole in the pasture. It's for the sheep but, yeah, that's okay." She laughed, "I'm sure Maud and Ella would enjoy the company."

So, all day, June worked in the garden picking fresh vegetables for the farm stand and pulling any weeds that had appeared overnight. The warm sun and the healthy garden pleased her. As soon as a basket was full, she would bring it out to the farm stand and rest for just a minute, sometimes for a glass of cold lemonade or ice tea, and then hurry back to the garden.

But, at the end of the day, she'd climb over the fence and head to the grove of trees. Off would come her boots and overalls, t-shirt and underclothes, and then she would wade into the pond – nude, joyful and at peace. Maud and Ella often wandered over to watch, eyes blinking as they stood in the trees.

Saturday was shopping day on the farm, and the Wife decided to take June with her to the grocery store. While the Wife shopped, June wandered the aisles, curious and amazed at the selection. After bundling everything into the truck, they would head off for lunch.

One day, as they were leaving the coffee shop, June felt her heart stop and her blood run cold. She caught her breathe and hid behind the Wife, clinging onto her arm, afraid to look.

"What in the world?" the Wife said and pulled away.

"There's an NPF agent," June whispered.

A man was standing by the door, and when he turned his eyes fell on June. He was tall with short blond hair, and he wore a green uniform, a utility belt with a sidearm and handcuffs hung off his waist. His face was grim as he looked around.

Then he smiled, and his face lit up.

"Oh, for heaven's sake, that's Jeremy," the Wife said, "he's not NPF, he's an Environmental Officer, an EO. He's one of the good guys."

"Hi, Jem," she called.

"Hi, Eve," he called back and walked over. "Who's that hiding behind you?"

The Wife dragged June out from behind her and introduced them.

"This is June. She thought you were an NPF agent. She's a Climate Refugee, and she has bad memories of them."

Jem smiled down at June. "Who hasn't," he said.

Jeremy was a friendly fellow, but June hung back, not trusting the uniform and the weapon. He spent a few more minutes chatting with Eve, and then said goodbye and went on his way. June felt her heartbeat slow and took a deep breath. "I'm sorry," she said and felt ashamed, but the Wife smiled absentmindedly, and they headed to the truck.

"He's a good guy," she said, "and cute, too."

June began to see Jem in the Village more often, and the Wife always greeted him.

"Hi Jem," she'd say. "You back, again?"

And Jem would smile, and look at June hopefully, but he was too pale and too much like Bobby and the boys at home – blond and blue-eyed – and June couldn't forget the boy with his dark curls and smoldering eyes. She could still feel his hands on her body. I love him, she thought, I will always love him no matter who I meet, and she felt the familiar longing grip her again.

Chapter 30

The summer wore on, and the shadows grew longer. June began to feel at home on the farm. She enjoyed feeding the chickens and loved Maud and Ella, loved the gardens and the golden wheat field, but she feared the big Ion2 wheat thresher. It was a roaring yellow monster and appeared to float over the wheat as it gobbled it up, hissing and spitting out market-ready sacks as it went, leaving the chaff behind. The Farmer asked her if she wanted to ride with him, but she was afraid – afraid of the sound and the speed as its huge steel body swept across the field. She would rather dig up root vegetables and feed the chickens. She liked peaceful things, the ones that gave her time to think and dream.

"No, thank you," she said politely, "I'll try the tractor, though."

"You got a deal," he said and laughed. "I'll have you plowing up the fields in no time."

The farm prospered, and as the days grew shorter, June carried more early autumn vegetables out to the Wife. One time she had to turn back, as a black, NPF vehicle slid to a stop in front of the farm stand. She hid behind a bush by the side of the house and peered through the leaves. Two agents climbed out and began to help themselves, and June could see the look of disgust on the Wife's face. They just take what they want, she thought and felt her face warm with anger. She listened as they bantered back and forth and tightened her lips as they headed back to their car. They just won't take me, she vowed.

The nights were cool, and when she slept June liked to leave her windows open so she could feel the touch of an autumn chill. She was comfortable in the big, soft bed now, and before turning off the light, she would draw the blankets around her, curl up, and read the book of Rumi poems the Wife had given her. "This is my nest," she told herself.

"Beauty," she read out loud, "Love will come around." His words were lyrical and brought her comfort.

One early morning, she woke with the eerie feeling that someone was watching her.

It was barely light, but a shadow moved against the wall, and there was the sound of something stirring: creeping. June sat bolt upright in bed, and pulled the blankets up to her chin.

Another stealthy sound and her teeth began to chatter.

"Who is it?" she shouted, and something crashed to the floor.

There was a flash of white, as a large black and white cat leaped up onto the table by the window. It sat and gazed at her and then started to wash its face with a big, white paw.

"Come, kitty, kitty," June called softly, and her heartbeat slowed. "You scared me to death."

But the cat ignored her, then slipped out of the open window and disappeared

"A big cat was in my apartment last night," she told the Wife later. "It woke me up and scared me!"

"Oh, that's Samantha," the Wife said, "Don't worry, she's harmless. We had her mama before her. Adam says she's a Maine Coon cat, but who knows."

After that, the cat came more often, and she soon decided that June's apartment was home. Samantha would sit on the table and purr loudly when June brushed the long, soft fur, but she would never allow herself to be hugged. She liked to be stroked and made it known that now she was June's cat.

June was touched. She had never had a pet, but she had loved the Fox, and now, it seemed, the cat had moved in. The big black and white cat spent hours sleeping in a sunny spot by the front door, but come nightfall she always disappeared.

"I'll never leave you," June told her. "I had to leave Fox, but I'll not leave you." The big cat looked at June and blinked slowly then curled up in the sun and went to sleep.

The Wife was amused. "I see Samantha has adopted you," she said. "She's a good mouser, but now she's decided to live with you, June, you need to buy her some cat food, otherwise you may find a dead mouse or two beside your bed." She stood with her hands on her hips, looking at the cat.

"I'll show you what to buy in the village, and you must put down fresh water every morning. When you do close your windows in the winter, you need to let her out when she asks and … Oh, she *will* ask."

So, June owned a cat – a big black and white cat with a long, soft coat, and a loud, rumbling purr that sounded like the old truck's electric engine.

June named her Kitty and bought bags of kitty kibble and a hairbrush. She fed Kitty and filled a china dish with water, and she brushed her soft black and white fur every day. At night Kitty would slip out the window, but in the morning, June would find her curled up at the foot of the bed.

"I'm happy," she told Kitty one day. "I never thought I would be happy again, but this is good. It may not be what I wanted, but it's good."

Kitty looked at June, blinked slowly, and then started to take a bath, delicately lifting one back leg over her head.

Chapter 31

The cooler days brought autumn color. Maple trees wore red and gold, and orange pumpkins filled the field by the vegetable garden. Even the leaves on the trees by the watering hole turned a soft yellow. Like butterflies, June thought, and it reminded her of the Daughter.

The water was too cold for swimming, but she still headed down to the watering hole to daydream. Sometimes Sherpa came along and would sit next to her or tease Maude and Ella.

June passed the time reflecting on her new life, and she missed North Carolina. She thought about her travels through Virginia and Pennsylvania and the people she had known: The Illegals and the man who had loved the Woman – and then disappeared. She often daydreamed about the Son with his dark eyes and thick curls, and her heart would become heavy.

One day, she started thinking about January, and she longed to see her friend's pretty face and violet eyes again. I wonder if she's safe or if that cruel red-haired agent has finally killed her with his greedy body. "I wish she had come with me," she said out loud. The thought made her sad and then angry.

"I wish I had killed him!" she snapped. Sherpa perked his ears up and cocked his head.

Autumn was also a busy time at the farm stand. The Farmer showed June how to cut cornstalks with a long, sharp knife, and then tie them into bundles. He brought out a wooden wheelbarrow from the barn so she could load up the bundles and bring them out to the farm stand.

"Why is this?" she asked. "Old cornstalks?"

"People like to decorate their porches," the Farmer told her, and he helped her cut more.

June shook her head at such a strange notion.

She helped pick pumpkins and wheeled them to the farm stand, and she always took a minute to visit with the Wife.

"What's this all about?" she asked on one occasion.

"It's almost Halloween," the Wife said, "and it will be bustling. I certainly wish you could help me here, but I'm still afraid."

June wondered about that and was puzzled. How strange, she thought. "I think Halloween is evil," she told the Wife. "It's witches and Satan. It's ghosts and lost, haunted spirits!"

The Wife sat down in the open end of the wheelbarrow and took June's hands. A lock of her hair came loose, and she blew it away, her face serious. She realized June was frightened.

"Halloween is for the children up here," she said. "They carve funny faces out of the pumpkins and burn candles inside them. We call them jack-o-lanterns. The children dress up in costumes and go to all the neighbors for sweets. It's not sinning, June, it's fun! *Fun* isn't evil, and if you don't believe in Satan or witches or ghosts, then they don't exist!"

That gave June a lot to think about.

Every day, she helped the Farmer bring loads of pumpkins to the farm stand, and by nightfall, they were always gone. People lined the road to buy the cornstalks and pumpkins, and children ran loose around the farm, laughing and shouting. The Wife sold hot apple cider and donuts, and there was excitement all around them. June had never seen such a sight, but she wasn't entirely convinced.

Halloween came, and Halloween eve June stayed in her little apartment. She locked the door and sat in the dark. She thought about Halloween and Satan. She knew there was evil because she had seen it herself, as she crouched in the broom closet in January's store. But that wasn't Satan, it was the agent with the red hair and dirty words. So, now she was unsure. Was Satan some evil creature with horns and a tail, or was that just superstition? Maybe it's an old wives' tale. That's what Mama called it, something to keep people from sinning. Or maybe Satan is just something bad in people like the agent.

She was reminded of the people back home. They had stopped going to church before she was even born. The preacher had shouted about "Satan and Sin, Satan and Sin," until finally, they were afraid to go. Even her mother stayed away, and she was a good woman who taught June to read the Bible. She'd told June about going to Sunday School when she was a little girl, and about going to church on Christmas Eve. She wove stories about the Child in the manger and all the animals that had come to the stable. There is no sin there, June thought, and she was confused.

At the end of November, the People Upstairs went away for a long weekend and took Sherpa with them. The Farmer asked June to tend to the farm. By now he knew she was a very trustworthy young woman but thought about it before he said anything.

"You will be responsible for the chickens," he told her, "and if there is a hard frost, and the sheep come up to the shelter, please haul out some hay and alfalfa from the bales in the barn." He pondered for a minute, lost in thought.

"We won't be away for too many days, but be careful."

"Don't worry about me," June said and lifted her chin. "I know how to take care of myself."

The morning they left, the Wife brought June a turkey pot pie for her supper. Colored leaves and pumpkins decorated the dish, and there was a lovely, flaky crust on top.

"It's for Thanksgiving," the Wife said, and she showed June the section in her history book.

"See? Pilgrims and the Indians, our American Natives, sitting down for a meal and giving thanks for a good harvest." She patted June's arm and looked concerned for a minute.

"Will you be okay here on your own?"

"I have Kitty," June said. "I'll be fine."

Later in the day, the Farmer drove the old red truck up to the house and leaned out. "Take care of yourself, June," he shouted.

The Wife whistled to Sherpa, climbed into their old pickup truck with her husband, and they headed down the driveway, the dog leaning out of the window, his ear blowing backwards.

"Stay behind the house," the Wife called back, and June didn't need to be reminded.

It was cold, but there was no hard frost. The air snapped with an icy chill, but Maud and Ella stayed down by the trees. June hiked down and sat by the watering hole to keep them company. The leaves had fallen and were whirling around the pasture and skipping across the road in the wind.

June wore a new red jacket she had bought at *The Farm Bureau* the Saturday before, and she brought her history book to read to the two sheep. She spun stories about the Pilgrims and how the Wampanoag Indians taught them to grow corn, squash and beans that flourished there. "It saved their lives," she told them in a hushed voice.

She opened the book and found her place. "Because they had a good harvest," she read out loud, "they set aside a day of thanks, and later generations called this Thanksgiving." She stopped and thought for a minute. "Except we didn't have that at home because, well … I guess there were no Indians, or maybe it cost too many dollar coupons." She thought about home for a few more minutes. "Well, everyone was happy, anyway," she added.

The sheep lifted their heads at the sound of her voice and then went back to tugging at the grass and weeds as she read.

As evening fell, June popped the potpie in the oven and went out to feed the chickens. They were foraging in the grass, but set up a commotion and followed her into the henhouse, clucking and crowding around her feet as she tossed the corn. She closed the shutters for the night, and the hens quieted down, murmuring among themselves as they scratched for food. The rooster ruffled his feathers and made a "puck, puck, puck" sound and bobbed his head.

"Happy Thanksgiving, kind creatures," she sang. "This is the ancient day of Thanksgiving, giving thanks for a good harvest."

There was no interest in the henhouse, just clucking and scratching, so she trudged back to her apartment, huffing a white cloud in the cold air. Just be glad you're not turkeys, she thought.

A warm, delicious smell greeted June when she opened the door, and she set out a place for herself and poured a glass of milk. Chunks of turkey meat and vegetables filled the pot pie, and it warmed her inside and out. The idea of Thanksgiving made her happy.

Except, she thought, something is missing!

"It's too quiet," June said out loud, and realized there was always the sound of the People Upstairs moving about, Sherpa yapping, the faint sound of voices, and she missed them.

"I'm alone, again," she complained. "I'm always alone!" Then she said the bad word the Man had used, and that made her laugh. "Okay, okay, June, so you'll read!"

She got up and brought her book back to the table and read about the Pilgrims and the Indians while she ate. Kitty kept her company, curled up by the heater, and then asked to be let out for the night.

"I wonder if there still are Indians, do you think so?" she asked Kitty. "They certainly were smart; they knew how to grow corn."

Kitty made a soft chittering sound and then slipped out the open door and disappeared into the dark, icy night.

Chapter 32

The day after the People Upstairs came home, the weather turned frosty and cold, and the first week in December there was snow. Flakes whirled around and landed here and there like feathers, and at night they looked like moths as they floated in the street lights. The fields had turned brown with the autumn chill, but now they were covered in white. The Villagers spoke of a cold winter, but June knew what a *cold* winter was like – and this wasn't it.

But cold it would be, and during the dark autumn evenings, June had kept busy knitting sweaters for herself and the Wife, and she had finished a dark blue scarf and mittens for herself. The Wife's sweater was to be a surprise Christmas gift.

The Farmer and June locked the shutters in the henhouse and turned the warming lights on, and Maud and Ella wandered up to the barn. Their wool was thick and oily now, and June liked to pat their broad backs.

"You feel like fat sponges," she told them.

They looked up at her with their gold eyes and then snuffled around the floor of the shelter looking for grain.

The Wife decided it was past time for June to buy a warm winter jacket, so they went back to the *Farm Bureau* to buy winter clothes.

"You need a scarf and mittens, too," she said and picked up a pair of gloves.

June shook her head. "I already knitted them as soon as the weather turned chilly in October."

The Wife was impressed. "I'd forgotten that you knit, and you did this already?"

"Humph," June said, and she looked through the coat racks.

She liked her red autumn jacket and found a puffy down parka the same color. She thought it made her look like a red balloon with her blond head sticking out of the top, but that didn't matter; she loved it.

"This will keep me warm," she said, "and I love this bright color."

The Wife agreed. "Yes, goose down is really warm, and red looks good with your blond hair," but she hid a smile.

June paid with her new dollar bills and decided to wear it home. The clerk cut the tags off for her with a pair of scissors and then stood back. "It looks nice and cozy," she said and shook her head.

Such a young woman, she thought, always in her own little world, and now she looks like a puffball (the clerk was fixated on the mushrooms and puffball fungi she'd see on her walks in the woods). A red puffball, she added.

Jem was home again. For months he had been in the Mid-Western Region where dust and sand were devastating the countryside, but now he was waiting by the coffee shop, and *he* didn't hide his smile when he saw them.

"That's quite a jacket you've got there, June," he said. "I'm sure it will keep you warm as toast." He laughed and poked her padded sleeve.

"Thank you," she said politely.

June didn't know what to make of Jem. He was a very kind fellow, and she knew he liked her. He was very good looking, in a pale way, but she didn't approve of his uniform; uniforms made her nervous. He also talked in riddles, and she never knew if he was joking or serious. What did "quite a jacket" mean? Was it a joke or a compliment? She decided it was a compliment, and said "thank you," again, a shy smile on her lips.

Jem joined them for lunch, and the Wife asked him about his trip, her face filled with concern. "What's happening in the Mid-West? I've heard such awful stories."

"It *is* awful!" he said, "a modern-day Dust Bowl, the 1930s all over again. Everything is buried in dust and sand. Thousands of acres of farmland have disappeared, houses, barns, fields … gone! It looks like the Sahara Desert out there."

He shook his head in disgust.

"No regulations, so there's been a drought now for years. It makes me so angry. We spent twenty-four hours a day with our faces covered with scarves to keep from suffocating, just to help small farmers drive their livestock over the border. That endless wind was throwing dust at us in waves. The corporate farms are finished! And now what? How the Hell are we going to rehabilitate that? Where will the food come from? Private farms are too small for the amount needed," he added.

He gazed out of the window for a few minutes. "It's moving so fast! The whole Mid-Western part of the country is going to be destroyed, and where will all the people go? All they have are the clothes on their backs."

He sounded grim, and June started to listen intently. There had been no dust storms at home, but the sun had burned it up, anyway. She thought about her Fox, and that made her worry about the wild animals out west.

"What about the animals?" she asked, and her eyes filled with tears. "Are you helping them, too?"

Jem looked at her, and he felt his heart skip a beat. He had always felt drawn to this strange young woman, but now he realized just how much. He had a sudden desire to lean over and kiss her and felt his face turn red with embarrassment.

"The wild animals all fled before the dust storms started," he said. "They knew to head north to the border, and I'm sure they're all safe. It's instinct. People don't want to leave their homes, so some of them stayed too long, and we had to rescue them, dig them out of their houses."

June contemplated what she'd heard, houses buried in sand and animals running to the border.

"Where's the border?" she asked. She was thinking about the Illegals and how they had headed north to the border.

"Canada," Jem said, and he was a little confused with her change of subject. "And the Northern Kingdom, of course."

June smiled, and went back to her lunch, her pale hair falling and hiding her face. She thought about the northern border, but then she started thinking about Jem. The Woman had said her son was to marry one of his own. Maybe she should think about marrying one of *her* own, too, and that would surely be Jem. Perhaps it really was right and proper.

But, how do I know if he's joking or serious, she wondered. I don't even understand him, and I really don't yearn for him like I did the Son. She put her chin in her hand, deep in thought.

When she looked up, Jem was talking to the Wife, but he was looking at her, and his eyes were filled with longing.

Chapter 33

Snow fell in slow swirls and covered the fields and pasture in the purest white. In the frosty early mornings, June bundled up and plodded through the drifts to feed the chickens and tend to Maud and Ella. The hens stayed snuggled in their nesting boxes, shuffling the straw as she collected their eggs. The rooster would merely cast a suspicious eye her way, but he stayed huddled in his nest. Often, she found the sheep in the shelter covered in snow and contentedly pulling at the alfalfa in the rack.

"Silly Ladies," June would say. "Silly Maud and Ella, you're covered in snow, and you have snow hats again. Aren't you cold?"

The sheep would look at June and then go back to the alfalfa racks, the snow still piled on their broad backs.

Every day, the snow fell and covered the fields and pasture. Sometimes, a gust of cold wind would whip across the countryside, stinging noses and foreheads, but the Farmer was delighted.

"This means the soil will be moist and healthy next year," he told June. "There will be a good crop of wheat and vegetables, and the bees will have a well-deserved rest this winter.

The days were short and the nights long. June did her evening chores in the dark, then hurried back to her cozy apartment, putting the teapot on to boil as soon as she got in the door.

She finally finished knitting her sweater: light blue wool with a unique design her mother had taught her, twisting the yarn every few stitches. June was proud of herself. She held it up and then danced a few steps across the room to the mirror. "Very nice, June," she told herself. "Very, very nice."

The Wife was delighted when she saw what June had accomplished, and her eyes opened wide with pleasure. "Wow!

That's just beautiful. I had no idea you could knit like that." She reached out and touched June's sweater with one finger and shook her head. "Wow," she said.

June smoothed the blue wool across her hips and was eager to return to her wool and knitting needles.

The Wife's reaction was more than she'd expected, and it motivated her. The sweater she was knitting for the Wife was almost finished. It was deep red with a delicate stitch across the top and down the front, and she began to rush to get it done by Christmas. June knew it would be a special gift.

"Listen," the Wife said. "Maybe you could knit some sweaters from the wool I spin, you know, and we could sell them. Just think, you would be making sweaters from Maud and Ella's wool."

Maud and Ella's wool, June thought, and images filled her head. How magical!

"Maud and Ella's wool," she said. "I'd love to do that! I can knit sweaters of the sheep's wool and gloves with matching scarfs that would reach the floor." June was charmed by the idea.

As the days passed, the snow piled up around the house and covered the walkway. Every night, Kitty would ask to go out, and then quickly scratch to come in again. She'd be wet with snow and ready to curl up next to the Ion heater the Wife brought down.

"Make up your mind," June scolded her, but she'd stroke the soft, wet fur and lean down and kiss Kitty's damp head. The big cat had found a place in June's heart and had become a part of her life. I love her, she thought as she stroked the wet fur. I will never leave her.

Late into the night, June would join Kitty next to the heater and start knitting, the red wool trailing onto the floor. Now and again, the cat would raise her head, blink her eyes and then go back to sleep. June felt comfortable and safe in her home now, but occasionally she would feel a sense of unease, a little cloud in the back of her mind. Stop it, June, she'd scold herself and force herself to think of something else.

And the snow fell and covered the streets and houses. In the Village, little lights were being hung on the bare tree branches, and then decorations began to show up in the store windows. There was a sense of festivity in the streets when June and the Wife went shopping.

"Merry Christmas," people would call out. "Happy Holidays."

June knew about Christmas and the Holy Child, but she had never seen such celebration.

"People are so cheerful," she said on one snowy Saturday morning's trip to the Village. The truck huffed along in the cold and June frowned, "Christmas is a very solemn occasion, and very virtuous. I've never seen anything like this: all the laughing and singing."

The Wife shook her head and looked over at June. What a strange little person, she thought. My goodness, I never know what will come out of her mouth next.

"Christmas is a joyous event," she said. "It's a time to laugh and sing carols and give gifts." But her little passenger looked so solemn, the Wife decided to say no more.

For the rest of the trip, June sat quietly and looked out of the truck window. She knew about gift giving and was glad she had finished the Wife's sweater in time – all those late nights by the heater had worked their magic – but she still couldn't wholly approve of all the banter and laughter.

A life-size Santa Claus statue had appeared in the corner of the coffee shop, dressed in a red suit with a white fur collar and a big smile on his rosy plaster face. That puzzled June as well, but she liked it. He looked a little bit like the driver from the Green Mountain Water truck. Maybe that's what Sir looks like, she thought, and that made her feel better.

"Sir is Santa Claus and the friendly driver," she sang to herself.

June bought some green gift paper in the Village and wrapped the red sweater, finishing the package with a gold ribbon. A week before Christmas she presented it to the Wife as a gift. June knew the soft, deep red yarn would look lovely with her hair and smiled at the thought.

"Oh, God!" the Wife shouted, "this is gorgeous!" She held it against herself and then hurried to June's bathroom to try it on. "This is stunning," she shouted again. "Damn, June, you are a master knitter." The Wife reappeared and smoothed the soft wool over her hips. "And it fits perfectly! How in the world did you know my size?" She blew June a kiss and began to whirl around the room, her hands flying over her head.

June was embarrassed. She hadn't expected the Wife to be so rowdy, and after all, it was just a sweater. June had knitted so many for the Wealthy Ladies across the River and, Lordy, they never shouted or danced around the shop. They were too dignified.

"I just looked at you," she said. "It was easy."

"Well," the Wife said and dropped onto the couch, "I have a Christmas gift for you, too." She hopped back up and disappeared into the cold. "I have to show this to Adam," she called back over her shoulder.

June sat down next to the heater. "Well," she told Kitty, "I guess she really liked my gift. She's not very dignified, is she?"

The Wife came back with a small box. "This is an Ion6 radio," she said. "You can listen to the news or music or anything you want. All you must do is tell it what you want. It will always recognize your voice, anywhere in the room, and it never runs out of power … ever!" She took the radio out of the box and put it on the counter next to the refrigerator. Then she said: "*News!*" in a loud voice.

A voice blared out of the little object – shocking and urgent – and June put her hands over her ears. She didn't want this stranger talking in her apartment, she didn't *want* to know about fires devouring the West, or floods rolling over what was left of her home in North Carolina.

"Please, I don't want this," she whispered. "I'm sorry. I don't want to know."

"Oh, of course, I'm so sorry!" The Wife was embarrassed. "Damn, I'm so thoughtless," she scolded herself. "Let's try music, you like to sing. Sometimes I hear you. *Music*," she said.

The man's voice faded away, and the sound of an unfamiliar melody took its place. It was sweet with instruments that June didn't recognize, but she liked it.

"Yes," she said. "Thank you! Thank you for my Music." June smiled a secret smile as she listened. I have a radio like the Ladies from across the River, she thought and had a moment of guilty pleasure.

Chapter 34

The People Upstairs were going away again. The Farmer was already in the truck and anxious to get on the road. They always called it "going home," but that meant they were going to see her parents.

Well, isn't this her home now, June wondered.

"We're going home for Christmas," the Wife told her as if she'd read June's mind, "but we'll be back for New Year's Eve." She creaked open the truck door and climbed in.

The Wife was wearing the red sweater June had knitted for her. She looked beautiful with her hair twisted up on top of her head in a delicate swirl.

"You be very careful and stay hidden," she added. "I know it's cold, but those NPF agents are always lurking around now. I really don't know what the Hell they want! Well, maybe I do, but I just don't want to think about *that*!" She leaned out the window, "Merry Christmas," she said crossly, and she didn't look merry at all.

June nodded but didn't answer.

"You're in charge of the farm, again," the Farmer leaned over his wife and called out the window. "Remember, the sheep's grain is in that red bin in the barn, so make sure they have a share every day. And the alfalfa. Sherpa will be coming with us, so take extra care."

He opened the truck door, and the dog jumped in, his tail waving like a flag. The engine started up with a whirring sound, and the old truck lurched around the corner and down the road to town. Then they were gone,

A few snowflakes floated in the cold air, and June watched the truck disappear. She took a breath of cold air and hurried back to her apartment. June felt a bit uneasy but brushed it away because she had something else on her mind, something exciting. The Saturday before, she had found a notice in the village. Fancy black words were printed on white paper with a border of greens and red bows.

Christmas Eve Service, June read. *The Community Church ~ All Are Welcome ~ Service Begins at 9:00 PM*

June was curious and had shown it to the Wife.

"Oh, that's a church event every Christmas Eve," the Wife said, "with candles and Christmas carols, and it's fun because it's dark outside. I used to go when I was a kid. With my parents, you know? I don't go now because, well … Adam is an Atheist, and I don't like to go without him."

Not for the first time, June had wondered what an Atheist was, but she thought it was rude to ask. Now, as she picked up the notice, she made a decision. "I'm going to the Christmas Eve service," she told Kitty. June looked out at the snow as it whirled around the yard and nodded to herself. Kitty didn't stir from her place by the heater.

June admitted she was apprehensive, but she wasn't afraid to go alone. Surely it would be solemn, and, of course, she could sit in the back and slip out if the preacher started shouting about Satan and Sin, but the rest of the week June kept thinking about her trip to the village. She thought about walking in the dark alone as she fed the chickens and it scared and thrilled her. The idea she was going to the Village alone was exciting anyway, "but in the dark?" she asked Maud and Ella.

"Wow," June told Kitty. "I don't know if I'm afraid or excited." Kitty wasn't impressed and jumped up on the bed and went to sleep

Early Christmas Eve, June fed the chickens and scooped a share of grain for Maud and Ella.

"Merry Christmas, Kind Creatures" she sang. "Tonight, I walk to the village alone in the dark." The idea made June shiver. This would be the first time she had gone to the village without the Wife. But, she thought, so what! I never promised not to go. "Anyway," she told the sheep, "no NPF agent worth his salt will be roaming around on Christmas Eve. Even *they* must take time off to be with their families." She tapped the grain pail against the shelter wall, and the last of the morsels fell to the floor. "But, I'll tug my hat down over my head just in case," and she headed back to her apartment.

June pulled on her new blue sweater, a pair of tan wool pants that she'd bought at the *Farm Bureau,* and her red knit hat. She looked in the mirror over the sink, and a solemn face gazed back, long pale hair hanging in smooth waves, red hat pulled low. The blue sweater suited her, and the color almost matched her eyes. "Not bad, June," she told her reflection, "not bad at all."

It was a long, cold walk to the village, and June shrugged into her red down parka and wrapped the dark blue scarf around her neck. Bundle up, she thought and pulled on her mittens.

The shock of the cold hit her as she started out. The chill hung like a freezing mist over the countryside, but June found it exhilarating. It was exciting to be alone in the night, and she sang as she walked. The further she walked, the warmer she became, and soon she could see the twinkling lights of the Village ahead. She looked carefully but saw no NPF vehicles.

The church windows were alight, and candles lined the path to the door. A life-sized crèche was set up on the church lawn, and June was filled with awe. There were two sheep like Maud and Ella and even an angel. The statues reminded her of the tiny figurines her mother would set out on Christmas Eve – delicate porcelain figures that she carefully stored away on New Year's Day.

"This is a crèche," her mother had told her. "It belonged to my mother and her mother before her."

On that long-ago Christmas Eve, June was too young to hold any of the figurines, but she had touched an angel with the tip of one finger. "When I'm gone," her mother had continued, "this crèche will belong to you."

Now, both June and her mother were gone. That Christmas Eve was long ago and far away, and this was the first time June had given a thought to the tiny figures stored away in the dining room's cabinet drawer.

"Oh, Mama," she whispered, "I forgot to take the crèche with me." She gazed at the statues for a long time, and June felt utterly alone. People passed her, hurrying up the pathway to the church, but she didn't notice them. They were just shadows in the candlelight.

"They're all gone, Mama," she said, "All under the sea, but just look, here they are! And they're as big as I am."

Music started to play inside the church and June slipped in and found a seat near the door. She looked around nervously — shy but curious. This was the first time she had been inside a church. Oh, she'd seen the church in North Carolina. She'd even walked past it as the Preacher stood on the steps and beckoned to her. But here she was sitting at the back of a church in the Garden State.

It was dim but lit with so many candles June was dazzled: plain white candles, their flames lighting up the faces around her. Everyone stood up and started to sing. The tune sounded familiar, so June stood up and hummed along, feeling her heart lift.

After everyone sat down, the preacher walked up in front of the altar and started to speak. June stared, shocked. The preacher was a young woman with short dark hair that fit her head like a cap. She wore a white robe with a long red scarf embroidered with gold thread and June thought she looked like an angel. That woman is a preacher, she thought, and the idea astonished her. Preacher Pride would say she's a witch, June thought, but she sat still and listened.

The preacher told the Christmas Story in a soft voice; she talked about the donkey and the Mother and the stable in a strange land where her baby boy had been born. She spoke of love and kindness, and how people should remember the Family. "You should always welcome the stranger," she said, and she never shouted about sin and salvation.

June was moved by the words. She thought about the old Southern soldier with his lonely eyes. Would he be welcome here? Would the Illegals? And then she thought, yes, they would. She blinked her eyes hard, and a few people looked at her and smiled, and she smiled back. Everyone was at peace in this place, and June felt safe. No NPF would be attending this service.

After the preacher sat down, a large woman in a red, wool dress and pretty face stood up and sang. Her voice and the words were haunting, and it made June feel both sad and happy at the same time.

Then the lady preacher sent them away with a poem about love that sounded like she had found it in the Rumi book.

June left the church before the others had gathered their coats, and she found Jem waiting for her outside, his breath a cloud in the cold, frosty air.

"I saw you come in," he said. "I waited. It's dark, and I'll walk you home if you want."

June looked at him under her lashes and was relieved. He was wearing a red sweater and a puffy, green down jacket with a green and white patch on its sleeve. There was no uniform or gun, and he looked cute and kind.

"It's Christmassy," he said and opened his jacket. "Red and green," he added when he saw the puzzled look on her face. "Those are Christmas colors."

Okay, June thought and joined him on the sidewalk.

As they walked, she told him about the songs and about the preacher. "The preacher's a woman," June said. "And she told a nice story. People sang and looked happy." She puffed clouds into the night air. "I liked it."

June felt her eyes tear in the cold, and her nose began to run. She sniffed and rubbed her nose on her new jacket sleeve and flicked the tears from her eyes. "I liked this gathering, Jem. I really liked it. Everyone looked happy."

Large snowflakes began to drift down, and Jem took her mitten-wrapped hand. "Do you mind? Just to keep it warm," he told her, and they walked in silence for a while; then he started to sing:

> *"God rest you merry Gentlemen*
> *Let nothing you dismay ..."*

June laughed and hummed along with him. He's really a nice man, she thought and stole glances at him as they walked, but when they reached her apartment, June felt uneasy. I like you very much, Jem, she thought, but I don't yearn for you. I don't want to be alone with you in my home. They stood by the door and laughed as their words turned to little icicles, and then June pulled her hand away. She remembered what the Woman had told her as they sat by the old bridge, "You will find one of your own." *Jem* is one of my own, she realized, but I don't know. I just don't know.

"Thank you," she said and turned away.

From her window, June watched as Jem disappeared into the darkness. She pressed her forehead against the cold glass, "I think I really like you, Jem," she whispered. "But I just don't know."

Chapter 35

During the Christmas Eve service, a black NPF vehicle parked on a side street and sat humming to itself. Agent David Anderson slouched in his seat, his black cap tipped forward over his brow. He was cold, and he was bored. His smoky-gray eyes scanned the surroundings, but David resented the Sergeant taking him away from his warm Christmas Eve fire and Whiskey Sour. There was also a lonely girl who lived across the hall he had his eye on.

"For God's sake, Sarge," he bellyached, "it's cold as Hell out here, and the only people in that church service are a bunch of old farts."

The Sergeant stared straight ahead and didn't respond. What an arrogant ass this guy is, he thought, handsome but spoiled rotten.

David *was* handsome, but he also *was* an arrogant ass, and the combination drove the Sergeant wild. What a spoiled shit, he thought again and grunted.

David was from a pleasant, small, mountain town, born to a couple who should have been enjoying retirement, but when he arrived, his mother had clasped her hands in prayer.

"A son," she had whispered, and tears filled her eyes. "A beautiful son, a child, at last, we are *blessed*."

His father wasn't so sure. "Whatever makes her happy," he told his buddies down at the Broadway Diner.

David was an only child. No more siblings arrived on the scene, so he became the apple of his mother's eye. There was nothing she wouldn't do for David, and nothing she wouldn't give to him. His father told her she was spoiling him rotten.

He was also a beautiful child: dark curls, smoky-gray eyes with thick lashes, and a perfect face. Sometimes, his father would wonder from whom he had inherited the good looks, but he had to admit his son was a stunner.

"What a beautiful child," ladies would say, as they stopped his mother in the street. "Oh my," they'd croon, "You will grow up to be *so* handsome and a real heart breaker!" David would smile and simper, and all the while he'd think, "What an old bag!"

When he was in eighth grade, David and half his class caught the virus that was plaguing the East Coast. "I'm dying up here," he'd shout. Then his Mother would climb the stairs to help her suffering son: water for his parched throat, Calamine lotion for the blisters, and ice packs for his swollen groin. It's a wonder his father and I didn't catch this thing, she'd think. When the fevers and swellings had passed, the boys in his class dropped their pants and peered down at themselves. They had heard the rumors and wondered if the virus had affected their manhood. Everything seemed to work, but they wouldn't know until they wanted to start a family.

David hoped it *had* affected him and started eyeing the girls in his class. "All play and no pay!" he told himself. For his sixteenth birthday, his mother bought him a new, bright red e-car, and the girls began to do more than eye him back. He became high school junior football captain and had his first back-seat experience with the most popular cheerleader in the senior class, a sassy blond with long legs and big boobs.

"A senior," he bragged to his teammates and leered. They milled around him, filled with questions, and he was delighted to tell all. It was the last time the cheerleader spoke to him, but he'd gotten what he wanted, anyway.

All through high school, David played the girls against one another until he got what he wanted – a night of rough sex in the back seat of his e-car. "Thank God for the virus," he thought. "I can screw my brains out with no consequences."

One evening over supper, David cleared his throat, and his parents stopped eating. "I will never get married," he told them. "Just too many tasty fish in the sea." He smiled and looked from one to the other.

His mother was delighted. Heaven only knows, she thought, what would I do if he brought some bride home, or even worse, bought his own house far away from me.

His father figured his son would be a skirt chaser all his life and went back to his spaghetti and meatballs. Where did he get *that* from? he wondered.

David excelled and graduated with honors, but the day after graduation, he told his parents he'd joined the National Police Force.

"Just think how good I'll look in that black uniform and shiny boots," he boasted, "and I'll carry a weapon!"

His mother was horrified, but his father felt a rush of relief. I love my son, he thought, but he'll be gone. No more girls crying to their parents or beating on the front door.

A week later, and with anticipation, David left home to become an NPF agent.

Now, he slouched down further in his seat. It was freezing in the vehicle, and the two agents watched as the people left the church bundling up in their winter coats and hats. Old farts, David thought, but then he noticed June and sat up in his seat. I want that girl, he thought and nudged the Sergeant.

"I want that girl," he said. "We can pick her up like the others."

"For God's sake, Agent," the Sergeant snapped, "it's Christmas Eve! Can't you keep it in your pants for one night?"

They argued loudly but settled back when Jem took June's hand. David narrowed his smoky-gray eyes and tightened his lips. I want that girl, he told himself and shifted uncomfortably in his seat. I don't know how long it will take and I don't care, but that one's a keeper!

The week after the New Year, David and his partner were posted to Southwestern Pennsylvania and then even farther West. They spent the next year away from the Garden State, but David never forgot the girl with the long, fair hair, the beautiful face, and the red goose-down parka.

Chapter 36

June knew when the People Upstairs had come home. First, she heard the truck hissing into the yard, and then the two of them moving around overhead, a bump, and Sherpa barking. A door banged, and the dog dashed outside.

It must be New Year's Eve, June thought and felt a bit safer. She had to admit, it had been a quiet week after her cold, shadowy walk to the Village Christmas Eve service. No NPF agents had been lurking around, but once again, June was glad the People Upstairs were home. She'd been lonely.

Every day she'd fed the chickens and sheep, cleaned her apartment and hung out. The high point was the Christmas Eve service. She thought Jem would come by again, but he didn't appear. "I think I insulted him," she told the chickens one night, but, of course, they continued to peck and scratch for food and didn't bother to look up. Damn, I'm so lonely I'm talking to the chickens, she thought, but she did find herself thinking about Jem more often, and she daydreamed about the Christmas Eve walk home.

Now, June glanced at the ceiling as the bumping continued. "I like him," she declared loudly. "And he's one of mine."

A little while after her noisy return, the Wife came down to visit, dropped onto the couch and sighed. "Long drive," she said and stretched her tall body out comfortably. She looked up at June with interest. "Was somebody here? I heard voices. Not that it's any of my business, just wondering."

June was embarrassed. She didn't want to tell the Wife about her walk into the village on Christmas Eve, and she really didn't to want to share her feelings about Jem. "Just talking to myself," she said and then wondered if the Wife would think that was odd, but the Wife changed the subject.

"I'm having a party tonight, and you're invited," she sat up and brushed her hair back from her face. "We have invited a few of our friends, good folks, uh … and I would love to have you come, too." The Wife looked hopefully at June. "I have lots of food and Adam bought a bottle of champagne for midnight."

June had never been to a party. She was tempted and was curious about *upstairs*, as well. Would it be like visiting one of the houses across the River that the Wealthy Ladies owned? She wanted to ask if Jem would be there but quickly decided it was a terrible idea. A Party with champagne! For a moment, June thought about sin and salvation but pushed the thought away.

"Yes," she said. "I have no party dress, but I can wear my blue sweater and tan pants."

"Righto," the Wife bounced up off the couch, and it was decided; June would wear her blue sweater, and she'd come upstairs through the front door for the first time.

"I'll come after my chores and knock," she said.

"You will be a guest, June," the Wife said, "not our hired farm hand. Just come on in."

At dusk, June fed the chickens. She watched as they settled down, and then climbed up on the beam. She remembered being a little girl when everything was normal. Her mother would fix her a treat for New Year's Eve – a cake or some cookies and milk, and they'd say Happy New Year, World. Thinking about her mother made June sad, and when she reflected on all that had happened since she'd left home, it made her head swim. She shifted on the beam, letting her legs fall on either side. So many memories, she thought. It was almost too much to bear. June watched the hens bobbing around for a while and then dropped down and headed to her apartment.

"Happy New Year, Amazing Creatures!" she sang and closed the door to the henhouse.

The hens just kept on scratching and pecking, but the rooster ruffled his feathers and made his "puck, puck, puck" sound.

June showered and changed into her tan pants and blue sweater and then looked in the mirror over the sink: the same face and long fair hair, a pretty face but not a party face. She found a stub of eyeliner from some long-ago student farmhand, studied it curiously, and said, "huh … like the Wife uses." Then she carefully drew thick, dark lines across her eyelids. When she looked again, her eyes seemed larger and bluer and more like a party face. Good, June decided, bundled herself into her red parka, and ventured around the house and onto the front porch.

A wreath of greens and red berries hung on the front door, and tall candles in the windows threw shadows across the porch. June could hear music and see people moving around inside, laughing and dancing. She stood still and looked through the window searching for a familiar face – the Wife or maybe Bob and Barbara from the store, but they were all strangers. She watched as they swooped and spun to the music and she knew she didn't belong.

I can't go in there, June thought. I don't even know how to dance.

"Well, aren't you a cutie!" A tall, well-dressed man moved out of the shadows: blue shirt, open collar, dark pants. "No smoking in Eve's house," he added sarcastically and held up a cigarette. He puffed a plume of smoke through thick lips and leered at June. "So, are you coming in or are you just watching the fun through the window?" June was speechless and horrified. The man moved closer and slipped his arm around her padded waist. "You're so damn cute. I could kiss you right here and now." His face loomed over hers, lips pursed, breath thick with alcohol. "Com'ere girl," he whispered and pushed himself against her.

That was more than enough for June, and she broke free and fled back to her apartment, locking the door behind her, scared and then furious.

"I wish I had punched him!" she told Kitty. "He looked like one of those fish the Son caught, googly eyes and big, flabby lips." June made kissing sounds. "I wish I had punched his ugly face! I will never let anyone do that, again. Not *ever!*"

Kitty looked at June and slowly blinked her eyes, then started washing one paw, her tail curled around her body.

"What a good girl," June told her. "You don't argue or laugh, and that is what I really needed right now, not someone telling me to forget it or get over myself."

She sat down on her bed and hugged her knees to her chest. "So that was a party … huh! Gentlemen down south didn't act like that. That man put his *hands* on me, oh yuck!" And June was outraged all over again. "Well, the Southern men didn't act like that *before* the virus struck," she added. "I guess they caught the sickness up here, too."

June got up and shrugged back into her red parka and boots. She walked down to the pasture fence where the snow was smooth and clean. The moon was almost full, and its light fell over the field like pale honey. She took a deep breath of the cold, fresh air, and then she squatted down and wrote 2060 in the snow with one finger.

Chapter 37

The Wife never mentioned the New Year's Eve party; neither did June. She just hoped they would never run into the Disgusting Man in the Village, and she wondered if the Wife knew what had happened. Was she embarrassed? Whenever the Disgusting Man popped into June's mind, she said the bad word out loud. She couldn't forget the feeling of his hands on her body, even covered by her parka, and over and over she vowed she would never allow it to happen again.

A few weeks into the new year, the Wife brought down a basket filled with woolen yarn and dropped it on the table.

"Look at this, June, it's all from Maud and Ella. It's washed and carded, and now I've spun it into yarn so you can start knitting sweaters for next year if you want." She sat down at the table and picked up a small bundle of the wool. "I'll bring more down as soon as I'm done," she said with pride.

The wool was thick and soft, the color of cream, and June buried her hands deep in the basket.

"Oh, how beautiful!" She felt her fingers itching to take up her knitting needles as they touched the soft yarn. "It's so soft, and knitting is just what I need during these dark months."

So, every night June fed the chickens and closed them in for the night, hauled alfalfa for the sheep and locked the barn door. Then she would curl up on the sagging brown couch and pick up where she had left off – knitting sweaters for the Villagers, some with intricately stitched decorations, and one for herself.

"I wanted to knit myself a sweater from Maud and Ella's wool," she told Kitty and slipped it over her head. "This way I'll always remember them."

June didn't question why she had said it, but the statement troubled her. "We will always be here," she told Kitty firmly and wouldn't allow herself to think otherwise.

Before she took up her needles, June would ask for *Music*, and her little radio would click on and play softly in the background. Now and again, she thought of Jem as she knitted, but she didn't yearn for him.

"I'm not sure how I feel about Jem," she told Kitty, "but I should really think about marrying him. He's one of my own, you know, and that is right and proper." She bit off a piece of yarn. "And he's a nice man, a handsome man." Kitty blinked her eyes a few times and then curled up and went to sleep. June liked the memory of Christmas Eve, of Jem taking her hand on their walk back to the farm, but she felt no longing. "It's likely he has gone back to the Midwestern Region ... wherever that is," she added, "but now I know I *will* see him again." She wondered when that would be, but then she forgot about him.

The days grew longer, and the snow melted in the pasture. Icicles dripped in the sun, and June took a walk down to the watering hole. A few small pieces of ice were floating on the water, and new grass was pushing through the patches of snow. Pretty soon Maud and Ella would leave the shelter and find their way back to the pasture, and June looked forward to it. She loved Maud and Ella, but her back was complaining from hauling the alfalfa into the shelter.

However, April was fickle.

After a week of warm weather that brought everyone outside to chat and laugh, an icy squall blew across the countryside and turned the pastures white again. The Saturday shopping trip to the Village was grim, and the diners at the coffee shop slurped their hot coffee sullenly. Huh, June thought, they don't even know how lucky they are!

The following week, the road to the Village was lined with clouds of yellow forsythia and the trees wore a green haze of tiny leaves. The sun was warming the earth, and now and then a stray shower watered the new grass. The Villagers stood around chatting, and this time they were sure.

Finally, Spring had come to the Garden State.

Eve worried about June. She was afraid one of the NPF agents would spot her – and that would be the end of that.

"They just take what they want now," she told Adam one spring evening. The weather was warm enough to sit on the front porch, and she was rocking slowly in her chair. "June is so dainty, and with her long blond hair and pretty face, oh, and that sweet, soft drawl she has? Well, that's just what they like, isn't it? They make me sick!" She glared at the front road where an NPF vehicle was drifting by. "And what the Hell are they doing up here, anyway?" she added, angrily.

A chilly evening breeze tossed the leaves and brought the sweet smell of new grass from the fields. Eve wrapped herself in her shawl and took a deep breath. She relaxed as the NPF disappeared around a turn in the road, but it had slowed down as it hummed past the farm. And it was happening more often – morning, noon, AND night!

"Go AWAY," she shouted after it.

"June may look dainty," Adam closed his eyes and let his mind wander, "but she's strong as an ox and smart as a whip. She learned to drive the tractor in one afternoon, and now she's handling it like, well, just … like a man." He sat up and looked at Eve. "And, for Pete's sake, she traveled all the way from North Carolina alone. She must know how to take care of herself." He settled back down in his rocking chair, "You worry too much, Eve."

But Eve still worried. She worried endlessly about June. She remembered June's reaction to the news on the radio and knew she would never want to watch TV. She hadn't appeared at the New Year's Eve party, and Eve wondered about that, but didn't ask, so she figured June certainly wouldn't want to come upstairs to a dinner party either. How would June find a husband or even a boyfriend?

"I guess she wants to stay in her own little world," Eve said out loud.

She also worried about the weather. The snowy winter had left the fields ready for planting, but the weather reports were troubling. Every day she heard more alarming news on the radio, and that added to her distress. She had not seen Jem for months and wondered where he was. What awful event is he was facing, Eve asked herself. Tornadoes were hitting the Midwestern Region, hurling dead trees across the ruined countryside. It was an empty land where nobody lived: no farms, no homes, no towns. The Southern Region was now entirely covered by water as the tides moved in, and North Carolina was under the sea. But Eve kept that information from June.

Sometimes, Eve let fear take over and wondered what they would do if the relentless climate changes moved into the Garden State. She would gaze out over the fields, rest her eyes on the trees and hills, and her throat would feel tight. Eve was afraid she was losing her country – piece-by-piece.

When she became overcome with fear, Eve would tell herself, "Of course, Mom and Dad have a farm up north in the Commonwealth, and we can pack up the chickens and sheep in the pickup and head there," but the idea was overwhelming – just leave home?

"And what about June?" she asked herself. Could she sit in the back with the animals? She couldn't squeeze in the front with them. There was barely room for Sherpa.

Then Eve would drag her morbid thoughts away and keep herself busy, but she found herself watching obsessively as June drove the Ion tractor across the wheat field, the big sun hat perched on her head. She wished Jem would come home, because he was interested in June and he could keep her safe, maybe even marry her. But Eve would sigh, it appeared June wasn't interested, and she would start to worry again.

Chapter 38

June knew the Wife was worried and it confused her, but she felt the Farmer would help. He was her husband, after all. Maybe he could tell her to turn off that darn television she had upstairs and stop listening to the news every night. She could hear it through the ceiling of her apartment; angry voices droned on and on. June didn't know what the voices were telling the Wife, but the more she listened, the more worried the poor woman became. June refused the Wife's invitation to watch any television. She thought it was … well, not a good thing to do.

However, June was enjoying herself. She loved driving the tractor, and after the first moments of fear and hesitation, she felt quite at home. She had finished plowing the vegetable gardens, and the moist soil was turned over and ready for the seeder. Now she was working in the wheat field and felt as though she were flying, hauling the plow behind as it churned the soil. It had been a long time since she had felt this happy.

It was a warm spring with a hot summer predicted, so the Wife had taken June to *The Farm Bureau* to buy shorts.

"It's too hot to wear these dungarees," she complained, "and it's going to get hotter." She pawed through the summer clothes bin, picked out two pairs of khaki shorts to try on, and handed a pair to June.

June hung back, embarrassed, but she finally took the shorts behind a curtain and pulled them on. When she looked at herself in the mirror, she felt her face turn red. They hugged her waist and her long, pale legs stuck out like a water bird's. When she turned sideways it was worse, her bottom was barely covered. The swimming suit was one thing. June was alone at the watering hole, and she usually didn't bother to put it on — but this?

"Oh, please, I can't wear these," she begged. "I feel like I'm in my underclothes and look at my white legs!" June pulled back the curtain and crept out

"You have such pretty legs," the clerk said – she had legs like a piano and felt annoyed and envious. She looked June up and down and shook her head. "You should feel proud, young lady, not embarrassed."

Eve didn't bother to look in the mirror, she just pushed the curtain aside and handed a pile of shorts to the clerk.

"We'll take them all," she said. "June, I'll give you lotion and you'll get a tan." And that was that.

Now June felt comfortable in her shorts. The sun hat shielded her face, and as she maneuvered the tractor across the wheat fields, she could see her legs and arms were, indeed, turning dark in the sun.

Sometimes, June would see one of the black NPF vehicles slowing down on the back road, but she felt strong and fierce on the tractor and never looked their way. They think I'm a boy, she thought, and it made her laugh out loud.

It was warm enough now, and June began to hike down to the watering hole late in the day. She undressed in the trees, then slipped into the cold water, ducking underneath and then floating on top, looking up at the trees, watching as the leaves grew green and full. Maud and Ella grazed nearby, and they kept her company. Occasionally, she heard the hiss of a vehicle as it passed, and then she would duck under the water. June knew she was hidden by the trees, but she didn't want to take a chance, especially with her bathing suit carefully folded and lying on the bank.

One day she thought she heard footsteps and rustling in the brush and her breath caught in her throat. Ella lifted her head, but then it was quiet, and June relaxed. This was her private place and she loved it. The idea someone would be lurking in the bushes was unthinkable. When she finished her swim, she climbed up on the bank. The water flowed down over her body, puddling at her feet. With a shock, June realized she wasn't a skinny girl, anymore. Her breasts were full and her legs long. She had a small waist and rounded hips, and when she leaned over, she could see where the tan stopped, and her pale skin started. She traced a line down over one breast and stopped at the curve of her hip. She thought of her mother sitting on the grass by the river back home, watching a five-year-old June whirling around, singing nonsense.

"Always stay young," her mother had said. "Always stay as young as you are today, Sweetheart."

"I wanted to Mama," June said now. "I wanted to stay young, but it was the *hate*." She realized something had changed as she had cowered with the brooms in January's store. I hated that cruel man and what he did to January. She was my best friend, and it was *ugly!* "I hated him!" she said out loud. "That's when I stopped being young, Mama. I wanted to kill him!"

June went and sat quietly in the trees and felt herself relax as she looked up at the leaves. She thought about the changes in her body and wondered how the Son would feel about her now. Would he demand that his mother allow her to stay with them? Could she be the woman he held, the woman who had his babies? She touched her breast again and felt a moment of longing that almost broke her heart. "Not one of his own," she reminded herself.

A warm breeze sent little ripples across the water, and she thought of Jem. "How would Jem feel?" June looked down at her nakedness. "Of course," she told the sheep, "if I marry him, he will see me like this." The thought embarrassed her, but she missed him, longed to see him again. Is that yearning, she wondered. She remembered how the Son had made her feel, how her body had responded to his touch and June realized the memory was fading. "It hurts," she whispered. "It hurts so much, but I imagine it is right and proper."

Maud and Emma glanced up, and June felt eyes on her, again, but then the two sheep went back to grazing. June pulled her clothes on and headed up the field without looking back.

Chapter 39

The Wife's concern turned out to be more than a figment of her imagination. It was, indeed, a very hot summer. The heat shimmered on the highway to the Village, and the air was ominously still without a whiff of breeze; but the crops grew in abundance, surprising and delighting the Farmer.

As June kneeled among the tomatoes and peas, she marveled at how sweet they were, and how many beans filled the vines. Every now and then, she would sample a few raw peas, and when she carried baskets of vegetables to the farm stand, she could see cars lining the road in front of the house. The bees were busy in the wildflowers, and the chickens foraged through the brush next to the henhouse. Occasionally, a rainstorm would blow up out of the north and soak the ground. Nothing seemed out of the ordinary, but June felt anxious again.

One Saturday morning, as the red pickup grumbled into town, June spotted Jem standing in front of the coffee shop and her spirits lifted. I'm glad to see him, she thought, even in his uniform.

"Welcome home," the Wife said and felt a wave of relief. Thank God Jem is back, she thought and gave him a hug.

June said hello and smiled at him, and her smile was genuine.

She smiled at me, Jem thought and felt his heart hit his stomach. He remembered the last time he'd seen her, how they held hands, and how cold it had been in the snow, but how warm he'd felt. I think I'm in love, he thought and was embarrassed. All the horsing around with his buddies and the locker room stories they shared. The rowdy way they unwound after the horrors of each day … the bragging, the women and the drinking. It seemed awful now. What would they think? he wondered and looked away for a minute.

The Wife was blissfully unaware and headed into the diner.

They found the table near the window that overlooked the main street, and June scooted her chair a bit so she could look out. The hazy sun hung over the Village, making little puddle-mirages on the asphalt, and the trees were dense with leaves. Villagers strolled by, stopping to chat in the shade and fanning themselves. June relaxed in her chair. I'm glad Jem is home, she thought. He likes me, and he makes me feel safe.

Jem and the Wife spent lunch discussing the Upper Southern Region and farms in Pennsylvania, things June didn't want to think about. He was talking about the countryside she had traveled through with the Illegals ... and the Man slipping away at night to steal eggs and honey.

"They are suffering from the ongoing drought." Jem said, and his face was serious, "but there is still water in the reservoirs and lakes. EO is just investigating small fires and damage. We also must nag the farmers constantly. They are refusing to rotate their crops. It's a constant problem, and after what we saw in the Midwestern Region, well ..." he shook his head in frustration. "But it's nothing to worry about up here," he quickly added.

They sat in silence for a few minutes, concentrating on their lunch, and the Wife thought about fires and damage. We rotate our crops; it's what farmers do! She looked out the window and started to worry. She felt sick and cursed herself for spoiling a good lunch.

"I feed the chickens in the evening," June said. "Why don't you come on by and help me, Jem."

The Wife was shocked. She had had vague hopes about Jem and June, but she was sure June would never be interested, especially as Jem wore a uniform ... *and* he carried a gun. What in the world would bring *this* on? To her knowledge, June had never even said one word to him. She glanced at June, sitting innocently across the table from her.

"Please do come," the Wife added, and she took in Jem's stunned expression with amusement, her worries forgotten. "June takes care of the chickens around six o'clock."

"Six o'clock it is," Jem agreed, and he had a sudden urge to laugh out loud. Well, I'll be damned, he thought.

June looked out the window and smiled.

The sun was dipping over the trees when Jem arrived at June's door. He had taken extra care and wore a pair of new jeans and a plaid shirt. His arms and face were tan from the burning hot days chasing down rebellious, angry men on their deteriorating farms. Many more farms were falling into this condition. The dust that had swept across the Midwestern Region would soon start to blow across Pennsylvania, but it seemed people still scoffed at the agents' warnings.

"No regulations," they shouted. "You guys can't tell me what to do with *my* farm! Screw you, anyway, who do'ya think you are?"

What the Hell is wrong with these people, Jem wondered sourly as he waited for June to come to the door.

June was happy to see him and his mood lifted. She had shocked herself with her boldness and knew the Wife was shocked, too, but June had been afraid he was insulted on Christmas Eve and had wondered if he would ever come back. The least I could have done was give Jem a cup of hot chocolate, June thought, and realized she had used his name. She felt uneasy but quickly pushed it away.

They walked across the yard to the henhouse without a word, but the hens rustled out of the underbrush and gathered around their feet, murmuring and clucking among themselves as they waited to go inside, and that made them laugh. "Cheeky critters, aren't they," Jem said. "and just look at that handsome rooster fellow."

Once inside, June scooped up a container of feed, and Jem took handfuls and tossed it around the floor.

"I grew up on a farm," he said. "This brings back memories."

The rooster made his "puck, puck, puck" sound and ruffled his feathers threateningly, but Jem said, "hah!" and ignored him.

June felt herself relax, the sound of the chickens as they scratched around the floor and the warm quietness of the henhouse was her safe place. Jem was strong and kind, someone she could trust, and June was glad he was with her. She watched him as he tossed the feed, his tan arm moving back and forth and realized how little she knew about this man whom, she believed, was the man she would marry. He is a Northerner, of course, but he's a familiar man with light hair and sky-blue eyes, a kind man who grew up on a farm. He's an Environmental Officer who carries a gun for his own safety. Other than that, June thought, I know nothing at all about Jem.

"Come," she said and pulled herself up onto one of the beams. "It's nice up here." She leaned against the wall and looked down at him. "Can you do that?"

Jem swung up on a facing beam and straddled it like a horse. "Yup," he said. "Nothing to it."

This is good, June thought. I'm comfortable with this nice guy.

"Where's your family?" She asked, her curiosity overtaking her shyness.

Jem was a private person, one who carried things inside, and it was difficult for him to talk about himself, but this was June, the woman he knew he was in love with.

"My mom still lives on the farm. It's up north in the Empire State. Dad died in the War when I was a kid, and Mom has taken care of everything ever since. She's done well with the farm, kept it going." He paused. "Someday I'll have to move back and take over. The farm has been in the family for generations." Jem shifted on the beam, lost in memories

"My Daddy died in the War, too …" June started and then stopped short. She didn't know what to say and had an odd urge to laugh, or maybe cry.

Jem stared at her, realizing what war they were talking about. My father and her father, he thought. My God … enemies!

"Why?" June asked. "Why the War?"

"It was a long time ago," Jem said softly, "I was just a little kid."

June sat very still. "Do you remember him?" she asked. "I mean your daddy, what he looked like and how he acted? Did he pick you up? Did he sing to you? I was just a baby, but I have memories, too."

"He was a good dad," Jem said. "He used to take me to the barn with him, show me how to take care of the stock. He taught me how to ride the horses and how to throw a fastball, even when I was a little kid." He paused for a minute, deep in thought. "People say I look just like him. I don't know, maybe I do, but he was very tall."

June smiled, "Well, you're very tall now, Jem. You're a grown-up, not a little kid."

She shifted her weight on the beam, "Mama would never talk about my Daddy," she said. "But I think I remember him. I think he used to pick me up and sing silly songs that made me laugh, but now I think I just made all those memories up. I don't even know where he died," she added, "just Up Here in the North." June paused and looked at Jem, "Mama said my Daddy died for the South."

"I'm sorry," Jem said. "I guess my Dad died for the North. I don't know what else to say." Then he brightened, "But the South is beautiful, I know. My Granny and Grandpa had a cottage down there somewhere by the ocean. I never saw it, but my Mom said it was wonderful, the water was so clear and warm."

"You don't have to say anything, Jem," June said sadly. "The South doesn't even exist anymore, and it had nothing to do with your Daddy or my Daddy. I know the Wife wants to keep this from me, but I know it's gone. It's under the sea." She sighed. "I have known for a long time."

"Yeah, it is," Jem said. He found it odd, but rather exotic, that June would call Eve *the Wife*, maybe something southern, he thought. "I've been down there, and it's awful," he continued. "Towns and cities, just gone."

He stopped when he saw June's face and realized this was June's home he was talking about. "But, listen, maybe someday we can get married, and those memories will be forgotten. North and South … we can make it all good."

"That would be right and proper," June said solemnly, and she studied Jem, thinking about being with him and making babies. Jem didn't have dark curls and deep brown eyes, he had sun-bleached hair and blue eyes, maybe like her Daddy. That's the way it should be, she told herself, but she felt she was losing something, as if it were slipping away, something inside her she didn't want to lose – a part of herself.

Long after he was gone, June sat and thought about Jem, wondering what it would be like to have *his* hands on her body

Chapter 40

Over the next few weeks, Jem came more often to help June feed the chickens. As they sat on their beams, June told him about the things she had seen on the road and some of the people she had met. In her slow, soft drawl, June spoke of her home in North Carolina, and how beautiful it had been before the burning sun. She talked about the lonely bus ride, and they laughed about the little country store with the shaky porch and the couple in the bushes. As she sat on her beam, lost in her memories, June told him about the grey-green hills, and how all the Travelers had to hide from the NPF – and Jem gazed at her face and knew he was in love.

He listened in amazement as June told him about Bo John, the soldier who lived in a cave near Butternut Falls, and how the old man was shocked the war was over. "He was from the South, and he had been hiding from the Northern soldiers, living in that cave all alone. But that old man was clean, you know? He bathed in the waterfalls. He trapped rabbits and ate berries and greens. He even made me coffee from some bitter weeds." June held up her hand at the expression on Jem's face. "Wait, that coffee was good," she said.

Jem stopped her, "You can't live on wild animals and berries. He would be dead by now."

"Oh, yes you can," June said firmly, and Jem didn't argue. She was the one who had lived on the run, but here she was.

"I told him the war was over," she continued, "but I explained he couldn't go home because ... well, there was no home, anymore."

She paused for a moment and thought about Bo John and his friends. "He didn't want to leave his friends, anyway. He had built a memorial by the path, had stacked stones on top of one another. Each stone was one of his friends who had died back then." June shook her head, "It's sad, isn't it, Jem? I gave him one of my bars of cold-water soap, and he wasn't insulted, just pleased. He liked the smell."

June never told Jem about the beautiful juggler, about how he had wanted her to go into the woods with him.

She never mentioned the Illegals, and her longing for the Son, or her friend, January, how she, June, had hidden in the broom closet as the NPF agent raped her. After some thought, June decided not to tell him about her Fox, because she knew he wouldn't believe her. These were the memories she would hide from everyone, locked away inside.

Jem found it easy to talk to June as they sat on their beams in the henhouse. He told her how beautiful the Empire State was. "You would love it," he said. He reminisced about his horse, Sunny. "I owned him when I was growing up. He was so pretty, June, gold, like the sun, a Palomino. That's why I named him Sunny."

Gold, June thought about the Son but pushed the memory away.

Jem told her about his school, and how he had decided to be an Environmental Officer. "We studied the environment and the weather in science class," he said. "It was damn scary, and there was no time to lose. I wanted to do something to help. It's what I do every day."

June didn't know what science class was but was too embarrassed to ask; she didn't tell him there had been no school in her hometown, but she knew very well what the environment was, it had destroyed her home and driven her away. "The burning days," she said, "that's why I became a Traveler."

Jem thought about the destruction he had seen, but he didn't tell June what was happening to the Delaware Water Gap. The endless drought creeping up from the South had killed the leaves and wasted the river. Little by little the rushing water had slowed, then dwindled, and now it was just a weak stream in the riverbed. There were no waterfalls in the Delaware Water Gap anymore, because there was no rain.

"He was old, that soldier," June said thoughtfully and broke into his musing, "He may be dead by now, all alone where he wanted to be. I should go back there and add another stone to the memorial."

Jem was sure the old man was dead by now. He didn't say anything, but he hoped June's idea of going back was just talk.

August arrived, and a few brown leaves floated down in an occasional hot breeze. June brought sweet corn out to the farm stand, but the Wife sent it back.

"It's filled with worms," she said with disgust. "It's too dry."

However, the cabbages and root vegetables seemed to thrive in the heat, and pumpkins dotted the dry fields with orange.

June dug turnips and cut cabbages and rolled them in burlap. She pushed them into the hole behind the kitchen cabinet for the winter, and again, she felt uneasy.

"I'm not worried," she told herself – but she was. It reminded her of the freezing winter, and then the burning sun that had arrived the following summer.

Jem's unit was sent to the Far Western Region where National Fire Fighters were battling wildfires that were consuming the region. "The drought," the unit was told. "The fires are racing across acres of forests, creating wind tunnels that throw flames for miles. Nobody has seen anything like it before."

Jem listened in horror. Every day the flames were coming closer to homes and major cities, and nothing seemed to stop their terrifying journey. It was an emergency and, except for the NPF, all national agencies were called in to help. He felt sick at heart. There's just no end to this, he thought and set off to let June know.

"I hate to leave you," Jem told her and kissed her for the first time, and then he was gone.

The next week the wheat started to turn brown, and the big yellow thresher appeared in the wheat field.

"I'm afraid it will burn up if I wait," the Farmer said.

June and the Wife watched from the side of the field, and June felt her heart sink. She had loved seeing the breeze as it moved across the field and turned it into a sea of pale gold. It reminded her of the ocean of ferns in the forest where she and the Illegals had camped, but this year it was too dry, and the wheat would die.

The next day the Farmer decided to plow under the cornfield.

"We need to turn the corn into mulch, and that may help keep what little moisture that's left in the soil," he said. "Damn, it's the least I can do." He ran one big hand through his hair. "I'll buy commercial feed for the chickens this year, and people can make do with the pumpkins on Halloween. I guess all we can do is pray or whatever for a snowy winter."

He patted June on the shoulder as she settled into the tractor seat.

"It will be okay," he said. "I have faith in Mother Nature."

June had never heard of Mother Nature but figured it had to do with nature and science. Maybe it's something Atheists believed in, she thought, but she didn't agree. June was scared. She drove the tractor into the field and started plowing under the corn, hearing it crunch under the blades.

Every day she woke with a feeling of dread.

Chapter 41

Autumn remained hot and dry with no colorful foliage; a few brown leaves whirled across the countryside in the sultry breeze. The water in the pond was low, but it remained June's escape. She headed across the pasture every afternoon, anxious for a distraction from the troubling weather. Even though the water was not as deep as it had been, it was still cold, and June would toss her sweat-wilted clothes on the bank and splash in. She'd float on top and gaze at the sky, and as always, it brought her some peace.

The thick green leaves had become dry and paper-thin, and June could see the back road through the trees. She was always alert to the sound of approaching vehicles but still enjoyed her private moments. On these long hot afternoons, June thought of Jem and wondered what he was doing so far away. Fires, she thought. At home, we didn't have fires, but it burned up, anyway. Where Jem is, it's dangerous, she reminded herself, and she longed to see his face, to know he was alive.

"Please, Sir," she pleaded, "Keep Jem safe."

When June was at the pond, Maud and Ella always grazed nearby, searching for what was left of the grass and weeds, but by the end of September, they began to tug the leaves off the bushes – the grass had turned brown, and the weeds had dried up.

Sometimes the sheep looked at June as if to the ask, "Why?" and June would look back and think, "why?"

I don't like this one bit, June thought, it scares me, but she kept it to herself. The Farmer was anxiously poring over farming magazines, and the Wife was becoming fretful, offering a stream of colorful curse words as they made their way to the Village. Even Kitty kept her distance. The pond was June's escape.

"I don't know the answer," June told the sheep. "I don't know what to do, so don't look at me that way."

Now and again, June would hear an NPF vehicle on the back road and would duck under the water, and more than once she had a sense that someone was watching her as she dressed, but she never heard a vehicle stop. Neither of the sheep glanced up, so she shook it off. Just imagination, June told herself and never looked back as she headed across the pasture.

Finally, October brought a welcome change in the weather. The dried leaves spun off the trees and made little piles by the side of the road, and the countryside seemed to breathe a sigh of relief. With the cooler weather, the Wife's spirits rose, and the Saturday shopping trips to the Village were bearable. Kitty chased the whirling leaves and became sociable again, and June began to relax.

Two weeks before Halloween, the Farmer found a large piece of barn wood and attached it to two posts, pounding nails into the plank with enthusiasm. He painted *Pumpkin Patch* in large letters and then stood back and admired his work.

"What do you think of this?" he asked June. "I'm going to let people pick their own pumpkins this year. Save you the trouble of hauling them out to the farm stand." He seemed to have moved on from the farm magazines.

June was relieved and decided she liked the idea.

"Why not bring Maud and Ella up to the barnyard so the children can pat them?" she offered. "We can buy orange ribbons for the two ladies to wear."

The Wife joined in.

"Let's make a sign that says petting zoo," she said. "June can oversee the pumpkin patch and the petting zoo, and Adam, you and I can take care of the farm stand. There will still be root vegetables to sell."

June was relieved that things had returned to normal and watched as the Farmer squatted down and painted *Petting Zoo* on another piece of wood. He nailed it to the barnyard fence and looked at June. "Waddaya say, June?"

"Let's do it," June said and felt her mood lift.

The Wife gazed at June with surprise. She's changed so much over the year, she thought, and now she's making suggestions and even joining in with the celebration. My God, last year she lectured me about Halloween and the Devil! Maybe she's finally used to our ways. The Wife watched as June examined the sign, her pale hair lifting in the breeze. Maybe she and Jem will end up together, after all, she thought and shivered in the draft. Maybe it will be a snowy winter, and everything will be all right. Maybe, maybe, maybe! "What is happening to our world?" she asked herself.

The day before Halloween, June hiked down to the pond and lured Maud and Ella up to the barn with a small wooden bowl filled with grain. They had bought bright orange ribbons in the Village on Saturday, and she fastened them around the wooly necks, tying them in big bows. Neither Maud nor Ella seemed disturbed by their adornments, and they looked at June with their big, gold eyes, content to stay in the paddock with their share of feed and alfalfa.

"Good Girls," June said and patted their broad, spongy backs. I love these sheep, she thought. They're such gentle creatures. "You're my responsibility now," she said. "Little children will want to pat you, and you must be good." Maude turned her back and started pulling the alfalfa, and Ella nudged June's hand.

The Wife hung a sign on the vegetable stand, and cars began to line up in front of the house. June stayed in the pumpkin field and smiled at the families as they wandered through the pumpkins. She helped them with their choices, and loaded the pumpkins into the wheelbarrow; she counted their dollar bills and carefully made change with the American money. It reminded her of the Wealthy Ladies from across the River, and the *Knitting Shop* back home. June was overwhelmed with memories. "Mama," she whispered, but she swallowed hard and pushed the memories away.

A group of children asked to pat the sheep, and June held them as they leaned over the fence. They laughed when they felt the thick wool, "The sheep are like sponges." Their voices were high and sweet, and June laughed with them. People have children Up Here, she thought, the virus didn't reach them! As her hands encircled their tiny waists, she was filled with wonder. She watched as the little ones jumped down and ran off through the pumpkins and wondered if she could have children with Jem: little ones running and playing, little Jems and little Junes. "Wow," she said, and it amazed her.

Towards the end of the day, June noticed a lone man standing quietly in the pumpkin patch nearby. He was tall with dark hair, his eyes were the color of smoke, and his body was trim in jeans and a black t-shirt. That man would be very good looking if he didn't look so grim, June thought.

"May I help you?" She smiled shyly and brushed her hair back from her face.

The man stared at her and then shook his head, "I'm okay, now," he said and turned away.

June shrugged, went back to playing with the children and loading pumpkins, but she still was aware of the stranger with the gray eyes.

As the afternoon shadows fell across the pumpkin patch, the families headed home. June thought about closing the gate, but she realized the stranger was still there. And he was watching her. His eyes locked on hers as he wandered among the pumpkins, and it made her uneasy.

"May I help you select a pumpkin," she asked again, but he only shook his head and kept staring at her. Then he ran his tongue over his upper lip and narrowed his smoky-gray eyes.

June felt a sense of panic. The hair stood up on the back of her neck, and she shivered as a small breeze touched her cheek. She wanted to run, call for help, but what would she say? "Help! That man is looking at me!" She quickly turned her back on him, but she was confused. If she glanced back, he'd see her looking, but what if he came up behind her, maybe grabbed her? She felt as if his gray eyes were undressing her, touching her, owning her, and she thought, *January!*

June stood ridged and uncertain, and she froze when something brushed her leg, but it was Sherpa. The dog planted himself close to her and growled low in his throat. When June finally turned around, the stranger was walking across the lawn towards the road, and it occurred to her, that he had never bought a pumpkin.

Chapter 42

The autumn weather remained well into November. A few field flowers decided to bloom again, and the Wife started to complain.

"It's supposed to be cold now. Remember last year? This isn't normal, June. Just think how cold it was back in the nineteen-hundreds. Sometimes it even snowed, and people traveled around in sleighs. There's a picture in your history book. Now it's too damn warm for you to wear your red autumn jacket!"

The Wife shook her head and looked out over the fields. "It looks so bleak. It makes me want to cry. The country is in flames or buried in dust and the sea is going to cover up the whole world. I'm afraid now."

"It's going to be okay," June said, "this is the Garden State!" But she looked at the sky and worried. The summer heat had bleached it to a washed out blue, and wispy clouds hugged the horizon.

When Thanksgiving arrived, the Wife brought June her Thanksgiving turkey pot pie and added a pumpkin pie in a big silver pie pan for dessert. Maybe she'll invite Jem, she thought, and her spirits lifted.

"We're leaving tomorrow for Thanksgiving and will be back on Monday. We're thinking of leaving Sherpa here to keep you safe."

"I have Kitty with me," June said. "I'll be fine."

She wondered if the Wife had noticed the man with the gray eyes hanging around her in the pumpkin patch. Maybe she'd sent Sherpa up there, but June didn't ask. The man had never come back, and she hadn't seen him in the Village. Maybe he was a Traveler, June thought, and he's gone. She realized how lucky she had been, traveling with the Illegals. "A young girl shouldn't be traveling alone," the Woman had said, and now June agreed.

That evening the weather broke, an icy wind from the North swept in, and Jem arrived in time to help feed the chickens. The Wife breathed a sigh of relief, and June felt her heart beat faster when she saw him. He's alive, she thought and felt like hugging him. Maybe I do love him, she decided.

June stole glances at Jem as she finished her chores, and when they sat on their beam with the chickens finally murmuring quietly below, she told him about the pumpkin patch, and the sheep with their big orange bows. "The children reached down and patted them and laughed so hard when they felt their wool. It was great," she said. "I was in charge, and the farm made a bundle. All the pumpkins are gone."

June didn't mention the man with the gray eyes. She wanted to forget the feeling of eerie dread and the way those smoky eyes had consumed her. She gazed at Jem on the facing beam. His eyes were so blue and kind, like the memory of her Daddy. His face was open and honest, and she wanted to say, "Please marry me, Jem. Please keep me safe!" But June just asked him about the fires in the Far Western Region, and about the people and the animals, how the EO had rescued them all.

Jem told her about the destruction on the other coast, the fire-tornadoes, and the raging flames, but he lied when he assured her the people and the animals were all safe. He never wanted to think about the charred bodies lying inside the destroyed farms ever again.

"You're a hero, Jem," she said. But he didn't smile.

"The farmers had already started moving out because it was so dangerous. It was an inferno. We moved them all to the Northern Border, and I don't think anyone or any animals were left behind."

Jem watched June as she shifted on her beam – her trim body, pale hair, and pretty face, and he wanted to hold her, tell her they would be married one day, have their own children.

He longed to say that everything would be all right: no more fires or dust storms, no floods or burning days, but he kept it to himself. How unfair, he thought, to promise so much when I honestly don't know if I believe it. Instead, he told her about his plans.

"I have to go back after Christmas. All our units will. The only agents that won't be grubbing around in that mess are the NPF guys. The fires are contained, but we need to decide what to do with what they left behind, find out if anything can be salvaged." His face was filled with concern. "I think all of us need to be alert now," he added. "I don't know what is happening with this weather. It worries me." He saw her expression and leaned across the space between their beams and kissed her, his lips just brushing hers.

"Wait for me," he said. "That's what will keep me going."

June touched her lips with the tip of her finger and felt safe for the first time in a month.

Jem came by every evening when June was feeding the chickens. The big house felt empty without the People Upstairs, and she was relieved Jem was there. On Thanksgiving, as they herded the squabbling chickens in for the night, June invited him to share her turkey and pumpkin pies. She had given the invitation much thought, but she trusted Jem now, she thought she might love him, so it was time to invite him into her home. "It's not much, but you're alone, and I'm alone, and so … you know, it would be nice." She tossed corn to the chickens and gave him a quick glance. Oh Lordy, what if he says no!

Jem had been tempted to invite himself and had no intention of saying no. He filled his bowl with corn and nodded. Hell yes, he thought, and that was that.

Before they left the henhouse, June stood at the door and sang, "Happy Thanksgiving, you Mighty Creatures and good night!"

Jem shook his head. "Wow," he said softly. "I'm in love with a crazy lady!"

He followed her through the door to her apartment and looked around with interest. "It's cute in here. It's cozy," he said and glanced over at her big bed, tucked into the corner by the side window.

"Sit," June ordered, and Jem sat. She slid the potpie into the oven and set two places at the table. Some late daisies were stuck in a glass jar and sat on the table as a centerpiece. The plates were spotless and the silverware shining, but nothing matched. Jem gazed at the daisies drooping in their water and was touched. Oh, June, he thought. You do so much with so little.

The turkey potpie was worth the wait, and June admitted the Wife had made it, "Oh, and the pumpkin pie, too," she added. She served the pie and Jem lingered over his coffee. He longed to end the evening in the bed by the back window, and his mind wandered as the sound of her soft, Southern drawl rose and fell in the background.

"Jem, *hello*," June raised her voice, and Jem jumped. His gaze had been fixed on June's bed, and he hadn't heard a word she'd said. He felt his face warm with embarrassment as he dragged his attention back.

"I need to feed my cat," June repeated, and Jem drew a blank.

"Cat," he said.

"Yes, my cat. Kitty is my cat." June was getting exasperated.

"Yes, you have a cat." Jem refocused. "I guess I'm tired, June. I'm sorry, I was just drifting away, and everything is so warm and, you know … cozy here." He looked around hopefully, and June noticed.

"Kitty! Food! Now!" June said, and Thanksgiving ended with a kiss goodbye at the open door. Kitty strolled past them without a second glance, her tail switching from side to side. Jem was familiar, he didn't deserve a sniff, and she wanted her dinner.

June leaned on the back of the couch with her elbows on the window sill. She watched as Jem disappeared into the dark, but this time she knew he'd come back. "I'm beginning to believe he'll always come back," she told Kitty.

Kitty gazed at June, and her eyes said, "food."

Chapter 43

Days! June thought, days and weeks and months sliding by like the river I crossed. She'd been living at Natural World Farm for more than a year and found it hard to believe. June felt at home, but she never felt entirely safe, not really.

During the Thanksgiving weekend, an NPF vehicle had hummed past the farm more than once. June made sure she was tucked away inside the hen house or hidden in the back yard. Just the sound of their vehicles made her nervous, especially now the house was empty. June realized she hadn't felt this way the year before, and she didn't understand why.

"Maybe it was all too new then," she told Kitty. "Or maybe I'm still afraid of that man in the Pumpkin Patch." June ran her hand over the cat's soft fur. "But you can keep me safe, won't you? You're my Watch Cat." She repeated it and laughed. "And Jem is here," she added. Kitty closed her eyes and rumbled contentedly.

And then something happened that frightened her and upset Jem.

The Sunday after Thanksgiving, June and Jem were sitting on their beams in a comfortable silence. The hens scratched at the floor, their heads bobbing as they searched for corn, and the rooster ruffled his feathers and settled down by the door. A cold front was moving in, but it was warm and peaceful in the henhouse. June was just telling Jem about the circus wagon with all the fancy ladies, when a passing vehicle slowed down and stopped in front of the house. June froze and then dropped down and flattened herself behind the hens' cubbies by the back wall. The chickens set up a racket, flapping their wings against the walls, and it was hard to hear anything through the din. For a moment, Jem was stiff with shock.

After a minute, the vehicle pulled away, and except for the hens chattering and the rooster ruffling his feathers, it was quiet again. June heard Jem's soft voice as he knelt and tried to calm her, and when she looked at his shocked face, she realized it was time to tell Jem what had happened to January, all those months ago.

"I have to tell you something," she said and was filled with dread. "I don't want to," she whispered and turned her face away. "I don't *want* to. I don't want to even think about it but I have to tell you, I know."

"Come," Jem said, and he sat June down with her back against the henhouse wall. "It's okay, June, come on!"

June felt the rough boards on her back and heard Jem's breath as he sat close; she clenched her hands and hid them in her lap, and then she told Jem about her friend, and what had happened to her.

"When I was a Traveler," she began, "there was a girl who owned the little store where I shopped. We became best friends. Her name was January and mine is June. It was like a joke, you know? June and January." She smiled at the memory. "There was a big, wooden table in the center of the store, and we always sat there with our tea. We'd gossip like old ladies."

June looked at Jem and twisted her hands in her lap. "She was so small and so very pretty. Dainty, you know? She had big eyes, dark blue, almost like purple. She was a Citizen, Jem, an American Citizen like me!"

As she talked, June remembered how much she had loved January, like the sister she'd never had, and how her friend had sung her funny song when she saw June arrive: *June and January, January and June.* With a sick feeling, she remembered she had called her by her name – January!

"She was my friend," June said and choked on the words. "I loved her!"

And then she took a deep breath and told Jem about the NPF agent with the red hair and cold blue eyes, how she, June, had been warned by a Traveler's whistle while she was shopping.

"I knew what that whistle meant," she said. "I wanted us both to try to escape, but January ordered me to hide in the broom closet and not to come out. I was so frightened, and I hid behind the mops and brooms." June started to tremble, and Jem put his arm around her, but he didn't interrupt.

"The agent, he came in alone, they *never* come alone, and he locked the door. His eyes were like … uh, narrow, and his voice was rough, low almost like a whisper. Then he grabbed January and threw her on the table, *our* table." June's voice shook as she talked. "He tore off her clothes and hit her so hard when she cried. And then … I closed my eyes tight and covered my ears! My friend, I let him do that to my friend!" June put her hands up, and her face crumpled like a baby's. "He raped her, I *know* what that is, he did that, and I didn't do anything! I wanted to kill him, but I hid in the closet! It was my fault!"

Jem stiffened as he listened and his face hardened. It sounded too familiar, but now June was taking the blame.

"It was not your fault, June! But then what happened?" His voice was like ice, and June turned her head and stared at him, her tears drying on her cheeks. She was shocked at his expression. He looked like a stranger – his blue eyes as cold as the red-haired agent's, and his jaw stiff, his lips tight.

"I helped her," she said and looked away. "I crept out of the closet, and I helped her. I made coffee for her and mended her torn clothes with safety pins. There was blood on her face, and I washed it off. She was ashamed, Jem, *she* was ashamed!"

June wiped her nose on her shirtsleeve and rubbed her eyes with the palms of her hands. "I asked her to come with me, but she wouldn't leave. It was her store, you know? Her *heritage.*" She paused and looked away. "But January told me something bad, something *really* bad. She told me he would come back to her store; he would always come back, again, and again and do … *that!*"

June swallowed hard. "She said to me, 'never let an NPF agent touch you, June, or he will own you, just like *he* owns me!' The next day her store was closed!" June tightened her lips and lifted her chin. "I was ashamed! I didn't help my best friend, and I should never have called her by her name."

Jem didn't understand what she meant by her last comment, but he took June by the arms and turned her around. "Did you tell Eve?"

"No, I don't want to talk about it, and she worries too much, anyway." June shook her head and pulled away.

"Well, then what did you do ... afterward? I mean. You were traveling. How in the world did you stay safe? How can you stay safe *now*?" He shook his head. "Jesus, no wonder you were afraid of my uniform!"

June looked at Jem's grim face and decided she'd never tell him about the Illegals. "Look," she said, and her voice was firm. "I traveled all the way from North Carolina to The Garden State alone. I can take care of myself."

"Why are you so stubborn," Jem shot back. It wasn't a question, but he didn't push it, and he didn't look happy.

"This is a secret between you and me, Jem, not anyone else. You have to promise!" June held his eyes with her own, and he nodded, but when he left, he didn't look back.

June walked out to the edge of the cornfield. The moon was full, and she could see clouds boiling up from the horizon, cold weather clouds that coiled around each other like fat snakes. She stood and gazed across the empty acres and willed herself to relax, but she was still shaken.

Now what have I done, she thought. I brought all those memories back, things I never wanted to think about again, and I probably made Jem angry. June watched the clouds as they heaved and rolled and let her mind drift. She wondered about the vehicle that had stopped by the house and trembled. Then she thought about Jem.

"Jem, with those cold eyes you looked like a stranger," June whispered. "I hardly recognized you." Then she felt angry and insulted. "What do you think I am, too damn weak and pitiful to take care of myself? A *child?*"

She shouted the bad word out loud, and that made her feel better.

An icy wind started to blow out of the North, tossing the few remaining leaves around. The sound of a dog's bark was carried in on the wind, and she shivered and hurried inside

Along the horizon, cold weather clouds were rolling up out of the north, but June was thinking about Jem as she closed and locked the door.

Chapter 44

The next morning June woke to the sound of a door closing and footsteps upstairs. She heard Sherpa's claws clicking across the floor, and felt a wave of relief. She stretched, yawned loudly, and then relaxed. I didn't know how scared I was, June admitted. She rolled over on her side and gazed at the window shade. The sun was shining, but it was chilly, and she pulled the blanket up to her chin. She thought about the night before, and the memory bothered her. It wasn't like Jem to be angry. His face was so stern, and it had frightened her, but at the same time, June was insulted he would imply she was such a helpless kitten. Although she had to admit, the vehicle stopping in front of the house had terrified her.

She hoped Jem would keep her secret, but as soon as June tumbled out of bed, she forgot about Jem – the floor was like ice under her feet. The cold weather had arrived in the night, and when she pulled the shade up, the world outside her window was covered in a hard, white frost.

It was late, and June pulled on her warmest clothes and headed to the barnyard. Her boots crunched on the ice-covered grass, and she shivered. "Damn," she said and huddled into her parka.

Maud and Ella were nestled together in the shelter, their wool stiff with ice. They turned and looked at her, and June felt guilty. "I'm sorry, ladies," she said, and hung over the fence and picked the ice off their backs.

With the bang of a door, the Farmer appeared on the back porch and dashed across the barnyard, his parka zipped up to his neck, and a wool cap pulled down over his ears. He pushed open the barn door and disappeared inside, and a few minutes later opened the back doorway to let Maud and Ella inside.

June still felt ashamed. I should have gotten up and checked, she scolded herself. I saw those cold weather clouds coming up out of the north, but I stayed in bed, and they were out here in the cold. She tightened the scarf around her neck and grumbled off to feed the chickens.

The Farmer headed back to the house and June stopped him as he crossed the barnyard. "Look, I'm sorry I didn't get up earlier and let the sheep in," she said. "I saw the clouds coming up last night, but I didn't know the weather had already changed until I stepped on the floor this morning."

The farmer huddled in his parka. "It happened so fast! Who would have known? I've never seen anything like this. One minute it was mild and the next … this!" He waved one gloved hand out over the frozen barnyard. "I already fed the sheep, but we need to keep breaking up the ice in the water trough." He frowned and hurried back to the house, his shoulders drawn up to his ears. June watched him for a minute and then turned away. "I should have known," she said. "I knew what those clouds were."

When June opened the henhouse door, she found the chickens tucked into their cubbies murmuring to themselves. They soon started fussing and clucking around her as she tossed the feed, their feathers fluffed out in the cold.

June turned up the warming lights. "Stay warm, my little darlings," she sang. The rooster started his "puck, puck, puck" sound and ruffled his feathers at her threateningly, and June waved him away. "You, too – you big bully," she added, and he settled down.

The window shutters were closed tightly, but June double checked them before she pulled her blue wool hat down to her chin and hiked across the field to the pond. Overnight, the water had frozen solid, and the shoreline grasses were stiff with ice. June stood on the bank and felt sick. It's too familiar, she thought. The sudden cold, the icy haze hanging over the sun, and the deep silence? It's so familiar and so frightening. "Damn!" she said and slid down the bank.

The ice was as smooth as glass, and June gingerly duck-walked out on the pond. She leaned over and tried to see the leaves below, but the water was too dark and the ice too thick. She stood up and felt her feet slip out from under her, sending her skidding until she sat down hard. It hurt, and June said the bad words out loud as she inched her way back to the bank, slipping and sliding as she crawled. Her bottom smarted, and she started to cry in humiliation. She felt as if a thousand eyes had seen her fall and were laughing at her as she stumbled up the bank. "Damn you," she shouted at the bushes.

June's tears froze on her cheeks, and the grass crunched like broken glass under her boots as she headed back to the farm. Nothing moved – no breeze, no birds, no vehicles on the road. The trees were covered in ice, and the wheat chaff was a sheet of white spread out across the field. Now and again, she would hear a tree branch groan, but that was all. The freeze had immobilized everything.

After lunch, the Wife came down with a large Ion heater and another canvas bag of yarn slung over her shoulder. The heater looked like a small version of the old fashion stove June had seen in her history book. It reminded her of the coal she burned at home, the dust that had made her sick, and how it turned the furniture black. She sighed and pushed the memory away. Instead, she visualized the glass meadow: the solar panels that captured the sun and turned it into heat and light, the heat that would warm the Ion heater.

The Wife shivered. "I'm glad to be home, but I've never seen cold like this! We need to keep the sheep in the barn now, and, oh, keep the shutters tightly closed in the hen house." She dropped the bag of wool on the floor and rubbed her hands together. "I brought you more yarn. I bet people will want to buy sweaters if this keeps up. We can bring some scarves and hats to the Village on Saturday." She looked nervously out the window. "I hope this is just a short cold spell, but I'm giving you this stronger heater just in case. It has enough power to heat the whole apartment, and it's very light. You can move it around if you want."

June didn't say a word about the cold, the idea was too frightening. She took the bag of yarn over and dropped it on the couch. "Thank you, and I'm glad you're back," she said. "Jem and Kitty kept me company, but the house was too quiet. Do you want some hot tea?"

The Wife smiled absentmindedly, her mind still on the weather, and headed out the door. "No, thank you. Jem's a good guy," she said and disappeared around the side of the house.

Jem, June thought, she wouldn't even recognize you.

That evening he arrived while June was in the henhouse, and he was the same familiar Jem she knew – the man she thought she might love.

They huddled on the beams in their down jackets and wool hats and tried to convince each other everything would be all right. Outside the air was filled with ice crystals that sparkled like diamonds but cut noses and cheeks like little knives. Inside it was warm, and the chickens scratched around contentedly below.

"Well, at least it feels like winter," June said, but she didn't mention the freezing winter at home – the winter before the burning days, the frozen haze that covered the sun, and the cold dry air that froze the inside of her nose, turning her words into frosty clouds. This cold weather felt ominous. June didn't tell him the pond in the pasture was frozen solid, that it had started freezing while they were discussing her friend the night before. January was something June didn't want to bring up, again, ever!

"It's a cold snap," Jem said, but he didn't mention the dust storms, the fires, the floods and the droughts he'd seen. He didn't tell her he was afraid they might all freeze to death now. He just couldn't understand this weather. In University, he'd never learned about the earth rebelling like this. Not so soon, anyway! It was supposed to be in more than a million years. Of course, there were footnotes about serious climate discussions and rebellions in the past, but they had died down in the Civil War. Why now, he wondered.

"I'm leaving for the Empire State tomorrow," he said. "I need to make sure my mom's okay." He stared into space for a minute. "I want to spend Christmas with her, but I'll be back here before I head to the Far Western Region again. We can spend New Year's Eve together."

A whole year has passed, June thought. Wow! She remembered the New Year's Eve party the year before, and the man who had tried to kiss her. Ugly person, she thought, and said the bad word out loud.

"What?" Jem turned and stared at her.

"I said I'm glad you'll be back for New Year Eve," June said. "I like that."

At her apartment door, Jem hugged her and kissed her goodbye. June thought he felt like a pillow but kissed him back, her lips stiff with the cold. I think I might love you, she thought, but she didn't say the words. And then he was gone.

Chapter 45

June spent the next week knitting scarves and mittens, hats and a sweater with a simple design. Every day, she curled up on the couch in her warm apartment, and her fingers found their familiar rhythm. The needles flew through the soft wool, and she worked deep into the night. June knew that by the end of the week, they would have a bag full of knitted goods to take to the Village.

The cold weather hung on, and it seemed to drop another few degrees. June and the Farmer took turns breaking up the ice in the trough for Maud and Ella. Even with the heating light turned up, the chickens huddled in their hay-filled cubbyholes, and they only came out when June fed them. For once, the rooster was quiet. It was so cold, Kitty took one trip outside and came back with her soft fur standing on end, frozen stiff.

June laughed when she opened the door. "You look like a bush on four legs, Kitty Girl." The cat pushed past her and headed to the new heater. Without a whisker of greeting, she curled up and refused to move. From then on, Kitty would slip outside for a moment or two and then hustle back in again.

June worried about her cat squatting out in the cold and decided to do something about it. She asked the Wife for some newspaper and filled an old roasting pan. The Wife stood and watched. "You need to buy a litter box and a bag of litter," she said. "Remind me when we're in the Village." Then she looked hopeful, "Maybe this cold snap will be gone by then, and Kitty will be able to stay outside."

June nodded and kept shredding the paper and said nothing. She was afraid, but she didn't want to admit it. She believed there would no end to the bitter cold until Spring. June had seen it before.

Then what, she wondered. What happens then?

The following Saturday, the old pickup groaned and lurched its way into the Village with the Wife and June huddled inside, a bag of knit goods on the seat between them. They were bundled into their down jackets and mittens, with wool scarves wrapped around their necks and wool hats jammed down over their ears. The pickup's heater was hissing angerly, but it wasn't providing much heat; the windows rattled in drafts of cold air. Words turned into puffs of ice when they spoke, so June sat quietly and looked out the window. The panels at the Solar Farm looked like a sea of ice, and they gleamed in the pale sun as the pickup passed. June craned her neck and looked back. The Solar Farm fascinated her, and she thought it looked mystical with its coat of ice. "It beautiful," she said, and her comment turned into an icy cloud.

Winter had come with a vengeance. It was colder than it had ever been in the Garden State, and the Villagers discussed it endlessly, their chilly faces filled with confusion. No one was able to stay outside in the street, so they crowded into the coffee shop.

When the Wife and June arrived, there was a line waiting for tables. Everyone was wearing bulky sweaters under their warmest coats, and some of them were debating the way to wear layers.

"Ah ha," The Wife said and joined the conversation. "Look what I brought to sell. They're wool from our own sheep." She opened the bag full of knit goods and spilled everything out on the counter. June piled the hats and mittens in neat piles and folded the sweater beside them. The crowd gathered around to look, fingering the warm wool and nodding among themselves. By the time there was a table free for the two women, every scarf was wrapped around somebody's neck, and every hat was jammed on somebody's head. The sweater had been stuffed into a woman's backpack.

"See," the Wife said, "I knew these would go like hot cakes. Now, let's eat!" She settled in her seat with satisfaction.

June smoothed her napkin over her lap and looked around.

More Villagers had arrived and filled the coffee shop with banter. They stopped by the Wife's table to chat. "I hope there'll be more scarfs and hats next week," they said. "We want sweaters, too. This cold weather is just awful."

They gossiped about the water freezing in their pipes and agreed they had to let the taps run. "The damn pipes will burst if we don't." They leaned on the counter, and an old man said he had to put blankets over the hood of his car at night. "The damn car won't start in the morning if I don't. So much for new technology!" And they agreed they'd never seen anything like it before. "It's just awful – Never seen anything like this – What the Hell is going on?" The words rolled out, and heads nodded. Coffee was served, and outside it got colder.

June listened, but she didn't say a word. She just drank her hot chocolate and ate her sandwich, and she felt sorry for everyone.

The next week the temperature dropped another five degrees, and the sun rose in a haze of frost. A cold wind blew shards of ice into people's faces, sharp as glass. More than a few Villagers sported Band-Aids, and everyone wrapped their new wool scarves around their faces. They looked up and wondered when they would see snow; but day after day, the sun would rise and hang in the sky, shrouded in the icy, gray mist. The trees and brush froze solid in hard shells of ice. They looked like sculptures, but nobody thought they were pretty.

There was a run on large Ion heaters, and one by one, villagers bought heaters for every room in their houses. Pretty soon there would be no heaters left in the Village. The solar panels shone back at the icy sun and provided power to the Village.

Nobody bought coal to burn.

The frigid weather settled in to stay, and in the middle of December, the town decided it was too cold to put the little lights in the trees for Christmas.

"They might freeze and break," the Mayor said. "Let the stores decorate inside this year.

The Villagers agreed. The storekeepers along Main Street hung Christmas lights in their windows and painted Christmas scenes on the insides of the glass. They hung green and red Christmas balls, silver glass horns, bells, and twinkling lights from their ceilings. The owner of the coffee shop gathered greens and made garlands to hang along the edges of the counter. The statue of Santa Clause appeared in the shop, standing in a corner by the front door, and June was happy to see him.

"He reminds me of someone who was very kind," she told the Wife. "Someone who brought us water."

The Wife frowned and changed the subject. "When you talk about things like that, it frightens me now," she said. "It's too cold and scary."

The last Monday of the month, the church members met for a meeting and decided it was too cold to set the crèche up on the church lawn. It was the first time in memory.

"It's never happened before," complained Mrs. Trumble in a loud voice. She was the oldest person in the Village, and had attended the church since she was a child; of course, she believed she'd have the final say. "It shouldn't happen now. Not because it's a little cold," she scolded and pulled her shawl around her shoulders.

But the church board was afraid the statues would freeze and crack, and that was the end of the argument. Instead, they decorated the windowsills with greens and big red bows, and they put tall white candles in every window. "In time for Christmas Eve service," the minister said. "There *will* be a service," she repeated firmly, and an announcement was hung in the coffee shop window.

June hoped the statues would be set up inside the church where it was warm and decided to brave the cold to attend the Christmas Eve service. She thought about the singing and the lady preacher with the soft voice and kind words. She remembered how peaceful it had been, and how it had touched her heart, and it reminded her of Jem. He'll be with his mother in the Empire State, she thought, and the Wife will be gone, too. Nobody would know.

"I don't care how cold it is," she told Kitty, "I'm going to that service."

Chapter 46

A few days before Christmas, the Wife arrived at June's door snuggled up in her warm parka with two wool hats pulled down to her chin. She was carrying a canvas bag of wool, and a small package wrapped in colorful paper.

"Damn, it's cold," she grumbled through a cloud of frosty air. "It's even too cold to travel up North, so we're staying here for Christmas. I am *so* disappointed, but Adam is afraid the truck won't make it." She held out the package in her mittened hand. "This is for you."

June was glad to see the Wife, as always, but her heart sank. "Thank you," she said and turned abruptly to put the kettle on for tea. Oh, Damn, she thought, I bet she's going to have a problem with my walking into the Village at night. I just know it! I just *know* it! Nobody has spotted an NPF agent since the weather turned, but she'll still worry. I bet she'll go on about agents running wild. June tossed tea bags into two mugs and frowned at the steaming pot. She was annoyed. Why should I sneak out? I'm a free person. I traveled all the way from North Carolina to the Garden State, so what's the problem with my walking to the Village alone? Why does everyone think I'm so damn fragile? It makes me feel like a stupid child ... well, it ends here!

June turned around, raised her chin, and tightened her lips. "I will go to the Christmas Eve service," she announced. "I went last year, I bundled up and walked into the Village alone, and Jem walked me home. It's cold, but I'm sick of being coddled. That place made me happy, and I want to feel that way again!"

The Wife stared at June and carefully set the gift down on the table. My God, she thought. I never knew. So *that's* when she got together with Jem. She felt laughter bubbling up and put her hand over her mouth. She remembered June asking about the Christmas Eve service the year before, and showing her the piece of paper with the announcement printed in red and green. It brought back memories from her childhood. I used to love going to that service, she thought. Late at night after my bedtime, the candles and Christmas songs. It was fun! I wouldn't mind going again. I wonder …

Then she made up her mind and decided, what the Hell! "Would you mind if I went with you? We could go to the service in the truck, and then come back and have supper upstairs by the Christmas tree. Adam won't go, you know, but you and I can go. It would make me happy, too."

June considered it for a few minutes before she answered. She wasn't sure if the Wife simply wanted to keep her safe by joining her, or if she really wanted to go. She remembered the Wife talking about going as a child, how she had loved the candles. June knew the Farmer was an Atheist. He didn't want to go because he believed in Mother Nature instead of religion. Not fair, she thought. He should go anyway. June liked the idea of having supper upstairs and remembered the decorations and lights through the window on New Year's Eve, the year before. Then she came to a decision.

"Yeah," she said. "I'd like that." And it was decided: They would bundle up and take the truck into the Village on Christmas Eve.

The Wife pulled out a chair. "Adam can trim the tree, he likes that stuff, and I'll make chili for supper, oh … and a chocolate cake for dessert." She looked happy for the first time in a long time. "I can even decorate the cake with red and green frosting. It will be so much fun, June, you and me going out after dark!"

Chili, June thought. She had never eaten chili, she didn't even know what it was, but the Thanksgiving potpie was good, so she thought, yeah, chili would be good, too. The more she thought about it, the more she liked the idea, and it seemed to make the Wife happy. June gazed at the Wife's animated face as she rambled on and realized her landlady hadn't smiled in a long time. The Wife worries, she thought, she hears terrible things on the radio and that television. It scares her and makes her sad.

"Wait," June said and rummaged around behind the couch where her knitting basket was. "Here, this is for you." she handed the Wife a deep ruby colored hat and scarf. "I made them for you, for Christmas."

The Wife held the softness against her cheek, and the worry lines faded away. "I love them. And look, they will match my sweater!" She touched June's hand for a minute. "I'm so glad you're here," she said. "You're like a member of the family, like my daughter or something." She tucked her hair into the hat and wrapped the scarf around her neck, then hopped up and went to admire herself in the bathroom mirror.

"So pretty," she said, and June felt a sudden fondness for the woman. I had a mother, she thought, but this is kind of nice. I like it.

June watched as the Wife headed back to the front of the house, her breath frosty in the air. She was almost hidden in her parka, and the new scarf was wrapped around her neck, the red hat pulled down over her ears. June knew the Wife was scared and realized that she was frightened, too. The Wife didn't understand, but June did. She had seen all this before.

A wind gust made a low moaning sound, and the windows shook. Kitty looked up from her spot by the heater, and her eyes were round and dark. Ice was forming on the windowpanes, making strange patterns, and June scratched a line across the ice. An Arctic wind out of the North had picked up and was shaking the house. We're *all* scared, she thought, but if candlelight, statues, songs, and a lady preacher can make two of us happy for a while, then a freezing trip in the old truck is worth it.

June remembered the little package the Wife had given her and sat down at the table. She touched it with one finger and moved it closer. "This is a Christmas gift," she told Kitty. "And it's not a radio."

She carefully unwrapped it, smoothed out the colorful paper, and opened the box. A small, silver pin, in the shape of a sheep, rested on cotton inside. Curls of wool were etched into the side, and there was a small drop of gold for an eye. June picked up the pin and held it gently it in her hand. She had never owned jewelry. At home, only the Wealthy Ladies wore jewelry: diamonds and rubies, sparkling on their fingers and around their necks, silver and gold pins on their ample bosoms.

"I love this," she told Kitty and pinned it on her sweater. "Just look at the wool. It's like Maud and Ella, see the golden eye?" She yawned and added, "I'll always keep this close to my heart."

Kitty yawned back and looked suspiciously at the window, turned around a few times, and settled down by the heater.

The windowpanes shook a few more times, and then the wind died down and blew back to where it had come from.

June went to sleep that night thinking about chili and chocolate cake. The pin was safe in its box on the bedside table, and Kitty was curled up at the foot of the bed.

Chapter 47

Christmas Eve was icy and clear – so cold the stars had dimmed and almost disappeared. A waxing moon hung low in the sky, pale and washed out, but it still gave out a faint light. June put on her warmest sweater and pinned the little silver sheep over her heart.

The Wife arrived, bundled up and wearing her red sweater with the matching hat and scarf. June hunched into her heavy parka, and both women started out, laughing at the idea of heading into the cold night.

The truck had been parked inside the barn with a heavy wool blanket covering the hood, but when the Wife crossed the barnyard with June, her husband stood in the window and watched, worried that it wouldn't start up at all.

The truck doors creaked and complained, and the seats were freezing, but when the Wife slid in, she giggled like a little girl. June laughed out loud, puffing a white frosty haze into the dark.

"Well," the Wife said, "let's see what happens," and she huddled down in her parka and turned the key.

After a few grumbles and groans, the engine turned over with a hiss and a roar, and the old truck shuddered out of the barn and lurched off down the main road. June stared through the frosty windshield and realized she could never have made it to the Village on foot. The asphalt surface had turned a flat white in the cold, and the sides of the road were lined with motionless trees bent low with ice. The truck was enveloped by a silence so complete, she could hear every tick as the truck's engine turned over. Her breath burned her nose with a wash of ice crystals that hung in the air. I would have turned back, she thought and then said it out loud, "I would have turned back."

The Wife glanced over and nodded her head. "I'm sure you would have. This is beastly!"

June remembered the year before: Jem walking back with her in the snow, the soft flakes just starting to fall. Maybe I love him, she thought and gazed across the frozen field. The Solar Farm gleamed though the dark, making sparkles in the cold. Perhaps that's what is right and proper.

The Wife pulled up outside the church with a rattle. June could see people hurrying up the walkway bundled in padded parkas and wool scarves, their hats pulled down covering their ears. There was no conversation or greeting among neighbors, just grim determination.

"Let's go," the Wife said, and they wrestled the frozen doors open and spilled out onto the sidewalk, laughing icy clouds into the air.

The walkway to the church was lined with small candles that flickered in the dark, and in the windows, tall tapers threw dim light across the lawn, but June and the Wife didn't stop to admire them. Their fingers were freezing inside their mittens, and tears froze on their cheeks.

It was warm inside and, little-by-little, familiar faces emerged from hats and heavy hoods. Candlelight flickered and cast shadows in the corners and, sure enough, up by the altar, the statues gazed down at the congregation. Somewhere, an organ started to play, and everyone stood up and began to sing. June had never learned the words after all, but she hummed along and glanced over. The Wife's hair looked like gold in the candlelight, and it fell in waves over her shoulders; her hands, rough from farming, held the hymn book, but she wasn't looking at the page as she sang. She seemed carefree and somehow at peace.

The Wife knows the words, and she's happy, June thought, and she wanted to reach out and touch her. Eve, she thought, that's Eve, and softly she called out her name. The Wife looked over and smiled at her, and that was the last time June thought of Eve as the Wife. Somehow, it made her happy and sad, all mixed up together.

As they drove home through the icy night, the truck's heater finally kicked over and wheezed out a bit of heat. Eve sang the Christmas carols so June could learn the words, and June sang along, memorizing them for the next year. This was nice, she thought, but she missed Jem holding her hand. "I miss Jem," June said, and it made Eve laugh out loud. "He'll be back," she said. "He'll not leave you, June."

Not far behind, a black NPF vehicle, its headlights dimmed, followed them back to the farm, but neither Eve nor June noticed. Inside the cruiser, it was cold and uncomfortable. The sergeant blew on his hands and cursed himself and the occupant beside him. "Okay, Agent," he said as he turned back. "Are you satisfied now?"

David Anderson smiled to himself but didn't bother to answer. Hello, pretty lady, he whispered.

"By the way," the sergeant said with malice, "we're heading back to the Far Western Region the end of the month. Merry Christmas, David," he added at the look on Agent Anderson's face.

Chapter 48

An icy wind blew leaves across the countryside, and it froze fingers and faces. Eve decided there would be no New Year's Eve party; it was too cold, and nobody wanted to come, anyway. Aggrieved, she came down to tell June and fussed about the weather.

"I can't even have a party," she said and sounded like a petulant child. "This damn cold weather, it just goes on and on!"

June nodded but admitted to herself she would just as soon stay in her warm apartment. She patted Eve's arm. "Spring will come," she said sympathetically, but she had no idea what *that* would bring. Worry hung over June day and night, and she couldn't shake it off. When she huddled in her bed at night, she began to fear the dark. What will happen next, she wondered but never said it aloud.

Jem returned the week after Christmas, and arrived on New Year's Eve as promised, bundled in white. An Arctic Weather Lab in the Far North had sent down white arctic overalls, jackets with fur hoods, and thermal boots for the EO agents, and Jem felt ridiculous. I feel like a damn snowman, he thought. But it kept him warm.

When June saw him, she felt a sudden sense of relief. The oppressive cloud of worry lifted, and she laughed when she let him in. All she could see was his face, peering out at her like a polar bear cub in a den.

"You look like you could use some hot tea," she said and felt giddy. She put the tea pot on to boil and glanced at Jem. "Whatever that is you're wearing, it looks warm."

Jem shed his arctic outerwear and sprawled on the couch with a sigh of contentment. "Come sit by me." He patted the seat next to him, and June turned the flame off. She sat down at the other end of the couch, but little by little, she moved closer. "I have something for you," Jem said and handed her a small box. "A late Christmas gift."

I didn't buy him a gift, she thought and felt guilty, but she took the box and carefully opened it. Inside, a gold pearl ring rested on a little velvet cushion, the stone glowing with a soft luster. June sat very still, staring at it, and felt her eyes fill with tears. She didn't know if this meant they would be married or if she would allow him to stay overnight – or what. She had never had a ring from a boyfriend before, just a jug of milk, and now she had a silver pin *and* a gold ring, and she felt so overwhelmed she didn't know what to say.

"That's your birthstone," he said puzzled. "It stands for joy."

June slipped the ring on her finger and held her hand up. The pearl shone with a strange luminescence – an almost mystical light. The Daughter would say this was magical, she thought, and the memory hurt her heart.

"It looks like the moon," she said. "It looks like the moon *used* to look," she corrected herself. "It will remind me of you when you're gone, bright like the moon, beautiful like the moon. Thank you." Then, overcome, she started to cry.

Jem was confused, but he let her cry. He stroked her pale hair and kissed the top of her head. He thought he knew why she was crying: the dim moon would eventually fade away like the stars had. *He* knew what was going to happen, and he believed she knew, too. June had told him about the Southern Region, about the frigid winter and then the burning sun and why she had left home, so he understood her tears. He also knew, whatever *it* was, it was moving further and further North.

"We are alive now," he said. "We have time to live, so let's live and love while we can. Let me make you happy, June. Let me keep you warm in your lonely bed."

June rested her head against Jem's chest and, faint as a whisper, she could hear his heartbeat. She remembered her swim in the Quarry, how she believed she was going to die there alone in the woods. And she remembered what she had thought as the dark water pulled her down: "I am going to die before I have even lived."

June trusted Jem, and she thought she might love him, and now she had his ring, this beautiful little moon on her finger. I want him to make me happy, she decided, I want him close to me tonight, and she closed her eyes.

"Yes," she said and pressed close to him, letting his hands touch her in secret places, his lips on hers and his breath in her ear as he showed her what it was like to be loved: the pain, and the almost unbearable pleasure. Later, they snuggled under the bedcovers, and for once June was not afraid of the dark.

Early the next morning he was gone, wearing his white arctic outerwear and heading to the Far Western Region, but he had kissed her lips hard and held her in his arms one more time before he dressed, reluctant to leave her side.

"You're so beautiful," he'd whispered, "so innocent," and he buried his face in her pale hair, pulling her close. This time, she had put her arms around him and held on.

After Jem was gone, June rolled over in her empty bed and curled up where he had slept, breathing in his man smell. She buried her head in the pillow he had used and gently touched the places he had touched; then she looked at the pearl on her finger and smiled. I must love him, she thought.

Chapter 49

Winter seemed to hang on forever. Frost covered the field and ice cycles hung off the barn roof. Every day June bundled into her parka, yanked her hat over her ears, and headed out to the henhouse. The poor creatures stayed huddled in their nests, only venturing out when she came to feed them, murmuring and shaking the straw off their backs.

"You aren't such a smarty pants, now, are you?" she teased the rooster as he halfheartedly fluffed his feathers. Poor old rooster boy, she thought, he doesn't like this anymore than I do.

June took turns with the Farmer breaking up the ice in the water trough, but every morning it was solid again. Sometimes after the ice ritual was done, she'd spend time with Maud and Ella, stroking their soft noses and thick wool.

"I have a silver pin that looks just like you," she told them one day. "It even has a gold eye." Maud and Ella stopped rummaging around the barn floor and looked up as if they understood her every word. "Don't worry, Ladies," she told them, "very soon you'll be back at the watering hole, and I'll be there, too, floating around and looking at the clouds." The idea charmed her.

As January dragged by, June started climbing up on her beam in the henhouse again. It was a warm, private place, and reminded her of Jem. When she thought about him, her heart beat a little faster. I liked it, she thought, I really liked what we did, but it reminded her of the red-haired agent. She cringed when she remembered his assault on her friend, his slapping and brutalizing her.

"Oh, January," she'd say over and over, "it doesn't have to be like that. It never had to be like that."

The memory was so distasteful, she tried to push it away, but it made June angry all over again. I should have hit him, she thought and tightened her fists. She couldn't seem to forget.

"I should have killed him," she said loudly, and the rooster made his "puck, puck, puck" sound. "I will never, *never* let anyone do that to me, ever! I promise you!" The hens shifted around uneasily, and a few of them clucked in alarm. But June had made a vow she would never break.

June missed Jem, but she wouldn't wear his ring during the day; she knew Eve would make a big fuss about how wonderful it all was, and the idea was embarrassing. But, she thought, what would Eve say about Jem staying overnight and doing, you know, what we did? The memory made her shiver.

So, the pearl ring stayed safely in its small box, and when June closed her apartment door at night, she would slip it on her finger. The pearl glowed with its own light, almost brighter than the moon, luminous and secret. "Jem," she would whisper, "this means joy, and that reminds me of how you made me happy." Her breath would catch in her throat, and she would run her hands down over her body, remembering!

In February, Eve brought the last of her wool down to June's apartment. It was still cold outside, but now and again, the sun broke through its frigid haze and started to melt the ice.

"I guess we won't be bringing more warm knit goods into the Village after this," Eve said, and her voice was light with relief. "At least I can breathe now without my nose burning."

June had to agree, but she was still worried. Once the cold broke, she wasn't sure what would come next. Would it be a normal blue sky with occasional downpours, rows of fresh vegetables in the garden, and wheat in the field, or would the sun burn everything up like it did in North Carolina? She held her tongue around Eve and the Farmer and never told them her fears. June knew they wouldn't understand.

Every morning, while June and the Farmer broke up the ice in the water trough, he'd gossip and worry about the crops. "Not a flake of snow," he said over and over. "I just don't understand. Why would it be so cold and dry? The crops need moisture. I don't *get* it!" And every morning, June would shake her head. "I don't know," she'd say and then turn away. I think I do know, she thought, but she never said.

Then one morning, it was so warm the ice cycles started to melt. Tiny drops of water slipped down and disappeared before they hit the ground. The air was fresh with a hint of spring. The Farmer smiled at June and rubbed his hands together as he looked out the barn door.

"Once the ground is defrosted, we will start to till the fields and hope for the best. I'll get the tractor out for you when it has warmed up enough to soften the soil." He looked at the frosty barnyard for another minute, "You'd like that, wouldn't you? Back out there in the fields?"

Then he stopped smiling, "You know, June, spring can't come soon enough!" The Farmer stood gazing out the barn door for another few minutes, his eyes scanning the frozen field, but when he headed back to the house he didn't look hopeful, he looked defeated

June watched him go and sat down on a bale of hay next to Maud and Ella, her chin cradled in her hands. "I don't know what to tell him," she said. Maud turned and looked at her with her gold eyes. "Maybe if I think good thoughts hard enough it will be alright: the vegetables will grow, and the wheat will flourish." She closed her eyes and thought about last year's garden with its sweet red tomatoes and leafy greens. She thought about the tractor breaking up the moist soil, and the sea of wheat that rolled across the field in the summer. She closed her eyes tighter and tried to visualize the farm the way it had been, and she tried to remember how it felt to sit high up on the tractor seat with the sun hat shielding her face.

But June couldn't help thinking about the summer she had left home. Ugly images forced themselves into her mind. She remembered the dry earth and leafless trees, the dust and the trickle of filthy water in the river. The memory made her heart sick, and she almost gagged.

"Please, Sir," she begged and closed her eyes tight. "Please make things normal. Even *okay* is good."

She shivered and opened her eyes again. "If you don't, Sir, if it happens here, then I'll have to keep running."

June was angry. She looked around the old barn and felt as though it was for the first time: the rusted stanchions where cows once stood, the haymow, and the gray barn walls that rose up so high the birds darted in and out making nests in the rafters. She noticed an old harness hanging on the wall and the familiar feed bins. This is home, now, she thought, and I don't want to leave. Small rays of sun filtered through a loose board and made warm puddles on the worn floor.

"I don't want to leave," she told the sheep, "I don't want to leave my apartment, and Eve, and the Farmer. I don't want to leave those silly chickens, and I don't want to leave *you*!"

She thought about Jem, somewhere in the Far Western Region. "He knows," she said. "He knows and he'll come back for me." Maud and Ella raised their heads and then went back to pulling at the alfalfa, their jaws working back and forth.

I'm too young to *think* things into reality, June thought sadly. "I'm sorry, Sir," she said. "I'm sorry if I insulted you. I'm just afraid."

Chapter 50

That evening Jem arrived. June had slipped on her moon ring and was about to turn on the oven when she heard the soft tap at her door. She felt her face flush and a flutter in her belly when she let him in. He looked tired but fit and when he hugged her, she felt how strong his arms were and how hard his body had become.

"The Far Western Region must have been good for you," she said and leaned back to look at him. He was so familiar, so dear. "You're bigger and stronger than you were, but I missed you so much. It was bitter cold here and everyone was scared ..." June realized she was babbling, but Jem looked so serious and stern she was frightened. Something is wrong, she thought.

"I'm tired of this, June," he said but he didn't look at her, and her heart seemed to skip a beat.

"I'm tired of seeing destruction," Jem let her go and slumped down on the couch, "only destruction: farms buried in dirt, towns and cities drowning in the ocean, homes and business burned to the ground, and people dying, animals dying, *everything* dying!"

June stood still and gazed at him. His eyes were empty and sad, his shoulders drooping. She sat down close to him, touching his arm, leaning against him for comfort, but she didn't know what to say. She didn't know if she could tell him she was afraid, afraid that she might have to run further to the North if there was no rain and the Garden State began to burn up, afraid of the NPF that seemed to be everywhere now. And how could she say she was afraid he didn't want her anymore?

"I want to quit this job," Jem said. He took June's arms and turned her around to face him and now his eyes were bright, burning as if he had a fever. "I want to quit this job and marry you. We can buy a house here or move north but we will be together." He kissed her hard on the mouth, holding her by the arms and forcing her lips apart.

"I have one more mission back in the Far Western Region," he said, "and I leave tomorrow. I won't be back until late summer … and then I am *done*! We can get married and if I can't find a job here, I'll take you to the Empire State and work the farm." He ran his hands over her body, and she felt herself melt, almost faint with relief.

"I want you," he whispered, "Please? I missed you so!" and now his eyes were eager. June nodded, unable to say a word as he slipped her overalls off, his hands gentle but his body urgent.

They left their clothes in a pile on the floor and crawled under the covers on her bed, a bed that was special now, a place where Jem loved her and made her happy, her safe place.

"You're so beautiful," he said softly and touched her face. "Wait for me," he whispered as he pulled her close.

"Don't let anyone else touch you like this." He ran his hands over her body and touched the secret places that made her tremble and burn inside.

"Don't let anyone else hold you like this, love you like this," he murmured as he buried his face in her pale hair and held her fast, finding a rhythm that was his own.

June felt cherished, safe. She liked what he was doing and she pressed her lips against his shoulder, responding, forgetting all the bad things that had happened: the frigid weather, the frozen fields and ice-covered trees, the black vehicle … just letting herself breath. "Nobody else, Jem," she whispered as her body arched under him, "only you."

Later, she turned the oven on and set out two places for supper. She felt as if she were dancing: her body aching and singing. She wanted him to do it again and she shivered at the thought. *This* must be yearning, she thought, this wanting-feeling must be love. Jem would be gone for one last trip and then they would get married and he would keep her safe. Maybe they would have babies, maybe the virus hadn't come here, but she was afraid to ask … maybe, maybe, maybe! At first, she had been afraid he didn't want her anymore, and then … this! She held up her hand and the pearl on her finger glowed with its soft, luminous light. Only you, Jem, she thought and felt alive. It was a vow she wanted so much to keep.

Chapter 51

NPF Agent David Anderson had been delighted and relieved to be back in the Garden State, even for the few weeks he was home, and he didn't even mind the soul-numbing cold weather, the frozen countryside, or the icy wind that brought tears to his eyes. Awesome, he thought, it keeps everyone off the streets and makes my job easier. The months in the Far Western Region were almost more than David could tolerate. He'd come close to quitting, but after spending a suffocating Christmas day with his parents, the idea of being without a job and moving in with them put a stop to that idle thought.

Now he was back in the Burn with the smoke and ashes, and his unit was tasked with identifying the bodies found in the ruins of houses and barns across the desolate landscape. It made him nauseated.

"For God's sake," he complained to his Sargent, "how do we ID people, we can't even find them?" He turned a burned log over with his boot.

"Shut your face and do your job, Agent," his Sargent said angrily and turned away with a scowl on his face. "This guy is just too damn much," he muttered to himself. "All he does is whine!"

Occasionally, the earth would roll and heave like waves on the ocean. The idea of the ground under his feet giving way terrified David, and he'd feel seasick from the motion. Enough of this crap, he thought but didn't say it out loud.

Of course, David had to admit, there were the ladies – refugees from the fires who lived in tent cities away from the destruction. Ah yes, the ladies, he thought, some willing and some not so much. But it didn't matter to him. He'd just have his way with them and then walk away. It was an itch that always needed to be scratched. However, he found it wasn't as satisfying anymore. Once the physical thrill was over, David felt empty, and finally, he faced an uncomfortable truth: he couldn't forget the girl in the Garden State, the one with the pale hair. Her face would intrude at the most inconvenient times, and it caused several embarrassing moments. "Damn," he told himself, "This is not good at all. I'm here, she's there, and I can't get my hands on her."

Then, something unexpected happened. David's unit was staying in a barracks at the northern border of the Far Western Region, working five days on and two days off. It was the end of his fifth day, and David was tired and spent, but when he arrived back at the barracks, he took a look around the bar on the first floor. A beer would hit the spot, he thought and stepped inside. It was a miserable place, just thrown together by the Environmental team – a large empty room with small, smudged windows and gray paint. A few tables and chairs had been tossed around, and the dingy bar took up a wall by the door. One scruffy man slouched on a stool, a glass and bottle of beer on the bar in front of him.

Ugly, *hideous* place, David thought, and was almost ready to head up to his room when he realized the man slumped at the bar was the blond girl's boyfriend, the Environmental Officer. His hair was singed, and cinders smudged his face, but it was the same fellow. David was sure. He had seen him more than once – with the girl he couldn't get out of his head. Whoa! He thought. Now, here *he* is, the boyfriend, looking miserable and staring at a glass half filled with beer.

David made a hasty decision. Luck like this didn't come along every day. He sidled over and slid onto the stool next to the boyfriend, ordered a beer with a whiskey chaser from the slovenly woman behind the bar, and cleared his throat. "Terrible business," he said and turned around with a warm smile on his handsome face.

"David Anderson," he said. "Bring the man what I'm drinking," he added loudly and stuck his hand out. The poor slob, he thought as Jem turned to look at him. This will be easy.

Jem was exhausted. He'd spent hours on the road north to the barracks and wanted to drink his beer in peace and then head up to his bunk. The last thing he wanted in the world was to share a beer and whiskey with some NPF officer.

He sighed and glanced over. "Jem," he said and took the offered hand. What the Hell, he thought, he looks friendly, and we're in this mess together.

David was clever. He knew how to get his way with the ladies and figured he could do the same with Jem. After all, he only wanted information. Who knew, maybe the poor guy would go back out into the smoke and cinders – never to be seen again. So, David started a conversation, sly and friendly, picking and prying out what he wanted to know.

"Where are you from, pal?" He leaned on the bar and took a sip of beer.

Jem tasted the whiskey, made a face and mumbled some kind of thank you answer.

"You have family back there?" David's glance was sympathetic.

Jem shook his head and leaned his chin on his hand, his eyes half closed, feeling exhaustion overcoming him.

David looked over at him. "I'm sure you have a girlfriend, a good-looking guy like you?" He turned around and pretended to look out the window, then glanced back furtively and saw the boyfriend light up, a gentle smile on his face. Gotcha, David thought and listened intently as Jem began to spill words.

Little by little, as he consumed a few more beers and shots, Jem became loquacious, occasionally rambling off on tangents, and David carefully steered him back to the girl. In the end, Agent Anderson found out what he wanted to know. He gave Jem a little shoulder rub, slid off his stool, and walked out of the bar.

The girl with the pale hair was named June, and she lived on a farm outside of the Village, the same farm where he'd seem her driving a tractor. He knew because he'd insisted they follow the truck she'd been riding in after the Christmas Eve service. Now, he learned June was from the Southern Region and had been a refugee on the road – and Jem wanted to marry her. David also discovered a few things about their private life, things he didn't want to know that angered him.

"But," he told himself later in his room, "it doesn't matter, Jem, because when I leave this place and go home for good, I'm going to take June away from you, whether she wants to go or not." And with that in mind, he rolled over and went to sleep.

Chapter 52

June was impatient. March brought back the bitter wind. It shook the trees and flung dust around the barnyard and across the fields. In the Village, people became sullen, snapping at friends and family members alike. "Will this never end?" they complained, but the second week, the sun seemed to shed her frosty veil, and the Villagers were finally happy. They turned off their dripping water faucets, folded and put away the heavy blankets that had covered the hoods of their cars. Icicles started to melt again, and large drops of water plopped onto the unsuspecting as they ventured out. But nobody cared at all, they just wiped the water away and laughed.

Eve and June drove into the Village the second Saturday in March, passing the wheat field with its pools of melted ice. June gazed at the glass meadow shining in the sun and felt a faint sense of relief. The sky was a pale blue, but a few ragged, misty clouds still hung around the sun.

"At last," Eve said. "I hope we never have a winter like *that* again!" She rambled happily on about the vegetable stand and the gardens, throwing a comment over to June now and again.

June's mind wandered as she looked out the window. She noticed the trees and brush had lost their ice jackets, and they seemed to be showing a faint haze of green. Maybe, she thought, maybe everything will be okay. "Please, Sir," she whispered, "make it okay. Just *okay* is really good."

The Village was alive! People were shopping and gossiping in the street. They ducked the melting icicles as they headed here and there, enjoying the warmer weather.

"People here, people there, people, people everywhere," June recited to herself, and it reminded her of her mother.

"Finally," the Villagers told each other. "I hope that's the end of this freezing Hell." On the corner, a small group of men gathered to chat. "Awful!" They said. "Too damn cold! We're not Alaska, after all!" They leaned towards each other and laughed at a joke, glancing around to make sure nobody else could hear. The group had shed their heavy coats and scarves and wore short sleeves and tattered jeans. Women with toddlers smiled and nodded to each other as they dragged their fussing children into the stores. "Ah, freedom," they called, and ignored the group of men on the corner.

It was exciting to be back in the Village, and June looked for Jem. It seemed like months since he'd shared her bed, and she shivered at the memory, searching the street and hoping he was back from the Far Western Region. Maybe he's waiting at the coffee shop, she thought, but all June could see was the front end of a black vehicle almost hidden in a side street. She felt her breath catch in her throat and pulled Eve into the doorway.

"Wait!" Eve said, pulling her arm away. "It's too early for lunch!" She was waving and smiling at Mr. Scott and glanced sideways at June.

"I think NPF is here," June whispered, and Eve stopped smiling.

"Where?" she whispered back, and they peered around the edge of the door, holding onto each other, but the car was gone. The street was empty except for a stout man in a Trilby hat walking a bulldog and looking nervously around.

"Everyone but that man has disappeared," June whispered. "They saw them, too!" She was still shaking, her breath catching with every word.

"I think everyone has the heebie-jeebies," Eve said, "and I think you're seeing things, June." With that conclusion, she decided they should have hot chocolate to celebrate the end of winter. "Come on, June, let's sit down. Forget about the NPF; they were called out to the Far Western Region, anyway." Eve dropped into a chair and picked up a spoon.

"Happy days are here again ...," she sang and tapped her spoon on the table to keep time.

June gingerly sat down and put her chin in her hand. She watched as people filled the street again, laughing and talking as if nothing had happened. The men were back on the corner, and the women were heading into the stores. Thank goodness no NPF, June thought, but by now she had stopped looking for Jem, and she didn't even make a connection to what Eve had just told her.

Jem remained in the Far Western Region, and by the end of March, June had almost forgotten the night he had stayed with her. In fact, sometimes, when she sat daydreaming, she'd see the fire in the Son's dark eyes, and not Jem's cool, blue ones, but every night, she put her pearl ring on and watched as it came to life, its luminous light shining like the moon. Jem, she would think, you touch me and make me happy, and that is right and proper, but you need to be *here* so I can forget. Late at night, June would wake with tears on her cheeks, but she never knew what had made her cry.

The first week of April, the Farmer drove the tractor out of the barn and parked it in the barnyard. "I'm going to check the soil and see if it's ready to plow," he said and headed to the wheat field. "We can talk later," he shouted back over his shoulder and sounded hopeful. "I'll just take a walk around."

June climbed over the fence and set off to the watering hole. The grass was beginning to lose its drab, brown, winter look, and both Maud and Ella were browsing around searching for early spring weeds. The trees were still bare, but their branches had a soft, misty look. There were fat buds on the underbrush and June pushed through them to the watering hole. Patches of broken ice had drifted and piled up against the sides of the bank, leaving a few watery gaps. Here and there, fallen leaves were frozen into a ragged design in the ice.

"The watering hole is still here," June called to the Maud and Ella, and they ambled through the brush. The two sheep gazed at the ice-filled pool, blinked their gold eyes, and turned away, uninterested.

"Ladies, Ladies," June scolded them. "You're too used to us breaking up the ice in the trough!" Neither of them looked back at her and they started to nose the brown grass.

June slid down the bank and pushed the ice pack with her foot. "It won't be long," she said. "Pretty soon, I can come down in the afternoon and wash the garden soil off myself."

She hummed a song she'd heard and climbed back up the bank. Yes, she thought, and I can float around like last year. The trees will be dense with green leaves, the sky will be blue, and the sun will be warm. When she hiked back to the farm, she was holding that thought in her heart.

The end of April was warm enough to plow the vegetable gardens and wheat field. The Farmer attached the plow, puffing as he leaned over. "I need this exercise," he said, stretching his aching back and cracking his knuckles.

June pulled her sunhat down over her hair and climbed onto the seat. She always felt proud and strong when she sat up high on the tractor. Nobody can get to me, she thought, no NPF agents can touch me, I'm invincible. June liked the word, *invincible*, and she said it out loud. The Farmer hit the Power Mode button and stood back. "Yeah you are, Kiddo, you're invincible."

June sang to herself, as she turned the tractor towards the wheat field, "Nobody can own *me*!" It reminded her of Jem, and how it was right and proper, but then she kept singing, "No, nobody can own me, no way!"

The soil was indeed moist, and June maneuvered the tractor across the field, the plow blades churning and turning the earth over and over again. "Row after row," June sang as she moved the big tractor along. By the end of the day, the wheat field would be ready for the seeder, and she felt a sense of satisfaction. The sun and rain would do the rest, and by the end of the summer, the thresher would be sweeping down the same rows she was turning now.

As June rounded the far back end of the field, she heard the low hum of a vehicle as it slowed to a stop behind the woods that lined the road. The trees were bare, with just the hint of green, and the underbrush was still twiggy with the buds just beginning to open. June stopped the tractor and turned in her seat, her back straight, and head held high. She knew it would be an NPF vehicle, and it was. The sleek, black body was almost hidden in the shadows, its engine purring softly and black windows closed.

June pushed her sunhat down over her hair, crossed her arms, narrowed her eyes and glared. She felt someone staring at her through the black glass, but the window remained closed. After a minute, the vehicle continued on its way, but as it disappeared around the bend, June heard a laugh – a low, harsh sound that made the hair stand up on the back of her neck.

Chapter 53

Spring had finally arrived, but there was no rain nor clouds, just blue sky and sun. The first day in May, the Farmer and June stood outside the barn looking out over the wheat field, and his face was gray with worry. "I think we should leave it alone this year," he told her. "The field you plowed is already dry, just look at it! It's enough to make me sick." He ran a large handkerchief over his face and stuck it in a back pocket.

June watched a crow drop down and land on a fencepost, folding black wings around its glossy body. The bird watched them with beady eyes and not a feather moved. June looked back. What does he think, flying over the dry earth and feeling the sun on his wings?

"Nope, I'm not going to plant it," the Farmer said, interrupting her thoughts. "I'll just let it rest, and we can spend our time with the vegetable gardens. Seems like the veggies may be sprouting now. I don't want to take a chance with the wheat."

June had seen tiny green nubs in the moist soil, and she had to agree. The vegetables were breaking through: small but visible, but she was disappointed. "I worked so damn hard to plow the wheat field with all its awful dry chaff," she said, "and now I'll miss that big old gold sea this summer." The Farmer nodded, and they stood looking out over the land for a while longer. Then he turned away. "We need rain!" he called back as he headed into the barn.

The crow gave a harsh call and spread its wings, heading back over the dry field. June was suddenly filled with a sense of dread. "That's just a bird, silly girl," she told herself, but the shadowy black body seemed to be a bad omen of some kind. June shivered suddenly and turned away – and she didn't look back.

As May wore on, the sun rose every morning in a cloudless sky, an expanse that was blue from horizon to horizon. Blue, blue, blue, June thought, but we need rain. I want to see storm clouds rolling up from the North, clouds filled with rain! But as the days passed, there were no clouds filled with rain, in fact, no clouds at all, just blue sky and sun.

Maud and Ella strayed down to the watering hole to graze on new grass and June followed them. The sheep nosed around the pool and dipped their lips in the water. June watched them for a while and then sat down on the bank. The water was low, and tall grass was growing on the opposite side, but there was still enough water to swim in. June gazed at the watering hole, and her mind wandered. She remembered the Quarry and wondered if the water was low in that bottomless pit. She thought about getting married and about the future – her future and everyone else's. "Where are the Illegals," she wondered aloud. "The Son and Jem. I am here, but, where are they?"

A vehicle passed by on the road and June ducked down, but it kept going. She tossed a twig in the water and watched as it floated. It brought back memories of the whirlpool where they had bathed when she traveled with the Woman and her family. The current had taken her around and around as she watched the stars whirl overhead, the only stars she had seen in so long – pinpricks in the black, black sky. She thought about the Son and felt an ache in her heart. What was his real name, she asked herself, did it even matter? She wondered if he had married one of his own, and her body stiffened with envy. "Jem," she said out loud and sighed. "It's right and proper." Ella raised her head, then went back to searching for new grass.

Jem was in the Far Western Region, and June was busy, but at night, when she climbed into bed and curled up in the spot where he had slept, she was filled with loneliness and apprehension. I'm alone with Kitty at my feet, she'd think, and I always feel safe with Jem near me. June would bury her head in his pillow and try to find a faint trace of him there, but in the darkest hours of the night, there would be tears. And day after day the sun rose, and June would forget.

It wasn't long before the leaves filled the trees, and the underbrush was thick with new growth. June stopped worrying about the far end of the garden. Let them drive by, she thought, they can't see me; but she would think about January and, fuming, tuck her hair more securely inside her sunhat.

"I'd like to kick the side of their vile black vehicle," she told Kitty. "Punch out the window!" But June made sure she was hidden in the trees or behind the house when they drove by. NPF seemed to be everywhere – the back road, the road past the house, and even the road past the watering hole. It made her nervous. It reminded her of the clerk in the Food Shop, "What a bunch of creeps," she told Kitty and said the bad word. "I had to hide in a pile of underbrush!"

However, the Saturday trips to the Village were uneventful and even fun. No freezing, lurching truck rides or iced sidewalks, and no black vehicles hidden in a side street. Eve would ramble on as she drove, and June would gaze out the window, her mind miles away. The Village was always alive with gossip, and June listened as she followed Eve into the shops. She'd buy Kitty's food and help Eve stow the grocery bags in the back of the truck, and finally, there was lunch in the coffee shop. The frightening winter was forgotten, and everyone went about their business, chatted in the street, or conversed over coffee as they sat at the counter.

"How soon we all forget," Eve noted cynically, but she had put winter behind her, too. "With all this sun, we'll need to take a trip to the *Farm Bureau* in another week. It's about time to buy new shorts and t-shirts for the summer." She sounded happy and relieved, but June wasn't so sure.

Chapter 54

Occasionally, June and Eve would see Mr. Scott in the coffee shop. He'd greet them warmly and remind June how much safer her money would be in her account, but June still kept her savings in coffee tins inside the hole where she stored her winter vegetables. However, she did like to look at Mr. Scott. He was so well dressed and handsome, and he spoke like the mayor, smiling and spilling out wise comments about the Village.

"I've never seen anyone like Mr. Scott," June told Eve. "He's very special, isn't he?" She stopped and thought for a moment. "I don't understand, you know?"

Eve shook her head in wonder. After all this time, June is still so damn naive, she thought, and even after reading her history book all the time. Really, I have to do something. It's time she grew up and became a little more sophisticated.

Eve gave it some more thought and talked it over with her husband. "Well, there's the Village Cemetery," the Farmer said and laughed at the look on Eve's face. "There's history in that place, going all the way back to the Revolutionary War. You can tell her about the Civil War, too … *Both* Civil Wars," he added, and they decided June should go to the Village cemetery for a history lesson.

"No time like the present," Eve said, grabbed a light jacket and headed for the door. She pulled the truck out of the barn and found June in the vegetable garden. "You've lived up North long enough," Eve told her. "Hop in, I'm taking you for a history lesson, a *living* history lesson."

June was curious. She dusted herself off and climbed into the truck with Eve, and they headed down the road to the Village. Eve drove without a word, and June glanced at her with interest as they bumped along. A living history lesson, she thought. Huh!

Finally, Eve broke her silence. "We're visiting the Village Cemetery. This cemetery is significant to the Village because the neighborhood boys who went off to war are buried there. Even from the Revolutionary War in the 1770s, you know, *Northern boys*."

She paused and stopped at a crossroad. "In fact, Mr. Scott's brother is there. I think he died in 2045 or 2046 in the American Civil War. They were all heroes," she added. "All the way back to the nineteenth century."

As she drove, Eve told June about the Revolutionary War and the founding of the country. "Way back then," she said. "Like in your history book."

She told her about the Civil War in the 1860s and Abraham Lincoln, then searched her mind and rambled on about the World Wars and about Vietnam. She described her father's war in Afghanistan, the Longest War in the World, and what she remembered about the New American Civil War. "Before then," she said, "this was one big country."

Finally, Eve drew a long breath and glanced over at June. "Do you have any questions?"

"What's a cemetery?" June asked, and Eve stared at her.

"I'm sure there was a cemetery back there in North Carolina," she said. "You know, a graveyard? A resting place for people who died?"

"There was the Memorial to the Lost," June said, but she was thinking about Mr. Scott's brother and was distracted. "I don't remember a cemetery anywhere in my town. Maybe our boys didn't come home. My Daddy didn't, but I don't remember all that." She reflected for another moment. "I really don't know about any other people who died. Maybe they went into the field by the church. My Mama never talked about those things."

Eve frowned. "Maybe the Memorial to the Lost is like a cemetery," she said and turned up a hill. They passed the church, and on the right June saw a park with green trees and flowering bushes. There were rows upon rows of stones lined up across the grass.

"Look, Eve, there are lots of matching stones in that park," she said. "It's pretty."

"Those are gravestones," Eve said and pulled over. "Each of them honors a person who is buried there. This is sacred ground."

"The Memorial to the Lost is just one big stone," June said softly. "It's for all the people in my town who disappeared in the Great Flood in 2058. First, the stone was covered by vines, but now it's covered by the ocean." She gazed out at the cemetery and thought how peaceful it looked: grass and trees, flowers, and the stones lined up like the soldiers in her history book. "But that could never happen here," she added.

Eve turned off the engine and sat back. "That big stone memorial is like a cemetery," she said. "It honors the lost. It's sacred."

"My Mama was one of them," June looked back at Eve, "one of the Lost. Mama went to visit my Auntie Glory, Down South, and she never came home." June was quiet and stared out the window. "I would like to walk in that cemetery," she added. "Maybe my Daddy is in there."

Eve left the truck parked by the side of the road and sat on a bench. She watched as June wandered through the gravestones and felt a feeling of deep sorrow. She knew in her heart that June would never find her father. A Southern soldier buried in their cemetery? Never! But Eve didn't want to upset June, so she just sat and let her mind wander.

Eve had vague memories of the Civil War of 2045. She had been a little girl, and it didn't affect the Garden State. Her father was too old to go, anyway. He was a veteran of the Afghanistan War. Eve remembered him fuming angerly about "The Sectioning —" a law that carved the country into regions after the war ended. He shouted about protesters. He'd roared with anger at the new Privacy Laws, too.

"Where in Hell are the Protesters?" He raved on, "NOW is the time we need to hit the streets and PROTEST!"

Eve had run to her room in tears.

"We're the United States of America," he'd shout and raise his fist in the air. I fought for these damn freedoms! He brought home a large American flag and hung it from the front porch and started wearing his old army cap with the gold stars on it. "No TV, no phones, no computers, what the Hell kind of county is this?" he'd rant.

"Just ignore him," her mother said. "He'll get used to it." But he never did. A year later, her father sold the house and moved the family North to a farm in the Commonwealth.

Eve couldn't remember much more about those early days in the Garden State, but she certainly remembered the school in the Commonwealth and all her friends. They were excited when the new Civics textbooks arrived with their bright covers. They learned about the different Regions and what they were called. The books were filled with colorful pictures of mountains and beaches and new words to learn, but Eve never learned much about the war, because the only American History books had been stored away in a locked closet behind the school lunchroom.

Eve's teacher was a petite, cheerful young woman with red hair that she wore in a ponytail, and ankle-length, full skirts that floated around her feet when she walked. "We're in the Northern Region," she told them. "Be very thankful about *that!*" Eve laughed with her friends, but she didn't understand why. Actually, she was thankful she lived on a farm with her parents. She had a vague memory of the Sectioning and was clever enough to avoid asking her father what her teacher meant.

Life went on. Eve skied on snowy slopes in the winter and swam in a creek in the summer. It was a good life, and her father finally came to terms with the new era. Daddy, she thought and laughed out loud.

Eve leaned back and thought about meeting Adam at a Green Camp Festival when they were in college, and she smiled at the memory. They were hoisting hay bales into a wagon and fell in love immediately. "Ah, Adam," she said softly, "you are the love of my life."

They married the following summer, standing in the Green Camp's vegetable garden surrounded by beans and lettuce. Very Adam, she thought now. Getting married in a vegetable garden in blue jeans and boots.

The next year, Adam worked at a co-op garden, but he wanted a farm of his own. "Sheep," he told her, "I want a couple of sheep. And chickens, of course." So, maps, bio-farming books, financial spreadsheets, and tax forms covered the kitchen table for months. Finally, he decided they should move to the Garden State, start the Natural World Farm, and Eve returned to the state she had left as a child.

Sitting quietly on the bench and watching June, Eve remembered the first time she had seen this Village, driving right past the cemetery as they arrived in town. Such a place of history, she though now, and memories of too many wars, too many young men and, yes, young women – lost.

Eve loved the Village and the farm, and she sadly recalled her only disappointment – not having a family. "No babies," the doctor had told them, "The Virus, of course." They drove home without a word, and Eve sat in the barn and cried. But now she had June: strange, beautiful June with the pale hair and sky-blue eyes; the woodland creature who'd arrived at the pasture gate. A little too old as a daughter, she thought, but sometimes she seems like a child.

Eve's daydreaming was interrupted as June dropped down on the bench. "There are names on every stone," she said, "and dates. Too many young men, just boys ... and girls, too. I can do my sums, you know, so I figured it out." June gazed into space for a while, and Eve let her sit quietly.

"Even on the ancient old stones from 1770," June continued. "Just boys then! Can you imagine? Like my history book. And I found Mr. Scott's brother. His name was Ivan, and he was only twenty years old. He died in 2044, not 2045." She sat back and sighed, and then glanced over. "There were stars on some of those stones. Stars with six points. Why?"

Eve gazed at the cemetery and rested her eyes on the rows of headstones. "Those were Jewish boys and girls," she said. "You know, like Mr. Solomon, the old man with the dog. They were all heroes," she repeated.

June thought this over and then nodded. "I like Mr. Solomon. He's very kind and polite." There were other people, too," she added, "young people, children, and even old people. They all died at the same time and not too long ago. Why?"

"It was the Virus." Eve pulled on her jacket, and they headed back to the truck. "It was an old childhood disease, and it mutated, became virulent. People stopped getting vaccinations, so it hit everyone. I had it, Adam had it, but we were young. Adam's parents were in the hospital, and they both died. Many of the elderly people died. It was sad."

"No babies," June said. "We had the Virus, too, and the town herbalist was called in. Nobody died." She stopped and thought for a moment. "I don't think so, but then there were no more babies. After that, the men believed they could grab any girl and … you know, do things. So, girls didn't go out without a chaperon." She looked over at Eve, "But my town was beautiful," she added firmly.

My God, Eve thought, a town herbalist and men running wild? No wonder she ran away.

June was deep in thought on the trip back to the farm, and Eve was quiet. She reflected on the Virus and what June had said about the babies, and it made her depressed. She glanced at June and was reminded of something she had heard years before – a rumor about the war. It was something terrible, and Eve knew June would never find her father's grave. Because there wasn't one. What did we do? she wondered and wanted to weep.

I didn't find my Daddy," June said as if she had read Eve's mind. "Maybe one day," she added, and then she sat and looked out the window. Her mind was on the rows of gravestones. So many boys, she thought, so many boys and girls.

Chapter 55

After her living history trip to the Village Cemetery, June started dreaming about trees: Tall trees with sweeping branches that reached the sky, pine trees with sharp needles sending sparks into the air, ferns that covered the ground in waves like soft feathers, and bushes filled with berries. She dreamed of trees with thick leaves, green and lush, weighing down their branches.

One night, June dreamed about the wheat field. In her dream, the grain looked like a golden tide, sweeping across the land and then bursting into flames. Inexplicably, it seemed to be a beautiful sight, and June woke with a start. Why, she wondered, why beautiful?

She thought about the wheat field all the next day, and it troubled her. Some of her dreams soothed her but others bothered her, and this one was one of them, but her chores kept her busy, and the vision faded away.

June spent her days in the vegetable gardens, checking and rechecking the rows of brown soil with their tiny green nubs. She pulled a long hose through the plots, and a trickle of water dampened the rows. Now and again, the crow settled on the fence post nearby, cocked its head and watched her. June thought she could feel it's eyes on her, and one day, she jumped up and glared at him. "No sprouts for you, Mr. Crow," she snapped and waved her hands in the air. The big bird spread its wings and sailed across the empty wheat field, calling harshly back as it disappeared over the trees. It's the dreams, June decided. I'm tired. I just scolded a crow and called him Mister!

Then one night, she dreamed about the man with the gray eyes. At first, he was almost invisible, an eerie presence standing in a copse of white birch trees by the watering hole – handsome, cold, unsmiling. Suddenly, he was practically on top of her. "You're mine," he shouted, and in her dream, his voice was like thunder. His face loomed over hers, his lips parted like a fish, and he sucked the air out of her lungs while his hands grabbed at her. June woke up gasping for air and trying to scream, the dream hanging over her – stifling her. Kitty looked up from the foot of the bed, then curled up again and closed her eyes.

"It was only a dream," June told herself, "Just a bad dream!" But she wanted her mama there, to hold her the way she had when June was a little girl. "Mama," she whispered, and tears filled her eyes. She sat for a while holding her knees and then curled up like a ball, but it took her a long time to fall asleep again.

Just as quickly as the dreams started, they stopped. Now and again, there would be a wisp of a dream, a snippet that disappeared with the morning mist, but there were no more visions that haunted her days. June was able to forget the man with the gray eyes. "Ugly," she said and forced him out of her mind, but she wondered about the trees. She remembered traveling with the Illegals: the forest, the towering trees, the sea of ferns and thick foliage, and the Son with his dark eyes. Then she would look around her snug little apartment and gaze at her pearl ring, bright as the moon, and remind herself, "June, how lucky you are."

The weather grew warmer, and the little green nubs became shoots. June crept through the rows of vegetables on her hands and knees and pulled weeds, checking to see if the soil was still moist from the winter frost and the trickle from the hose, but she was worried. We need rain, she'd fret. But no clouds gathered on the horizon, and despite her work, the soil was becoming dry, cracks appearing in the rows of vegetables.

The Farmer worried, too. He'd stand next to June in the barnyard and look out over the fields. "We need rain," he agonized over and over until June shut her ears to his ranting. She would leave him and go back to her weeding, crawling along in the heat, the moisture running down her back and under her arms, praying for rain. "Please, Sir. Please send rain." But every day the sun would rise in a cloudless sky, hotter than the day before – and always, the crow would return.

The Farmer scared Jane with his talk, but in the late afternoon, she'd shake off her fears and head down to the watering hole, undress in the bushes and splash in. The water level was low, but she floated around anyway and glared up at the hot, blue sky.

One late afternoon, when June scrambled up onto the bank, she found Maud and Ella grazing in the trees. The sheep had been shorn, and their bodies looked smooth and delicate.

"Hello, Ladies," she called. "You're finally at the watering hole." They glanced up and gazed at her with their gold eyes and then went back to searching for grass.

June left them grazing and stood in the sun, tugging her fingers through her wet hair. The water ran off her body in rivulets, making puddles on the ground. She thought about Jem and touched her breasts with her fingers. Soon, she thought, soon he'll be back. It was quiet in the grove, and June daydreamed as she stood in the sun. Maybe someday they would be married and have a farm of their own. Her mind drifted as the sun warmed her body.

Then, the leaves moved, and a bird shot out of the underbrush and disappeared over the pasture.

Maud and Ella looked up, alarmed, their eyes fixed on the bushes by the road. Again, June felt a presence, but this time the sheep didn't drop their heads and graze again, they turned away, pushing and bumping each other in their haste. Frightened, June crouched and covered her nakedness; she remembered her dream: the man with the gray eyes, hiding and watching her. But she *knew* who it was, and narrowed her eyes. "It's NPF agents," she whispered and was filled with rage. "Damn them," she snapped, "I'm a citizen, how dare they?"

"You want to look at me," June shouted. "Well, here I am!" And she stood up and faced the bushes, her chin up, mouth firm. After a moment, she slowly slipped on her underclothes, her white t-shirt and finally her overalls, picked up her sandals, and headed back to the farm in her bare feet.

"I hope you had a good look," she called back over her shoulder and then added the bad words the Man had used.

Chapter 56

The month of June was the hottest on record, and the people in the Village were talking. First, Mrs. Robertson complained. She lived on the south side of town, and nobody listened. "She moans all the time," someone said, but then folks on the west side started to protest.

"The water smells bad," the homeowners grumbled. "It tastes like salt, and it's brown, no more than a trickle. A salty, brown trickle!"

Three of the Town Council members finally drove out to the reservoir to check out what was causing the problem – two men and a woman. It was almost an hour's drive, and they bickered all the way.

"What the Hell," Mr. Harold said. "Now what?"

"It's Climate Change," Mr. Scott said, and, as usual, that started the argument.

"No such thing," spat Mr. Harold. "It's just gossip. Why listen to those tall tales?" He glared at Mr. Scott and drummed his thumbs on the steering wheel.

"Mark my words," Mr. Scott shot back.

"Oh, hush, you two boys," Mrs. Grower threw in for good measure, but the argument continued until they arrived.

A parking area surrounded the central pumping station by the reservoir, and when they pulled in, Mr. Harold's van was the only vehicle in the lot. Sweat ran down their backs and soaked their shirts as they clambered out and looked around. It was eerie, totally silent without a breath of air, and the bickering stopped at once. The three Villagers puffed their way to the top of the embankment and looked down in horror. The fresh water was shockingly low – lower than it had ever been. Silt muddied what was left, and it smelled like the sea.

"Oh, my God!" Mr. Scott whispered. "All that environmental ruin down South is catching up with us now. Somehow the ocean waves have contaminated our drinking water." Mr. Harold was silent and white as a ghost, and Mrs. Grower started to cry in huge, gulping sobs.

Without a word, they climbed back down the embankment and drove back to the Village, their faces filled with dread. Mrs. Grower stared out the window and snuffled into a tissue, and Mr. Harold stared straight ahead, his hands frozen on the steering wheel,

"Climate Change," Mr. Scott said, but nobody else had a word to say. There were no more arguments, just a horrified stillness in the van and the sound of their breathing.

Mr. Harold pulled up at the Town Hall building, and the three members crowded through the door to the Mayor's office, shaken and full of fear.

One look told the Mayor what he had feared, and he stood up, sending his chair crashing to the floor behind him. "Get out," he shouted, and they filed back into the street, whispering among themselves. They were members of the Town Council, after all.

"What the Hell do we do now?' Mr. Scott demanded – and silence!

The following day, the Mayor called a meeting and announced he'd contacted the Governor of the Northern Kingdom. She had agreed to send water trucks to the area as soon as possible: fresh water until the crisis was over. "Meanwhile," he said, "we will supply bottled water to all villagers. The farms will be exempt because they have artesian wells." He paused and wheezed into an inhaler. "The water trucks are for the Village. Get that bottled water and the word out, now!"

So, the word went out. Members of the Town Council went door to door. They delivered cases of bottled water and flyers and put posters in store windows. The Villagers dug through attics and garages to find the largest containers they could find, and then they waited.

Eve came down to June's apartment to tell her the latest news.

"It's the water," she said. "Adam heard it from one of his friends who works for the Mayor. Luckily, we have an artesian well, so we won't have a problem, but it certainly is worrisome." She dropped into one of the chairs by the window. "You must keep watering the vegetables, June, but be very frugal." She looked out at the gardens, and her face was filled with dread. "Water trucks are coming down from the Northern Kingdom for the poor Village, but damn it! I want all this stuff to stop! I want to enjoy life again!"

June didn't know what an artesian well was, but she assumed the water was fresh. She didn't say a word as Eve rambled on but felt her heart sink. What *could* she say? "I know what is happening, and I know what the water trucks are for? I've lived through this before?" She sighed, put the teapot on to boil, and took out cups and tea bags. This is going to be a long, hot summer she thought, and sighed again.

Eve was still fretting when they drove into the village on Saturday morning. June sat next to her as the truck bumped along; she looked out at the empty wheat field and the glass meadow with its solar panels blazing back at the sun. Leaves on the trees were beginning to look faded, and the grass was turning brown. June thought about the watering hole and felt sad and frightened. It looked like a mud puddle; Maud and Ella were drinking out of the barn trough again.

"Keep the livestock hydrated," Eve broke in as if she was reading June's mind. "Keep fresh water in the trough and the chicken's water fountain." She slowed down and gazed out the truck window. "Oh, look, June, that must be the water truck. Look how big it is … it's *huge!*"

A familiar silver tanker truck was parked at the corner just outside of the Village, and June craned her neck as they passed. Green Mountain Water, like the ones at home! She could see no driver but noticed the grim faces of some determined villagers as they waited.

"See, see?" Eve clutched the wheel as they turned into the Village, and her voice was high with anxiety. "We need Jem to come back now. I don't know what to do! *Adam* doesn't know what to do!"

I know what to do, June thought … run! But she was quiet, looking out at the Main Street.

The Village was filled with worried people as they gathered in the street to gossip. "First that damn freezing winter and now this," they grumbled, their voices loud with worry. "When does this Hell stop and we can go back to normal?"

Eve parked, and they pushed through a crowd of anxious women milling around and talking outside the grocery store. The Water Truck poster was taped to the window, and a sign leaned on the counter: *No Bottled Water!* Cases of cola were stacked by the door.

What if there isn't enough water in those trucks?" Eve whispered. "Should we sell water from our well? What if our well runs dry? Maybe there will be a *water war* like in the Far Western Region." Her voice was rough with emotion as she tossed random items into her basket.

"There is always enough water in those trucks," June said with authority, but Eve was in no mood to listen. They loaded the groceries into the back of the truck, and June tried to ignore Eve's ramblings.

The coffee shop was almost empty, except for Mr. Solomon, with his bulldog, sitting at a table in the corner. The Trilby hat was gone, and wisps of white hair had taken its place. The bulldog lay under his chair, tongue lolling out.

"Come join us, Eve," the old man called out. "Lots of room at the table and Old Louie and I could use the company."

Eve smiled vaguely, chose her favorite seat by the window, and sat down, her face frozen with shock. June smiled at the old man. "Hello, Mr. Solomon," she said and took her seat. She thought about the dog and hoped there would be enough water for both of them.

The waitress dropped two heavy, white mugs on their table. "Enjoy your coffee and tea!" she snapped. Her hair was frizzed from the heat, and she had forgotten her makeup.

"One more coffee here," the old man called out cheerfully.

The waitress nodded and wiped her hands on a towel. With a sigh, she tucked it into her apron. "I just don't know how long we'll be able to serve it. With the water situation, you know … rationing. We just got these new mugs, too. Maybe we can serve cola in them." She shook her head and wandered away. "Let me know what you want," she called over her shoulder.

Mr. Solomon man tapped his mug on the table. "Don't forget my coffee, dearie." His dog looked up with rheumy eyes and then went back to sleep.

June sat and looked out the window. Villagers were standing in the street gossiping and arguing. She had grown to love this little Village and the kind, friendly people. These Northerners, she reminded herself. What will happen to them? She gazed at the bicycle store across the street and the *Farm Bureau*. Eve had recently bought them both new shorts, and June had picked out a forest-green t-shirt for a change. Down the block, the elegant Town Hall sat across from the Chase Bank where Mr. Scott worked … Mr. Scott, whose brother was buried in the Village Cemetery.

June felt like putting her head down on the table and going to sleep. Deep in her heart, she knew it was time to run and right there at the table with Eve grousing across from her, June began to plan. She would leave as soon as Jem returned: leave the Village, the farm, her cozy apartment. Leave Eve and the Farmer, her chickens, the sassy rooster, and Maud and Ella. It was almost more than she could bear, and all June could say was, "Everything will be alright, Eve, this is the Garden State."

Chapter 57

By the end of the month, the countryside looked drab and dry. Patches of burned grass grew larger every day, and the leaves on the trees were falling like brown slips of paper floating down in the hot sun. Some of the Villagers started to wear dark glasses when they ventured outside. The sun was so bright it caused an unbearable glare.

June stood on the bank, looking down at the watering hole and felt sick. There was no water left, just dry mud the color of ashes. Deep cracks were beginning to appear, and the tall grass lay wilted in a heap on the opposite bank. How could this have happened so fast, she wondered.

After a few minutes, she turned her back and continued on her way to the Village. She wanted to see if the Water Truck was still parked outside of town. That morning, Eve had driven them to the Village and passed it parked at the corner as usual. June had looked again but caught no sight of the driver, and she was curious.

She walked on the side of the road in case an NPF vehicle came into sight, but there was no one – just the hot pavement that stretched out ahead. As she crunched through the fallen leaves, June daydreamed about the Christmas Eve she had walked along the same road with Jem. The snow was falling around them like a curtain, and she remembered he had held her hand. I think maybe I love him, June thought. The memory hurt her heart, and she wiped her eyes with the tips of her fingers.

"Come back, Jem," she said out loud. "Come back, hurry!" But now, June was afraid she'd be gone when he arrived. She forced the thought away and kept walking, her eyes on the road ahead.

The Water Truck was still parked by the side of the road, and a line of Villagers was gathered at the side with their containers.

They gossiped among themselves as they waited, laughing now and again. How can they laugh? June thought, but she admired them for their tenacity.

The driver was crouched by the spigot, and June saw the familiar mane of white hair, the flash of his glasses and heard his laugh. For some odd reason, he made her feel hopeful, and she wandered over.

"I remember you," he said. "And here you are, older and still pretty!"

June felt herself blush. "This is the Garden State," she said shyly. "The burning days shouldn't happen here." She nodded at the brown countryside. "Why?"

A hot breeze threw a handful of wilted leaves at them, and the driver shook his head. "I have been driving this truck for years, and there's no end to this … no end at all! From the southern border of the Garden State on down, it's all gone. The ocean is taking the land." He paused and looked at June. "At least there are no more hurricanes. The waves are gentle, but they're relentless."

The driver stood up and pulled a large white handkerchief out of his back pocket and wiped his forehead. "People disappeared, Young Lady. Some moved up North like you did, but some stayed put. They didn't even leave their homes." He took his glasses off and dabbed his eyes. "And over East on the shore? Some families even camped on the sand and waited. It was crazy! They put up tents, but then they just stood there, day after day … on the beach." He put his glasses back on and looked around. "Well, all those people? They're gone now. The ocean took them!" He shook his head. "I'll just wait in the Green Mountains, Young Lady, that's where I'll wait."

June watched the Villagers, and her heart was heavy. She knew some of them: shopping in the grocery store, helping her pick out her clothes in the *Farm Bureau,* or gossiping over coffee in the coffee shop. They were filling their containers and talking among themselves, making little jokes, their eyes covered by their dark glasses. She watched as they laughed. They're just accepting this, June thought and turned to the driver, "When do you leave?"

His face brightened, "I'm staying here until all the water is gone, and then I'll head home. I figure early tomorrow morning." He smiled, and his glasses gleamed in the sun. "But, I'll be back in a week, Young Lady, parked right here on this corner, and other trucks will be coming before then."

He looks happy, June thought. Maybe, if Jem isn't home, I'll ask him to take me with him. I'm sure another week won't matter."

Before June left, the driver filled a glass of Green Mountain water. "This is my gift to you," he said, and she felt a moment of joy as she tasted the coldness on her tongue. "The mines in the Southern Region are flooded, Young Lady," he added. "Karma, I guess."

When June arrived at the farm, it was quiet. Kitty was sitting by the apartment door, cleaning herself, and she watched June for a few minutes and then slipped over the wall and disappeared. The Farmer had taken the truck into town, and Eve was in the house. She had drawn the curtains, shutting out the sun. More and more often, Eve stayed inside with Sherpa, and June missed her. She stood gazing at the garden, the shoots shriveling in the heat, and knew she had lost the battle. June crouched down in the dirt and felt guilty and empty. Everything had changed, and she knew why. "Jem, where are you?" she whispered.

After a minute, she looked over her shoulder, and her long, pale hair fell over her face. Upstairs in the farmhouse, a window curtain was quickly moved back into place. Sherpa barked somewhere inside but was quickly hushed.

How odd, June thought. What's with Eve?

She squatted down on her heels and picked up a handful of soil from the vegetable garden. Last year she had helped tend these gardens, and the earth had been moist and brown. She had plowed the wheat field, sitting high up on the tractor with her sun hat perched on her head, and the wheat had flourished and turned gold in the warm sun. All summer the farm stand was filled with sweet corn, red tomatoes, and mounds of greens; and in autumn, she'd been able to store her share of root vegetables and cabbages for the winter. But today, as the soil ran through June's fingers, small puffs of dust floated up from between her sandals.

The tender green shoots that appeared a few weeks earlier and forced their way up through the dry earth were dying in the hot sun. She sighed and gazed out over the acres of farmland that belonged to Eve and the Farmer – good people who gave her a living space in their basement apartment and paid for her work on the farm. Sometimes Eve had brought her honey from the beehives behind the barn, and she'd laughed because June was afraid of the bees. They always went to the Village on Saturday morning, rocking along in the old truck, and they'd share lunch in the coffee shop. But now Eve stayed in the house, afraid and depressed. The only time June saw her was on Saturday mornings, and Eve hardly said a word as they shopped.

June was worried. A sepia haze hung over the horizon, coming closer every day, and heat lightning flashed far away. Now last year's wheat chaff was burned black by the sun and lay in dusty heaps across the field. Every now and then, for no apparent reason, a small fire would start, little flames licking along the ground only to die as the dust smothered them. The cornfield was empty, and the bees were gone. A crow gave a harsh call as it beat its way across the wheat field, and then it was quiet. Damn crow, June thought.

She looked back at the garden, lost in thought. She had seen this back home. First, that dry, bitterly cold winter and then the endless sun, killing every living thing; vegetables, fruit, wheat, corn ... all gone. June felt a chill in the hot, still air. It was happening here, and she realized she would have to leave her little basement home – leave Eve and the Farmer, the chickens and Maud and Ella – leave and head further North. She was afraid she'd be unable to wait much longer for Jem, and she trembled at the thought. Unless he came home now, she would have to leave him behind and travel on alone.

June stood up and brushed the dust off her shorts. Her mind was miles away – making plans, thinking about Jem. Then, she turned and almost collided with the man standing behind her, so close she could have reached out and touched him. June saw the black boots and then the black uniform, the utility belt with the weapon and the handcuffs. Shocked, she looked up and saw the handsome face with the hard mouth and smoky-gray eyes. It was the man in the pumpkin patch, her nightmare, and he was standing right in front of her.

June was frozen with fear, a fear unlike anything she'd ever known, not when she'd left home, nor when she had cowered in the brush pile, or even in the dark water of the Quarry. It overwhelmed her now because she knew she was lost. Nobody was there to help her; the Farmer was gone, and Eve was hiding somewhere upstairs, quiet as a mouse, because *this* was the NPF. June felt faint as his eyes locked on hers.

"I've been watching you," the agent said, and her blood turned to ice. "For almost two years! I've seen you with the farmer's wife in the Village and on the tractor. You thought I didn't know it was you, didn't you!" He laughed, low in his throat. "Oh, and June, I've seen you with Jem." He smiled when he saw her shock. "Surprised? Well, I met Jem at the North Western border and heard all about you. Men become friendly out there in the Burn, all dirty and exhausted, and we like a beer and some company." His voice was a low mummer now. "Jem told me all about his blond sweetheart ... the same girl I want and *will* take away from him. If it hadn't been for that damn dog, I would have grabbed you in the pumpkin patch before I even knew your name."

June couldn't look away as the agent's eyes ran over her body. He smirked and moved closer. "I've seen you floating around in your little pool in the pasture, naked as a jaybird, and on the ice, when you fell on your ass. Oh, and I saw you with no clothes on, standing on the bank and daring me." He laughed again, an ugly sound deep in his throat.

June's fear turned to embarrassment, and thoughts flashed through her mind: the man in the pumpkin patch, the number of times she had felt someone watching her at the watering hole, and yes, even a few short weeks before when she stood on the bank naked and shouted, "Look at me!" June's face turned red with humiliation.

The agent ran his tongue over his upper lip and reached out and grabbed her arm. "Well, now I'm finally here, and you're mine!" He squeezed her arm hard. "Why don't we make this easy? We can go inside your apartment, and I'll show you what a real man is like."

January! June thought, oh *January*! She saw the agent with the red hair, remembered what he'd done, and she felt a wave of smoldering anger, as hot as burning coals. It filled her up until she thought she would burst. I hid in the broom closet then, she thought, but not now ... *not now*!

"You - are - mine!" the agent repeated and tightened his grip on her arm, dragging June with him, unaware of the expression on her face.

All the guilt and pain June carried, and the fear that hung over her like a cloud, became a rage she couldn't contain: a white, hot fury that consumed her and boiled over. "Never," June hissed. She took a step back, lashed out and struck him so hard it sounded like a gunshot. And then she spit the bad words right into his face.

The agent rocked back, and his face went ashen with shock, then red with rage. His fist came up so fast June never saw it coming; she just felt her head snap back – once, then twice – and then her knees weak. The world turned dark, and June saw swirling flashes of light as she fell back – and down and down in slow motion – right into the dying vegetable garden.

In the darkness, June felt him lean over her and knew she couldn't stop him. He tugged her shorts, and she heard the ugly words he hissed into her ear – awful things that made her feel faint.She tried to push him away, but he was too strong. And then, she felt him tear her underclothes and try to force his fingers into her secret places. Just as she sank into the emptiness, June heard an angry shout.

"Let her go, you moron. You're on duty." The voice faded, and the words were garbled. Then they came back, loud and clear, "Come back on your own time, Agent"

Then June slipped away.

Chapter 58

I'm dead! June thought. She was floating on an ocean of ferns: green waves in a forest and a breeze tossing her hair. It was quiet, and as the current carried her along, something soft as a butterfly's wing was touching her face.

June could open only one eye, and when she blinked it hurt. Golden light swirled around her making her head ache, and she was puzzled about that. Wasn't this heaven? An angel was leaning over, gently patting her face and singing. The angle's hair hung down in waves, and the light glowed around her head like a halo.

"I'm dead," June said.

She closed her eye, but the memory of the man with the gray eyes washed over her – the things he'd said and done. She opened her eye again and jerked up. Her surroundings spun around for a minute and then returned to normal. The garden, the wheat field, and the barn, they were all there. I'm not dead, June thought. She heard Sherpa barking and then realized Eve was sitting next to her, patting her face, and crying "I'm sorry! I'm sorry!" over and over again.

Why is she saying that? June thought, and then she leaned over and threw up in the garden.

Eve stopped crying and held June's hair back. She rubbed her shoulders until June was steady, and then helped her to her feet. As they stumbled back to the apartment, June clung to Eve's arm, her body trembling, afraid to ask what had happened.

"He didn't do anything to you, like ... you know," Eve said as if reading her mind. "Well, he did hit you and knock you down, but some NPF Sergeant came and told him to stop before he did anything else, and well, you know what I mean. You fell into the garden, June. I thought you were dead."

Eve started crying again. "I was scared, and Adam isn't home. I was afraid to help you. I was hiding in the house and I didn't stop that man. I'm so sorry!"

She sounds like me, June thought.

Eve slipped June's soiled shorts off and sat her in a chair. She found a soft robe and wrapped it around June's shivering body, rubbing her hands until they warmed up.

"I don't think he'll come back now. He knows it's against the law to come onto anyone's property, and for God's sake, you're a citizen! How dare he do that?"

June sat quietly as Eve gently washed her face and brushed her hair back. She winced as the cool washcloth touched the side of her face.

"That bastard," Eve said. "He gave you a black eye, and he even split your *lip*! How dare he do that?" she repeated.

"Ouch," June whispered.

"I'm so sorry," Eve said again. "What can I do? Can I make tea?"

Oh, he'll come back, June thought, but she didn't say it out loud. He touched me ... there. He watched me for two years, and now he's come for me and won't stop. The realization made her shudder. January had told her: If an NPF agent touches you, he owns you, and he will come back ... again and again. "Oh Jem," she whispered. "Now it really *is* too late." But, June didn't tell Eve. This is my problem, she thought. I'll have to take care of it myself, but that agent will *never* touch me again.

Eve brewed some tea. She set two places at the table and sat with June. "He won't come back," she said again. "That NPF sergeant was furious, and he shouted at him. I had to close Sherpa in the closet to keep him quiet." Eve's hand shook as she poured the tea. "It was awful!"

"He won't come back," June repeated, tasted her tea and winced again. "I hit him before he could take me away." Then, she whispered the bad words she had called him. Eve looked shocked, and then they both laughed, and they kept on laughing – but June felt like screaming.

Eve finally left, convinced everything was all right, and June stood up, looked around her apartment, and sighed. She slipped her pearl ring on for the last time and dumped the wool and knitting needles out of her carry bag. She pulled her backpack out from under the bed and stood looking at it, lost in thought, then she sighed again and started to pack.

June slid her mother's poem about the Pilgrims into the Rumi poetry book Eve had given her, glanced at her history book and then stuffed both books into the backpack. She carefully slid the Fox's silver stone in after them, and packed four t-shirts and two pairs of shorts, underclothes and the sweater she had knitted from Maud's and Ella's wool; on top, she added a package of kitty kibbles and her mother's picture. When she was done, she set the bulging backpack by the door.

June had never opened the little desk drawer before, she had never needed paper, but now she found what she needed. Stationary, envelopes, three pencils, and a pen were nestled inside, and she sat down and took out two envelopes and the notepaper. She hadn't written a word since leaving home, but she took up the pen and, carefully forming the letters, June wrote a note to Eve:

> *Dear Eve,*
> *I am sorry, but I will have to leave. You have been good*
> *to me, and I love you, but I know if I stay he will come back*
> *and I will bring dishonor to your home. Now, you and the*
> *Farmer will be free of his evil presence.*
> *Love,*
> *June*

She sealed the note in an envelope and wrote Eve's name on the front. Then she sighed again, pushed it aside, and started the second note.

Dear Jem,
I am sorry. I have to leave. I vowed to be true to you,
but if I stay, I will never be clean again. This I know.
Ask Eve.
I love you

June read the note over again and then slipped it into the envelope, wrote Jem on the front and kissed it closed. She held up her hand and gazed at the pearl on her finger. It glowed with its strange luminescent light, and she thought about Jem with his blond hair and warm blue eyes, his strong arms holding her as he loved her and felt a lump in her throat. She took off her ring and placed it on top of the note. As it lay in front of her, the pearl seemed to dim until it became opaque, dull, dead. June sat there for a few more minutes and then turned away.

"Kitty," she called and hung a pair of freshly washed jeans and the dark green t-shirt over one of the kitchen chairs. When she was done, June lay down on the bed and closed her one good eye. Kitty slipped in the open window and jumped up on the bed. She looked at June's face, and, then for the first time, curled up close to her.

June reached down and touched the cat's head. "I can bring you in the carry bag," she said. "I won't leave you behind." Kitty started her raucous purring, and June stroked the long, soft fur until she drifted into a restless sleep. She dozed until dawn, and sometime during the night, Kitty crept off the bed and out the window. In her sleep, June slid her hands between her legs, where the agent had touched her, and tears spilled down her cheeks.

Just before the sun touched the farm and the rooster's loud call woke the household, June dressed. She pinned the little silver sheep to her green t-shirt, and slung the backpack over her shoulder, picked up the carry bag, and left the apartment. Her face ached, but at least both eyes were open; she gazed around her little home before softly pulling the door shut behind her.

At the last moment, June made a detour across the barnyard and dropped her bags in the dust. She opened the henhouse door and watched as the hens headed for the underbrush. The rooster shook out his feathers and hopped onto a fencepost.

I can't believe I'll miss these chickens, she thought, all they do is cluck, eat, and poop.

"Kitty," June called softly and looked around, but the cat was nowhere to be seen. She gazed at the barn and then the house. "Kitty," she called again. "Come, Kitty, come. Where are you, Kitty?"

She waited for a few more minutes — and then the rooster crowed again. June picked up her carry bag and, with a heavy heart, she set off and didn't look back.

Chapter 59

Running

June climbed the fence and headed across the pasture. She felt the familiar weight of the backpack as she walked and her heart was heavy. At the watering hole, she found Maud and Ella grazing in the trees and dropped down next to them closing her eyes and gently touching Maud's back, memorizing the feel of the clipped, spongy wool. She stroked their soft noses and looked at them as they gazed back at her with their gold eyes.

"I never met sheep before," she said. "I wish I could take you with me." She bounced her hand off Ella's soft rump. "Look," she pulled her backpack over. "I'm bringing the sweater I knit from your wool. You two Ladies will always be with me." She rubbed the soft sweater against her cheek and felt her eyes fill with tears. "I don't want to leave," she said.

Unmoved, the two sheep went back to grazing, and June got to her feet, hoisting her backpack over one shoulder. She stopped on the bank of the watering hole and shook her head in despair. The water was gone, the pool a hollow pit of dried mud, and it reminded June of the mud plain at home.

"The Land of the Lost," she said, "where I stood waiting for Mama." It seemed so long ago now. It was hard to believe.

June let the backpack slide off her shoulder and walked around the watering hole. She squatted down where the tall grass had grown and tossed a small rough stone into the middle as a goodbye gift. June had loved this little watering hole. She missed those hot afternoons – floating on top of the water and gazing at the sky, her clothes folded on the bank. "Yes, naked as a jaybird," she said out loud and thought about the NPF agent with his gray eyes, hiding in the bushes. "He was watching me as I enjoyed my solitude," June said. She tightened her lips and lifted her chin.

"You will never own me," she shouted and jumped up. She made fists with her hands and shouted the bad words again and again. "You think you can do what you want with me ... ruin me with your body? Spoil my life?" She stamped her way back to her backpack. "You will never have me!" June slung her backpack onto her back and picked up the carry bag. "I am GONE!" she shouted and headed into the woods. Behind her, Maud and Ella looked up and watched, blinking their gold eyes.

The trees were filled with dried leaves and they were falling all around her as she walked, tossed by a warm, early morning breeze. They made rustling sounds under her feet, and June relaxed and let her mind wander. She stayed away from the road until she came to the Solar Farm, her Glass Meadow, then crossed to the other side of the road. The sun was just rising, and the solar panels caught the early rays, flashing them across the field like a river of gold. She had always wanted to walk through the Glass Meadow and now, at last, she would.

Gold, June thought to herself, and that reminded her of the Son and how he had touched her hair. "Gold," she said out loud and began to daydream. "Maybe I can somehow find the piece of myself I lost two years ago." The further she walked, the less she thought about the Natural World Farm. All of them: Eve and the Farmer, Maud and Ella, Sherpa, and the chickens were becoming memories – beloved but lost forever.

"Jem," she whispered, "you have been away for such a long time." For June, the reality of marrying Jem and being safe with him was just another memory. "June and Jem" was a Rumi poem, disappearing like dust in the sun. All gone except Kitty.

"Kitty," she called again. "Come, Kitty!" But the solar panels shone back at the sun, and the only sound was a bird call in the woods. June remembered the woman pushing her old dog in the baby carriage. Now I understand, she thought. I know why she couldn't leave him behind.

She didn't hear the vehicle but saw a flash of black through the trees and heard the bird's cry. In a panic, June squatted down and rolled under one of the solar panels, hugging her belongings against her body. The purring sound grew louder as it approached, and then it slowed down and the vehicle pulled over. June squeezed her eyes shut and held her breath, but a minute later the vehicle continued on and disappeared around a corner, and she crawled out and ran for the woods, her heart pounding in her chest.

"Please, Sir," she pleaded, "Please, Sir!"

The silver water truck was parked where it had been the day before, and several people stood in line waiting in the rising sun. June kept to the woods by the road and crept up to the passengers' side, keeping the truck between herself and the villagers. She could hear the driver talking and occasionally laughing with the people in line. June waited a few minutes, then reached up, grabbed the handle and carefully opened the cab door. Inside she could see a green jacket on the seat and a bottle of cola in a bottle holder. A doorway behind the driver's seat was closed. She waited until the next burst of laughter and then slipped inside, crouching on the floor of the cab. With one quick move, June pulled the jacket off the seat and over her. She knew if she slammed the door shut it would bring instant attention, so she left it ajar and prayed nobody would notice.

June relaxed and curled up on the floor of the cab with her head on her backpack. The driver's jacket smelled good, like pipe tobacco, and she breathed it in. The voices lulled her and she yawned and settled down. As she was drifting off, there was a sound by the open door and Kitty slipped through. The cat made a soft chattering sound and curled up close. June reached out and stroked her, running her hand over the long, soft fur. She heard the familiar ragged purring sound and sighed with relief. "Kitty," she whispered. "Oh, my Kitty." And then she slept.

Chapter 60

"What the Hell!"

June woke with a start. The Driver slammed the open cab door shut, and came around to his side, sliding into the driver's seat and staring, the sun glancing off his eyeglasses.

"What the Hell!" he repeated and poked the jacket with his pipe. "Who the Hell is crouching on the floor of my truck? Come on out, I see you down there." His voice was harsh, but he didn't sound angry, just surprised.

June crept out from under the jacket, and he recognized her at once. He saw the bruises and blackened eye, the fear in her face and her torn lip. The Driver's face turned white with shock, and he sat back, his hand falling by his side. "My God! It's you, Young Lady! Who did that to you? Who would do such a thing? Are you okay? No, wait," he interrupted her, "you don't even have to tell me." He added a string of words she had never heard, but she knew they were bad.

June sat up and held Kitty in her lap. "Please, please help me. Help us! I need to run. If I stay here, I will bring dishonor to Eve and the Farmer." Tears burned her sore eye and made streaks down her dusty cheeks. "I drove the agent off this time, but the Natural World Farm will never be free of the shame ... ever! I know."

"Bastard," the Driver said. "Of course, you can come with me! Here, you stay there under my jacket until I tell you it's safe." He sat back and filled his pipe with shaking hands. "I have to tell you, Young Lady, I am horrified. I don't understand this kind of evil."

June crouched down and pulled the jacket back over her. Kitty curled up by her side, and she felt the truck's engine vibrate as it pulled away from the curb. She thought about the farm: the people who had been so kind to her, the apartment, and working in the gardens. June remembered the big bed where she had learned what it meant to be loved … and Eve, so beautiful and so filled with fear now. June's tears fell, and she felt as if her heart would break. She thought of Jem – his gentle blue eyes and generous smile, how he had held her and made her happy. He would come back and find her gone, just a note and his ring left behind. But now it all seemed like a fairy story, something her mother might have told her. Jem will find someone else, and then he will be happy, she told herself, and his memory seemed to drift away and disappear. June's tears dried on her cheeks, and she felt as if she were floating, the feeling she had in the watering hole as she looked up at the sky.

The Driver broke his silence. "My name is Bill, and we are on our way to the Northern Kingdom," he said, "The Green Mountains, where the air is clear, and the water is clean. You can work for me, Young Lady, and you can help my wife on the farm." He stuck the pipe in his mouth but didn't bother to light it, humming as he changed gears.

June peered out from under the jacket as a gust of wind shook the truck windows. Dried leaves whirled around in the air, and it was quiet for a few minutes. I'll be alright, June thought. I'll be okay, and just okay is fine.

"Thank you, Mr. Bill," she began, "and my name is June because …"

"Stay down, stay down," the Driver shouted, and June heard the NPF vehicle as it hissed past, going in the other direction, fast!

"You stay down until we are out of this area," he said, and June crawled back under the jacket. "He is looking for you!" The Driver changed gears, and the truck seemed to lift off the ground. We're flying, June thought.

"It's a nice village up there where we're going," the Driver continued. "We don't turn travelers away in the Northern Kingdom, and the NPF agents are not allowed!" He laughed to himself, "I guess you'd call us by our old name: Sanctuary

State. Oh yeah, we fought *that* battle, you bet we did. But the Northern Kingdom won it!"

June sighed and curled up on the floor. Her eyes grew heavy as the smell of old tobacco filled the cab. "Illegals," she said, and sat up, wide awake, "do you allow Illegals?"

The Driver sucked on his pipe and thought for a minute. "Not too many of them up there where the snow flies," he said, "but we have a few Europeans. And I do know one woman who is from the Southern Border. She has two kids, a boy and a girl about your age. Good looking family and as nice as can be. They have a craft shop in the village. You'll meet all the people up there. Yes," he assured her, "you'll be safe in the Northern Kingdom, you and your big cat." He glanced down at June. "Safe as we can be, as long as Mother Nature lets us, but," he added, "we have hope. We *always* have hope!"

June rested her head on her backpack and relaxed. As she listened to the Driver talk, his words soft and sometimes hard to understand, she knew – knew in her heart that she would find the piece of her heart that had been missing for so long, the yearning that was always inside her. This time she would never push him away; this time, she would never leave his side.

"I will never leave you," he had said.

"I will never leave you, either," she whispered.

Oh Jem, she though with a fleeting pang of sorrow, I'm so sorry.

The truck turned onto the highway and headed North, and finally June closed her eyes and dreamed.

Chapter 61

The Garden State

Agent David Anderson pulled the NPF vehicle to the side of the road and stared at the Natural World Farm. He was filled with contradictory emotions: anger, pain, shock, and, yes, something he didn't understand – sorrow. He knew June was gone, and he didn't know where she was or how to find her. His whole life had been filled with women who desired him, loved him, and, at least, treated him with respect. David put his hand up and touched the bruise on his cheek.

"How *dare* June strike me," he whispered, his lips tight. "She should have been proud and eager that I chose her!" He slammed his hand on the steering wheel and cursed under his breath. "When I find her, well, then she'll know!"

Earlier, when the sun had just cleared the trees, David had grabbed a vehicle and headed to Natural World Farm. The sun hitting the panels in the solar farm was blinding, and he'd pulled over to darken the vehicle windows, then raced on. The front door to the farmhouse stood open, but David ignored that, stormed around the corner of the house, and found the farmer's wife standing outside June's apartment in tears.

"She's gone!" That's all the wretched woman could say. "She's gone!"

David demanded the poor woman open the apartment door, and he forced his way inside. He inspected every corner of the big room, peered into the refrigerator and bathroom medicine cabinet – but they were empty. Notepaper and a pen were neatly centered on a desk and a few clothes were folded over a chair. But that was all there was. He felt his heart drop and stared at the open door.

"Damn it, here, take this," the woman handed him a note, and as he scanned it, David felt sick. "She's gone," the woman repeated and burst into tears again as he headed back to his vehicle.

The huge Green Mountain Water truck was lumbering up the road as David headed back to town, and the driver gave him a wave as the truck headed North. David almost pulled him over, but somehow, he felt time was running out, and he continued on. The Village was busy, but no one had seen June, and nobody had any idea where she'd be. He looked for Jem – maybe he was back from the Far Western Region – but nobody had seen Jem, either. David felt like taking every single person from the Village into the NPF headquarters for interrogation, but he knew *that* would never fly. Finally, he turned the vehicle around and headed back to the farm.

Now, as the sun reached high noon, David parked across from the farm, just in case June returned. He looked over his shoulder, scanning the road back to the Village, sighed, and gazed out over the acres of farmland that belonged to the Natural World Farm. He'd never felt so confused and had an odd urge to put his head down on the steering wheel and cry. "Shit," he said, "I feel terrible! It *hurts*!"

David realized June would never have been a one-night stand. He wanted her forever, longed to hold her at night, and bring her gifts, find a home for them, and introduce her to his parents. Maybe, if he hadn't been affected by the Virus, they would have a baby together. Just do those things the other agents did.

The awful truth was, David didn't know how. It was like a foreign language. What would he have said? What would he have done? How could he make June love him? It was something Agent David Anderson had never had to do, so now, as he sat in his NPF vehicle by the side of the road, he felt sick at heart.

All that was left was the bruise on his cheek, and he touched it gently with the tips of his fingers.

A crow gave a harsh call as it beat its way across the wheat field, and then all was quiet. David felt a chill in the still, hot air, and finally, for the first time in his life, David Anderson began to cry.

Acknowledgement

I would like to acknowledge and thank my good friend and editor, Martha Phillips, who took June under her wing and finally brought her home. And to Deborah Persico Tostanoski, my very first reader, who gave me so much joy and encouragement. Finally, thank you Naomi, Leah, and Chris, and my wonderful Manhattan writers' group who, before the Shutdown, helped June on her way.